FEARLESS

A Mirrorworld novel

FEARLESS

A Mirrorworld novel

Written by

CORNELIA FUNKE

A story found and told by

Cornelia Funke and Lionel Wigram

Translated by Oliver Latsch

Little, Brown and Company
New York Boston

Little, Brown and Company

Hachette Book Group
237 Park Avenue, New York, NY 10017
Visit our website at lb-teens.com

Little, Brown and Company is a division of Hachette Book Group, Inc.
The Little, Brown name and logo are trademarks of Hachette Book Group, Inc.

The publisher is not responsible for websites (or their content) that are not owned by the publisher.

First Paperback Edition: May 2014
First published in hardcover in April 2013 by Little, Brown and Company

Library of Congress Cataloging-in-Publication-Data

Funke, Cornelia Caroline.
Fearless / Cornelia Funke.
p. cm.
Summary: "Jacob Reckless journeys to the Mirrorworld to tell his shapeshifting friend Fox that a fairy curse—a deadly moth in his chest—means he has only one year to live. The journey in the Mirrorworld turns into a search against time and against a Goyl treasure hunter for an enchanted crossbow, which is known to strike down any army it faces, and less well known for its healing power when shot by a loved one"—Provided by publisher.
ISBN 978-0-316-05610-6 (hc)—ISBN 978-0-316-05611-3 (pb)
[1. Fantasy. 2. Brothers—Fiction. 3. Adventure and adventurers—Fiction. 4. Magic—Fiction.] I. Title.
PZ7. F96624Fe 2013
[Fic]—dc23

2012028742

10 9 8 7 6 5 4 3 2 1

RRD-C

Printed in the United States of America

Book design by Alison Impey

For Ben, who is both
Jacob and Will.

—C.F.

To Paula, my Fox, who always
has my back.

—O.L.

40
30
20
Long. West 10
0
10
60
50
40
30
NORGA
SVERIGA
CALEDONIA
EIRE
ALBION
YURTLAND
Pendragon
LONDRA
Goldsmouth
Dunkerk
FLANDERS
HANOVER
PRUSSI
GOYL
WESTPHALIA
Saint-Riquet
LUTIS
Abbey of Fontevaud
Champlitte
Bluebeard's Mansion
BAVARIA
Dead City
HELVETIA
Valiant's Castle
VENA
LOTHARAINE
LOMBARDIA
LEONIA
CATALUNIA
ETRURIA
KORSO
THYRANNIAN SEA
APULIA
SMERALDA
CORDOBA CALIFATE
77
87
Longitude East

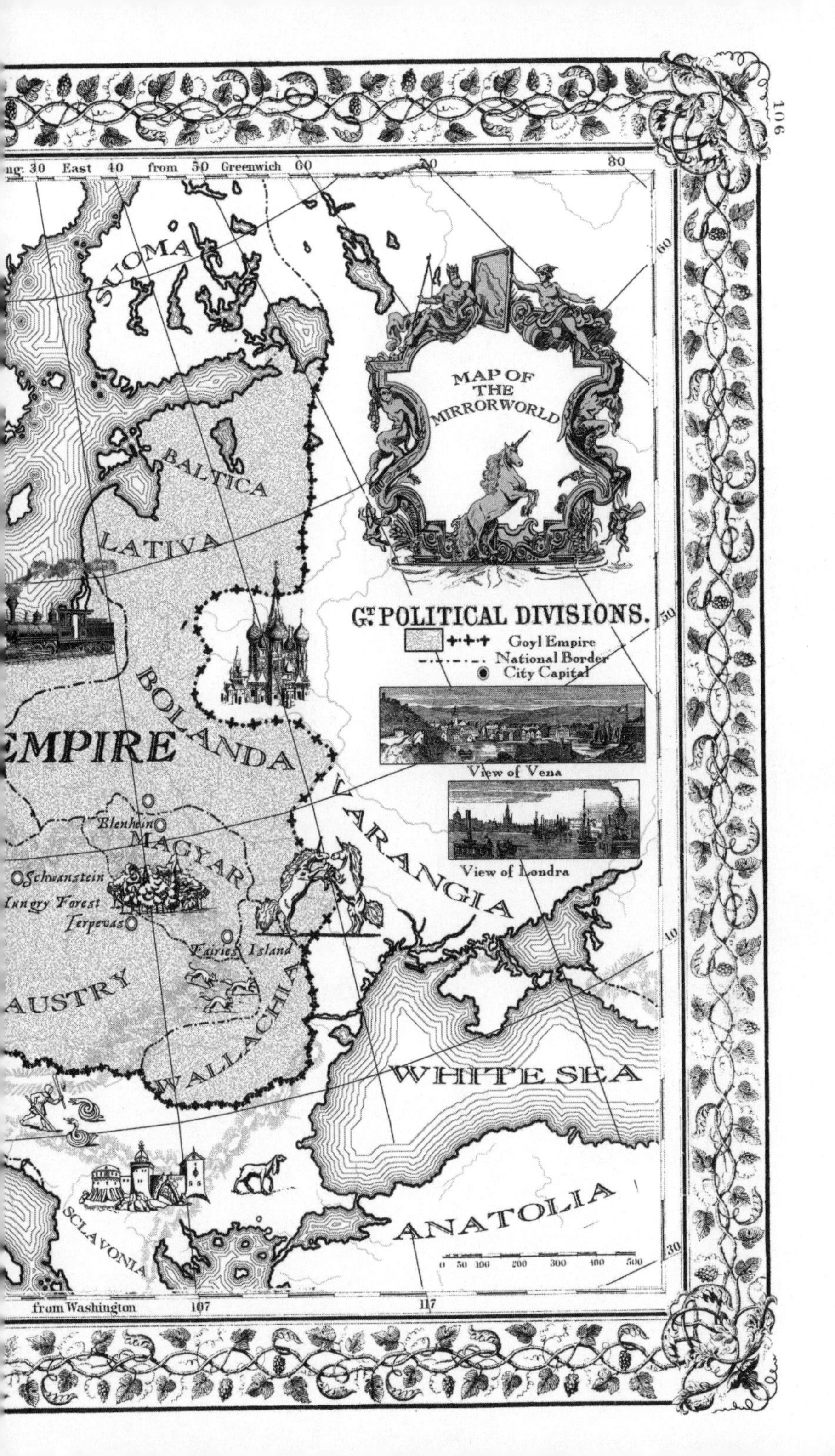

ng: 30 East 40 from 50 Greenwich 60 70 80
SUOMA
BALTICA
LATIVA
BOLANDA
EMPIRE
MAGYAR
Blenheim
Schwanstein
ungry Forest
Terpevas
Fairies Island
AUSTRY
WALLACHIA
VARANGIA
SCLAVONIA
WHITE SEA
ANATOLIA
MAP OF THE MIRRORWORLD
G^T. POLITICAL DIVISIONS.
Goyl Empire
National Border
City Capital
View of Vena
View of Londra
0 50 100 200 300 400 500
60
50
40
30
from Washington 107 117
106

1. WAITING

He still wasn't back.

"I won't stay long." Fox wiped the rain off her face. With Jacob, this could mean anything. Sometimes he stayed for weeks. Sometimes months.

The ruin lay deserted as usual, and the silence between the scorched walls made her shiver nearly as much as the rain. The human skin warmed so much less, yet Fox now shifted into the vixen ever more rarely. All too clearly she had begun to feel how the fur stole the years from her—even without Jacob reminding her.

He'd held her so close before he left, as if he wanted to take her warmth with him into the world where he was born. Something frightened him, though he didn't admit it, of course. He was still like a boy who thought he could outrun his own shadow.

They'd been way up in the north, in Sveriga and Norga, where even now the forests were still buried in thick snow and where hunger drove the wolves into the towns. Before that they'd traveled so far south that the vixen still found desert sand in her fur. Thousands of miles...cities and countries she'd never heard of before, and all supposedly to find an hourglass. But Fox knew Jacob too well to believe that.

At her feet, the first wild primroses were springing up between the shattered flagstones. She snapped off one of the delicate stalks, and the dew rolling off the flowers was still cold. It had been a long winter, and Fox could feel the past months like frost on her skin. So much had happened since the previous summer. All that fear for Jacob's brother...and for Jacob. Too much fear. Too much love. Too much of everything.

She tucked the pale yellow flower into her lapel. Hands...they made up for the chilly skin her human body came in. Whenever she wore her fur, Fox missed reading the world with her fingers.

"I won't stay long."

With a quick movement, she grabbed a Thumbling who'd pushed his tiny hand into her jacket pocket. He only let go of the gold coin after she shook him as hard as the vixen would a captured mouse. The little thief bit at her fingers before he dashed off, muttering insults. Jacob always tucked a few coins into her pockets before he left. He hadn't adjusted to the fact that she now managed quite well in the human world—even without him.

What was he afraid of?

Fox had asked him, after they'd ridden for days from one wretched village to the next, only to end up standing beneath some dead sultan's dried-up pomegranate tree. She'd asked him again, when Jacob had gotten himself drunk three nights in a row after they'd found an overgrown garden with nothing but a dried-up well in it. "It's nothing. Don't worry." A kiss on the cheek and that careless smile she'd been able to see right through since she was twelve. "It's nothing. . . ."

She knew that he missed his brother, but this was something else. Fox looked up at the tower. The charred stones seemed to whisper a name. Clara. Was that it?

Her heart still tightened whenever she thought of the brook and the two dead larks. Jacob's hand in Clara's hair, his mouth on her mouth. So ravenous.

Maybe that was why she'd nearly gone with him—for the first time. She'd even followed Jacob up into the tower, but in front of that mirror her courage had deserted her. Its glass seemed to her like dark ice that would freeze her heart.

Fox turned her back to the tower.

Jacob was going to come back.

He always came back.

2. THE WRONG WORLD

The auction room was on the thirtieth floor. Wood-paneled walls, a dozen rows of chairs, and a man by the door, who ticked Jacob's name off a list with an absent-minded smile. Jacob took the catalog the man offered him and went to stand by one of the windows. A thick forest of towers; beyond them, like watery mirrors, the Great Lakes. He'd only arrived in Chicago from New York that morning, a distance that would have taken a week by stagecoach. Beneath him, the sunlight glinted from countless glass walls and gilded roofs. When it came to beauty, this world could easily compete with the one behind the mirror, and yet Jacob felt homesick.

He sat down on one of the chairs and surveyed the faces around him. Many were familiar: antiques dealers, museum curators, art collectors. Like him, they were all treasure hunters, even though the treasures of this world possessed no magic beyond their age and beauty.

The bottle, which Jacob had tracked all the way to this room, was listed in the auction catalog between a Chinese emperor's teapot and the silver rattle of an English King's son. The bottle looked so innocuous that hopefully it wouldn't attract any other bidders. Its dark glass was protected by a much-handled sheath of leather, and the neck was sealed with wax.

BOTTLE OF SCANDINAVIAN ORIGIN, EARLY 13TH CENTURY, read the caption beneath the picture. Exactly the description Jacob had given when he sold the bottle to an antiques dealer in London. Back then he'd thought it an amusing move to render its inhabitant harmless that way. On the other side of the mirror, releasing him would have been deadly, but in this world he was as harmless as bottled air, a bubble of nothing behind brown glass.

The bottle had changed owners several times since Jacob had sold it. It had taken him nearly a month to trace it—time he didn't have. The All-Healing Apple, the Well of Eternal Youth...he'd already wasted many months searching for the wrong objects. And death was still embedded in his chest. Time to try a more dangerous remedy.

The moth above his heart was growing darker every day: the seal on the death warrant issued by the Dark Fairy for uttering her name. Her sister had whispered that name to Jacob between two kisses. No man was ever executed more tenderly. Betrayed love. The black moth's bloodred outline was a reminder of the crime he was actually dying for.

A dealer to whom he'd sold a carafe of elven glass many years ago smiled at him from the first row. (She'd taken it for Persian crystal.) Jacob used to bring many objects through the mirror, to pay for Will's school or his mother's doctor's bills. Of course, none of his clients had ever suspected that he sold them objects from another world.

Jacob glanced at his watch and looked impatiently at the auctioneer. *Get on with it!* Lost time. He didn't even know how much he had left. Half a year, maybe less...

The emperor's teapot fetched a ridiculously high price, but, just as he'd expected, the bottle didn't arouse much excitement as it was placed on the auctioneer's table. Jacob was certain he'd be the only bidder, when suddenly another hand rose a few rows behind him.

The other bidder had the delicate build of a child. The diamonds on his short fingers were certainly worth more than all the items in the auction combined. His short hair was as black as a raven's feathers, but he had the face of an old man. And the smile he gave Jacob seemed to know a little too much.

Nonsense!

Jacob had sold a handful of gold coins for the auction. The wad of banknotes he got for them had seemed more than enough. After all, he hadn't sold the bottle for that much in the first place. But each time he raised his bid, the stranger also raised his hand, and Jacob felt his heart grow angrier with every number the auctioneer called. A whisper went through the room as the bids surpassed the price for the imperial teapot. Another dealer joined the bidding, only to drop out as the price kept climbing ever higher.

Give up, Jacob!

And then what? He had no clue what else he should look for, be it in this world or the other. His fingers instinctively searched for the gold handkerchief in his pocket, but its magic was as powerless here as the creature imprisoned in that bottle. *Never mind, Jacob. By the time they realize you can't pay, you'll be long gone through the mirror.*

He raised his hand again, though the amount the auctioneer had called made him nauseous. It was a steep price, even for his own life. He glanced back at his opponent. The eyes looking back at him were green, like freshly cut grass. The small man adjusted his tie and gave Jacob another smile, and then he lowered his ringed hand.

The auctioneer's hammer dropped, and Jacob felt dizzy with relief as he picked his way through the row of chairs. A collector in the first row bid ten thousand dollars for the silver rattle. Treasure, on both sides of the mirror.

The cashier was sweating through her black jacket, and she'd put too much powder on her pasty skin.

Jacob gave her his most winning smile as he pushed the wad of money toward her. "I hope this will do for a deposit?"

He added three gold coins, which were usually a welcome currency even on this side of the mirror. Most dealers took him for a fool who didn't know the value of antique coins, and he always had some preposterous story ready for those who quizzed him about the Empress's head on them. The sweating cashier, however, just cast a suspicious look at the three coins and called over one of the auctioneers.

The bottle stood barely two steps away, together with the other sold items. Even from this close, the glass didn't reveal anything about the creature hidden inside. Jacob felt a brief temptation to grab it, despite the guards by the door. But then a quiet cough interrupted this far-from-sensible train of thought.

"Interesting coins, Mr.... I'm sorry, your name is...?"

Green eyes. His competitor barely reached up to Jacob's shoulder. His left earlobe was studded with a tiny ruby.

"Reckless. Jacob Reckless."

"Ah, yes." The stranger reached inside his tailored jacket and gave the auctioneer a smile. "I will vouch for Mr. Reckless," he said, offering Jacob a card. His voice sounded hoarse, and it had a slight accent Jacob couldn't quite place.

The auctioneer bowed his head reverently.

"As you wish, Mr. Earlking." He looked at Jacob. "Where shall we send the bottle?"

"I'll take it now."

"Of course." Earlking smiled. "It's been in the wrong place far too long, hasn't it?"

Before Jacob could reply, the small man made a quick bow. "Please give my regards to your brother," he said. "I know him and your mother very well." With that he turned and disappeared into the well-dressed throng.

Jacob looked at the card in his hand. NOREBO JOHANN EARLKING. Nothing else.

The auctioneer handed him the bottle.

3. GHOSTS

The wrong world. The security man at the airport scrutinized the bottle so intensely that, had this been the other world, Jacob would have put a pistol to his uniformed chest. His flight was late arriving into New York, and his taxi got so held up in Manhattan's evening traffic that he longed for a carriage ride through the sleepy streets of Schwanstein. The moon shone from the grimy puddles in front of the old apartment building. Staring down at him from the brick walls were the grotesque stone faces that used to frighten Will so much as a child that he ducked his head every time he stepped through the door. Since then the exhaust had eaten away at them, and they were now barely distinguishable from the stone vines that grew around them. Yet as he climbed the steps to the front door, Jacob felt their stony stares more intensely than ever before. His brother probably felt the same way. The contorted faces contained a whole new kind of terror since Will himself had grown a skin of stone.

The doorman in the entrance hall was the same man who had always dragged him and Will out of the elevator when they were children, riding it up and down too many times. Mr. Tomkins. He'd grown old and fat. On the counter where he kept the mail was the same jar of lollipops he'd used to bribe them to run his errands. At some point, Jacob had managed to convince Will that Tomkins was a man-eating Ogre, and for days his brother had refused to go to preschool because he was afraid to walk past the doorman on the way.

The past. It lurked in every corner of the old building: behind the pillars in the entrance hall, where he and Will used to play hide-and-seek; in the dark catacombs of the basement, where he'd gone on his first (and unsuccessful) treasure hunts; and in the elevator, which would transform into a spaceship or the cage of a Witch, whatever their adventures required. Strange, how the prospect of death brought back the past. It was as though every moment he'd lived was suddenly back, whispering *Maybe this is all you get, Jacob.*

The elevator door still jammed a little when it was pushed open.

Seventh floor.

Will had left a note for him on the door. WE'RE OUT SHOPPING. FOOD IN THE FRIDGE. WELCOME HOME! W.

Jacob tucked the paper into his coat pocket and unlocked the door. He was paying with his life for this welcome, and he would have done it again, just for the feeling of having his brother back. They hadn't been this close since the time when Will used to crawl into his bed every night—when he still believed that doormen sometimes liked to eat human flesh. Love was lost so terrifyingly easily.

The darkness that met Jacob behind the door was strange and yet familiar. Will had painted the hall, and the smell of fresh paint mingled with the scents of their childhood. Jacob's fingers still found the light switch, but the lamp was new, as was the sideboard by the door. The old family photographs had disappeared, and the yellowed wallpaper—which, even years later, had shown the spot where his father's portrait had once hung—had been covered by white paint.

Jacob dropped his bag on the well-worn parquet floor.

Welcome home.

Could it really be home again, after all those years during which all he'd wanted from this place was the mirror? A vase with yellow roses stood on the sideboard. Clara's signature. Before coming through the mirror, he'd felt slightly nervous at the prospect of seeing her again. He couldn't be sure whether the Larks' Water was still affecting him or whether it was just the memories that set his heart racing. But all was well. It had been good to see her, with Will, in the world Jacob hadn't belonged to for an eternity. She had obviously not told Will about the Larks' Water, but Jacob felt how the shared memory bonded them, as though they'd gotten lost in the woods and had found their way out together.

Their mother's room, like their father's study, was still mostly unchanged. Jacob hesitated before he opened the door. A few boxes full of Will's books were piled up next to the bed, and the family photographs that had hung in the hallway leaned against the wall beneath the window.

The room still smelled of her. She had sewn the patchwork quilt on the bed herself. The pieces of fabric used to be all over the apartment. Flowers, animals, houses, ships, moons, and stars. Whatever the quilt said about his mother, Jacob had never been able to decipher it. The three of them had lain on it together many times, when she'd read to them. Their grandfather told them the fairy tales he'd grown up with in Europe, full of the Witches and Fairies whose kin Jacob would meet later behind the mirror. Their mother's stories, however, were American. The Headless Rider, Johnny Appleseed, the Wolf Brother, the Magic Lady, and the Stone Giant of Seneca. Jacob hadn't come across any of them behind the mirror yet, but he was sure they existed there, just as his grandfather's fairytale folk did.

The photograph on the nightstand showed his mother

with Will and him in the park across the street. She looked very happy. And so young. His father had taken the picture. He must have already known about the mirror back then.

Jacob wiped the dust off the glass. So young. And so beautiful. What had his father sought that he hadn't been able to find with her? How often Jacob had asked himself that question as a child. He'd been certain she must have done something wrong, and he would get so angry. Angry at her weakness. Angry that she could never stop loving his father; that, against all better judgment, she had always waited for his return. Or maybe she'd just waited for the day her older son would find him and return him to her? Wasn't that what Jacob had fantasized about all those years? That one day he'd return with his father and wipe all that sadness off her face?

Behind the mirror were hourglasses that stopped time. Jacob had long searched for one for the Empress. In Lombardia there was a carousel that could turn children into adults, and grown-ups back into children. And there was a Varangian count who owned a music box that, if you wound it up, would transport you back into your own past. Jacob had often wondered whether such items changed the course of events or whether one ended up doing things the very same way one had already done them: His father would still go through the mirror, and he'd still follow, and Will and his mother would be left behind again.

Heavens, Jacob! The prospect of his own death was making him sentimental.

He felt as though for months now, someone had kept throwing his heart into a crucible over and over again, like a lump of ore refusing to take the right shape. If that bottle proved as useless as the apple and the well, then all of his efforts would have been in vain, and soon he'd be nothing but a picture in a dusty frame, like his mother. Jacob returned her photograph to the nightstand. Then he straightened the bed, as though at any moment she might step into her room.

Someone was unlocking the apartment door.

"Jacob's home, Will!" Clara's voice sounded nearly as familiar as his brother's. "There's his bag."

"Jake?" Will's voice had no trace of the stone that had tainted his skin. "Where are you?"

Jacob heard his brother walk down the hallway, and for an instant he was transported to another hallway, with Will's rage-contorted face behind him. *It's over, Jacob!* No, it would never be completely over, and that was a good thing. He didn't want to forget how easily he might lose Will.

And there he was, standing in the doorway. No gold in his eyes, his skin as soft as Jacob's, just a lot paler. After all, Will hadn't spent most of the past weeks riding through a godforsaken desert.

Will hugged Jacob nearly as hard as he used to in the schoolyard as children, whenever his big brother had saved him from yet another bullying fourth grader. Yes, this was well worth paying for. As long as Will never learned the true price.

Will's memories of his time behind the mirror were fragments from which he desperately tried to assemble the whole picture. Nobody likes living with the knowledge that he can't remember the most crucial weeks of his life. Whenever Will described places or faces to him and Clara, Jacob realized again how much his brother had lived through alone behind the mirror. It was as though Will had a second shadow, which followed him like a stranger and scared him every now and then.

Jacob couldn't wait to go back, but Clara asked him to stay for dinner, and who knew whether he'd ever see her or Will again. So he sat down at the kitchen table, into which he'd once carved his initials with his first penknife, and he tried to act as carefree as possible. But he'd obviously lost his knack for peddling his stories to his brother as the truth. Jacob caught more than one pensive glance from Will as he tried to explain his trip to Chicago as merely some Schwanstein factory owner's obsession for Djinns.

He wouldn't have even tried that story on Fox. During their endless searches for the wrong objects, he'd often been close to telling her the truth, but he was stopped by the prospect of seeing his fear on her face. He loved Will, but he would always and foremost be the older brother to him. With Fox, Jacob could simply be himself. She saw so much of what he tried to hide from others, though he didn't always like it, and they rarely spoke of what they knew of each other.

"Will, do you know a Norebo Earlking?"

His brother frowned. "Short guy? With a strange accent?"

"That's him."

"Ma sold him some of Grandpa's things when she needed money. I think he has a bunch of antiques shops here and in Europe. Why?"

"He asked me to send you his regards."

"Me?" Will shrugged. "Ma didn't sell him everything he was interested in. Maybe he wants to try his luck with us. He's a strange bird. I could never figure out whether Ma liked him." Will rubbed his arm. He often touched his skin, as if to make sure the jade was really gone. Clara noticed it as well. Ghosts...

Will got up and poured himself a glass of wine.

"What should I do if he makes an offer? The basement is full of old junk. It looks like our family hasn't thrown anything away since this house was built. There's barely enough space for the pictures we took off the walls. But Clara needs an office and..." Will left the sentence unfinished, as though their parents' ghosts were listening from their empty rooms. Jacob ran his fingers over the initials he'd once carved into the tabletop. That knife had been his first secret possession.

"Sell whatever you want," he said. "You can also use my room, if you'd like. I'm here so rarely, I can just sleep on the couch."

"Nonsense. You'll keep your room." Will pushed a glass of wine toward him. "When are you going back?"

"Tonight." Ignoring his brother's disappointment was no longer as easy as it used to be. He was going to miss Will.

"Is everything all right?" Will looked at him anxiously. Fooling him *definitely* wasn't as easy as it used to be.

"Sure. It's just hard work, living in two worlds." Jacob tried to make it sound like a joke, but Will's face was still serious. He looked so much like their mother. Will even frowned the way she used to.

"You should stay here. It's too dangerous."

Jacob looked down so his brother wouldn't see him smile. *Oh, little brother, it only became dangerous because of you.* "I'll be back soon," he said. "Definitely."

He still was a decent enough liar. The odds were a thousand to one that the bottle's inhabitant would kill him rather than save him. *A thousand to one against you, Jacob.* He'd beaten worse odds.

4. DANGEROUS MEDICINE

Back. The rain that whipped into Jacob's face as he stepped out of the tower seemed to be the same rain that had been running down his mother's window. His eyes scanned the crumbled walls for the outline of a vixen, but all they spotted was a Heinzel, hungry and haggard, as they always were toward the end of winter. Where was she?

It was rare for Fox not to be waiting for him. She often sensed his return days in advance. Jacob, of course, immediately thought of traps, or the shotgun of a farmer protecting his chickens. *Nonsense, Jacob.* She was good at looking after herself, better than he was. And he wouldn't have wanted her around when he opened the bottle, anyway.

After the noise of the other world, the silence surrounding him here seemed even more unreal than the Heinzel.

It always took his eyes a few moments to adjust to the darkness. The lights of the other world made him forget how dark nights here could be. Jacob looked around. He needed a place where the bottle's occupant wouldn't grow all the way into the clouds. And Jacob couldn't risk any damage to the tower, and the mirror inside.

The old chapel.

Like the tower, the chapel had been left untouched by the fire that had destroyed the castle. The building lay just beyond where the overgrown garden stretched down the slope of the hill. Jacob had to hack a path through it with his saber. Mossy steps, crumbling statues, marble fountains filled with rotting leaves. A few headstones still stuck out from the unmowed grass: Arnold Fischbein, Luise Moor, Käthchen Grimm. The servants' graves had been spared by the fire, while the mausoleum of the castle's owners had been reduced to a circle of sooty stones.

The wooden doors of the chapel were so warped that Jacob barely managed to open them. The inside looked desolate. All the colorful glass windows were broken, and the wooden pews had long gone to heat a few drafty cottages. But the roof was still intact, and the nave was barely more than twelve feet high. This would have to do.

A Thumbling peered over the rim of the dried-up font as Jacob pulled the leather sheath off the bottle. The brown glass was so cold that it nearly burnt his fingers. Its occupant was not from the south, where Djinns could be found in the markets of every desert village. The medicine

Jacob needed could be provided only by a northern Djinn. They were very rare and very vicious—which explained why the men who hunted them were often even more scarred than Chanute. The ghost Jacob was about to set free had given his captor such a fight that the man had died within hours of trapping it. Jacob had buried him himself.

He chased the Thumbling outside before his curiosity cost him his life. Then Jacob closed the doors.

"They are all murderers, Jacob, never forget that!" Chanute had warned him more than once about the northern Djinns. "They get locked up because they love to kill. And they know they have to spend the rest of their immortal existence serving every fool who gets hold of their bottle, so their only desire is to kill their master and take possession of the bottle themselves."

Jacob stepped into the center of the chapel.

The etched pattern on the neck of the bottle was what bound the Djinn inside. Jacob copied it onto the palm of his hand before he drew his knife. The only thing more dangerous than catching one of these ghosts was letting him out again. But what did he have to lose?

The seal on the bottle was that of the judge who'd sentenced the Djinn to an eternity behind brown glass. Jacob used his knife to peel the wax off the top. Then he set the bottle on the flagstones and quickly stepped back.

The smoke that rose from the mouth was silvery-gray, like the scales of a fish. The wisps formed fingers, an arm, a shoulder. The fingers felt the cold air and clenched into a fist. From the shoulders grew a barbed neck like a lizard's.

Careful, Jacob!

He ducked into the smoke still rising from the bottle. Above him, a skull with a low forehead and stringy hair was taking shape. A mouth opened. The groan it uttered made the chapel shudder like the haunches of a frightened animal. The cracked windows burst, and Jacob breathed the dust of broken glass. Colored shards rained down on him while the ghost above him opened his eyes. They were white, like the eyes of a blind man, and the pupils were like black bullet holes. Their lurking glance found Jacob just as he got hold of the bottle and closed his fingers firmly around its neck.

The huge body ducked like a cat ready to pounce.

"Will you look at that!" The Djinn sounded hoarse, as though he had lost his voice in his glassy prison. "And who are you? Where's the other one, the one who captured me?"

He leaned down toward Jacob. "Is he dead? I remember breaking his ribs. But that is nothing compared to what I will do to that judge. I've been picturing it all these years. I will pluck him apart like a flower. I will pick my teeth with his bones and blow my nose on his skin."

His hoarse rage flooded through the chapel, and the pattern on Jacob's hands grew icy crystals.

"Enough of the boasting!" Jacob shouted up at the ghost. "You will do none of those things. You will serve me until I grow tired of you, or I will take you to one of the prisons where they store your kind like bottled wine."

The Djinn brushed the filthy hair from his forehead. Each strand was made of flexible glass and was worth a fortune anywhere behind the mirror.

"That was not very respectful!" he whispered. His face was scarred, and the left ear was torn off. In their cold homeland, Djinns were often used in wars. "Well then, what are my master's wishes?" he purred. "The usual? Gold? Power? Your enemies laid out at your feet like swatted flies?"

The bottle was so cold that Jacob's hands were getting numb. *Hold on to it, Jacob!*

"Give it to me!" The Djinn leaned down so far that his glass hair brushed against Jacob's shoulder. "Give me the bottle and I will get you whatever you desire. If you try to keep it, I shall wait day and night for my chance to kill you. I have seen nothing but brown glass for a long time, and your screams would help drive out the silence that still numbs my ears." The idea brought a smile of pure delight to his sly face. Djinns liked to talk nearly as much as they liked to kill.

"You can have the bottle!" Jacob called out. The stench of sulfur emanating from the Djinn's gray skin was so strong that he nearly threw up. "For one drop of your blood."

The ghost bared his teeth, which were as gray as the rest of his body. "My blood?" His grin was pure malice. "What's killing you? Poison? A disease? Or is it a curse?"

"What is it to you?" Jacob replied. "Do we have a deal or not?"

The grin turned murderous. His kind of Djinn usually tried to bite off the head of whoever handed him his bottle. Jacob knew of two treasure hunters who'd died that way. Djinns had strong teeth. *You'd better be quick, Jacob. Very quick.*

The ghost offered his hand. "We have a deal." His little finger alone was longer than a human arm.

Jacob closed his fingers more firmly around the bottle, though the glass was scorching his skin. "Oh no. Your blood first."

The ghost bared his teeth again and leaned over Jacob with a sneer. "Why don't you come and get it?"

Exactly what Jacob had been waiting for.

He grabbed hold of one of the glass hairs and pulled himself up. The ghost snatched at him, but before the Djinn could reach him, Jacob had already rammed the bottle up his nose. The ghost howled and tried to pull it out with his massive fingers. *Now, Jacob!* He jumped onto the Djinn's shoulder and sliced the tattered earlobe with his knife. Black blood spurted out. Jacob rubbed it on his skin while the ghost still tried in vain to pull the bottle from his nostril. His grunts and groans sent ice crystals dancing through the air. Jacob jumped off the Djinn's shoulder. He nearly broke his legs landing on the icy flagstones. *On your feet, Jacob!* The chapel's roof burst under the pressure of the ghost's barbed back. Jacob slithered toward the door.

Go, Jacob!

He ran toward the tall pines behind the chapel, but before he could reach the protection of their branches, he was grabbed by icy fingers and lifted up into the air. Jacob felt one of his ribs break. Dangerous medicine.

"Pull it out!"

Jacob screamed with pain as the ghost tightened his grip. The huge fingers lifted Jacob higher, until he was close enough to push his hand into the massive nostril.

"If you drop it," the ghost whispered, "I'll still have enough time to break all your bones."

Maybe. But the Djinn was going to kill him even if he handed over the bottle. *Nothing to lose.* Jacob's fingers found the neck of the bottle. They gripped the cold glass.

"Pull - - - it - - - ooouuut!" The ghost's bloodthirsty voice enveloped him.

Jacob was in no rush. After all, these might be the final moments of his life. Up on the hill he saw the tower rising into the dark sky, and beneath it a marten was nibbling on the fresh buds of a tree. Spring was coming. *Life or death, Jacob.* Once again.

He pulled out the bottle and threw it as hard as he could against the remnants of the chapel's gabled roof.

The Djinn's enraged howl caused the marten to freeze. The gray fingers closed around Jacob's body so hard, he thought he could hear every one of his bones break. But his pain was penetrated by the sound of shattering glass. The huge fingers let go—and Jacob fell.

He fell far.

The impact winded him completely, but above him he could see the ghost's body erupt as though someone had stuffed him with explosives. The Djinn's gray flesh tore into a thousand shreds, which rained down on Jacob like grimy snow. He lay on the ground, licking the black blood from his lips. It tasted sweet and burnt his tongue.

He had gotten what he wanted.

And he was still alive.

5. ALMA

Schwanstein's gaslit streets had not seen a practicing Witch for years. Witches were part of the past, and the people of Schwanstein believed in the future. Instead of relying on magic and bitter herbs, they preferred the doctors who had moved there from Vena. It was only when modern medicine failed them that they found their way to the village on the eastern side of the castle hill.

Alma Spitzweg's house stood right next to the cemetery, even though her craft usually kept her patients out of it before it was their time. Officially, she ran a normal medical practice. Alma could splint a broken limb like any doctor from the big city. At times she even prescribed the same pills, but Alma also tended to cows and Heinzel with the same diligence she applied to her human patients;

her clothes changed color with the weather; and her pupils were as slender as the pupils in her cat's eyes.

Alma's practice was still closed when Jacob knocked on the back door. It was a while before she opened it. She'd obviously had an exhausting night, yet her face brightened immediately at the sight of him. On that early morning, she looked exactly as Jacob would have imagined a Witch would look like when he was a child, but he'd seen Alma with many different faces and in many different bodies.

"I could have done with your help last night," she said. Her cat was purring a welcome at Jacob's feet. "The Stilt from up by the ruins tried to steal a child. Can't you get rid of it?"

The Stilt. The first creature he'd encountered behind the mirror. Jacob's hands still bore the scars from its yellow teeth. He'd tried to catch it more than a dozen times, but Stilts were cunning, and masters at playing hide-and-seek.

"I'll try again. I promise." Jacob picked up the purring cat and followed Alma into the plain room where she practiced both the old and the new kinds of medicine. As he took off his coat, she noticed the black blood on his shirt and shook her head wearily.

"And what is this now?" she asked. "Couldn't you just once come here with a cold or an upset stomach? Will I regret to my dying day that I didn't stop you from apprenticing with that Albert Chanute?"

Alma had never liked the old treasure hunter. Too many

times had she given shelter to Jacob after Chanute had beaten him. And like all Witches, she didn't like treasure hunting. Jacob had first met her by the ruins. Alma swore by the herbs that grew there. "Cursed? Half the world is cursed," she had said when asked about the stories that surrounded the ruins. "And curses wear off faster than a bad smell. All that's up there are burnt stones."

She'd never asked what a twelve-year-old boy was doing all alone among the walls of a burnt-down castle. Alma never asked such questions, maybe, because she already knew the answers. She had taken Jacob home with her, given him clothes that wouldn't attract curious stares, and warned him about Thumblings and Gold-Ravens. During his first years behind the mirror, he could always count on her for a warm meal or a place to sleep. Alma had patched him up after he'd first been bitten by a wolf; she'd put a splint on his arm after he'd tried to ride a hexed horse. And she'd instructed him on which of her world's creatures were best given a wide berth.

She dabbed some of the black blood off his skin and sniffed it. "Northern Djinn blood." She looked at him, worried. "What do you need that for?"

She put her hand on his chest. Then she opened his shirt and ran her fingers over the imprint of the moth.

"Fool!" She punched her bony fist into his chest. "You went back to the Fairy. Didn't I tell you to stay away from her?"

"I needed her help."

"And? Why didn't you come to me?" She opened the cupboard where she kept the instruments for the less modern part of her practice.

"It was a Fairy's curse! You couldn't have done anything." Fairy magic was beyond the power of any Witch. "It was for my brother," he added.

"And your brother's worth sacrificing your own life for?"

"Yes."

Alma looked at him silently. Then she took a knife from the cupboard and cut a strand of Jacob's hair. The hair caught fire as soon as she rubbed it between her fingers. Witches could set fire to almost anything with their touch.

Alma looked at the ash on her fingertips—then she looked at Jacob. Her fingers were white as snow. She didn't have to explain what that meant. He'd cleansed himself of a curse before. Back then, the ash on Alma's fingers had been black.

The Djinn's blood had done nothing.

He buttoned up his shirt again. *You're a dead man, Jacob.*

Had the Red Fairy been watching him all these months, as he'd found hope after hope dashed? Was she watching him right now? The Fairies had many ways to see what they wanted to see. She'd probably been waiting for his death ever since she whispered her sister's name to him. *No, Jacob. Ever since you left her.*

"How much longer?" he asked.

The pity in Alma's eyes was worse than her anger. "Two, three months, maybe less. How did she curse you?"

"She got me to say her dark sister's name."

Alma's cat was brushing against his legs as though she were trying to console him. One never would have guessed that she could become quite vicious to visitors she didn't like.

"I thought you knew more about Fairies than I. Did you forget how big a secret they make of their names?" Alma went to her apothecary cabinet. Its drawers were filled with every remedy the Mirrorworld had to offer.

"I said the Red One's name countless times."

"And? Many things are different with the Dark One." Alma picked a root from one of the drawers. It looked like a pale spider with its legs drawn under its body. "She's more powerful than the others, but, unlike them, she doesn't live under the protective spell of their island. That makes her vulnerable. She cannot allow anyone to know her name. She probably hasn't even told it to her lover." She ground up the root in a pestle and poured the powder into a pouch. "How long have you been carrying that moth on your chest?"

Jacob pushed his hand under his shirt. He could barely feel the imprint. "The Red first saved my life with it."

Alma's smile was full of bitterness. "She saved you only so she could give you the death she had planned for you. Fairies love playing with life and death . . . and I'm sure her revenge will be all the sweeter for having made her mighty sister her unwitting accomplice." Alma offered Jacob the pouch with the powder. "Here. This is all I can do. Take a pinch of this whenever the pain comes. And it *will* come."

She filled a bowl with the cold water from the well behind her house so Jacob could wash off the Djinn's blood before it burnt into his skin. The water soon turned as gray as the ghost.

On Jacob's last birthday, he'd filled a sheet of paper with a list of the treasures he still wanted to find. He'd turned twenty-five. *You'll never get any older, Jacob.*

Twenty-five.

The towel Alma handed him smelled of mint. He didn't want to die. He loved his life. He didn't want a different one, just more of this.

"Can you tell me how it will happen?"

Alma pushed open the window to pour out the water. It was getting light. "The Dark One will use her sister's seal to reclaim her name. The moth on your heart will come alive. It won't be pleasant. Once it tears free from your skin and flies off, you will be dead. You may have a few more minutes, maybe an hour . . . but there can be no salvation." She quickly turned away. Alma hated for others to see her cry. "Jacob, I wish there was something I could do," she added quietly, "but the Fairies are more powerful than I. It comes with their immortality."

The cat looked at him. Jacob stroked her black fur. Nine lives. He always believed he'd have at least that many.

6. WHAT NOW?

Many of the graves in the cemetery behind Alma's house were from when large numbers of Trolls had migrated to Austry to escape the cold winters of their homeland. Their magical woodworking skills had earned most of them large fortunes, and a number of their grave markers were covered with gold. Jacob had no idea how long he'd been standing there, staring at a masterfully carved frieze depicting the deeds of a long-dead Troll. Around him, men, women, and children were going to work. Carts rumbled over the rough cobblestones in front of the cemetery gate. A dog barked at a junk man who was doing his rounds among the simple cottages. And Jacob just stood there and stared at the graves, unable to think.

He'd been so sure he would find a way to save himself. After all, there was nothing he couldn't find. He'd firmly believed that, ever since he became Chanute's apprentice. Since his thirteenth birthday, his only ambition had been to become the best treasure hunter of all time—it was the only name he'd wanted to make for himself. But now it seemed that the only things he could find were the ones other people desired. What were they to him? The glass slipper that brought never-ending love; the cudgel that slayed every foe; the goose that laid golden eggs; or the conch that let you listen to your enemies. He'd wanted to be the man who found them, nothing else. And he had found all of them. Yet as soon as he sought something for himself, he searched in vain. That's how it had been with his father, and that's how it was now with the magic that might save his life.

Rotten luck, Jacob.

He turned away from the grave markers and their gilded carvings. Most of them depicted tavern brawls or drinking games—the deeds that Trolls were proudest of were not always the honorable ones—yet some also showed the things the dead had crafted from wood: living puppets, singing tables, ladles you could leave to stir on their own. *What will your gravestone say about you, Jacob?* Jacob Reckless, born of another world, killed by the curse of a Fairy. He leaned down and propped up the tiny gravestone of a Heinzel.

Enough with the self-pity.

His brother had his skin back.

Suddenly, the wish that Will had never come through

the mirror became so overwhelming that it made him sick. *Find yourself an hourglass, Jacob. Turn back time; do not ride to the Fairy. Or just smash the mirror before Will can follow you.*

A woman opened the rusty gate in the cemetery wall. She placed a few flowering branches on a grave. Maybe it was the sight of her that made him think of Fox, for that was what she would do. Though it was more likely she'd put a bunch of wildflowers on his grave. Violets or primroses. Those were her favorites.

He turned around and walked toward the gate.

No. He would not search for an hourglass. Even if he turned back time, everything would just happen again, exactly the same way. And things had turned out well, at least for his brother.

Jacob opened the gate and looked up at the hill where the tower stood out against the morning sky. Should he go back and tell Will how things were standing with him?

No. Not yet.

First he had to find Fox.

It was to her he owed the truth, more than to anyone else.

7. IN VAIN

The Dark Fairy flinched. Jacob Reckless. She didn't want to see his face anymore. All the fear on it, the pain...she could feel death, drawn to him by her name, like a wound on his white skin.

This was not her revenge. Even though the pond that showed her his fear was the same one where he had turned her skin to bark.

Her red sister was probably seeing the same images, on the lake that had spawned them both. What was she hoping to gain from his death? That it would numb the pain of his betrayal, or heal her injured pride? Her red sister didn't know much about love.

The pond turned dark, like the sky it reflected, and then her face was all she saw trembling on the waves. They distorted it, as though her beauty was dissolving. So?

Kami'en no longer saw her anyway. All he saw was the swollen belly of his human wife.

The sounds of the city drifted into the nocturnal garden.

The Dark One turned around. She no longer wanted to see, not herself, nor her sister's unfaithful lover. At times she even longed for the leaves and the bark he'd put on her.

He looked nothing like his brother.

The moth that landed on her shoulder was like a sliver of night on her white skin. Yet even the night now belonged to the other. Kami'en now slept more and more often by the side of his doll-faced princess.

What did her sister want with all that fear and pain? They would never bring back the love.

8. CHANUTE

Along the road to Schwanstein, the workers were already crowding the gates of the weaving mill. Sirens were calling the morning shift to work, and as their wailing battled with the sound of church bells in the early morning, Jacob could barely calm the old horse Alma had lent him. The mare pricked her ears as though the Dragons had returned, but she was hearing only the modern times. The howling of sirens. The ticking of clocks. Machines wanted to run, and they ran fast.

Many of the men shivering in front of the gate looked up at Jacob as he rode past. The treasure hunter who always had some gold in his pocket, who came and went and did as he pleased, and who knew neither the toil nor the tedium that galled their lives. On any other day he would have understood the envy on their tired faces, yet on this morning Jacob would have gladly swapped with any one of them, even if that meant fourteen hours of hard labor for two copper coins an hour. Any life was better than death, wasn't it?

It was a ridiculously beautiful morning. The flushing trees, the fresh green...even the old mare's hide seemed to smell of spring. Pity. Dying in winter might have been a little less hard, but Jacob doubted he had that much time left.

A boy was sleeping by the side of the road, his bundle clutched to his chest so that the Thumblings didn't steal what little he owned. Jacob had not been much older when he first came to Schwanstein, but thanks to Alma he'd at least been better nourished.

The pointy gables had looked like one of the illustrations in his grandparents' yellowed fairy-tale books, and the coal soot in the air had smelled so much more exciting than the exhaust fumes in the other world. Everything had smelled of adventure: the leather harnesses on the carriages, even the horse manure on the grimy cobblestones and the butcher's scraps that were being picked over by some hungry Heinzel. A few months later he'd met Albert Chanute, and he'd lost his heart for good to the world behind the mirror.

The windows of The Ogre were still shuttered. Jacob tied Alma's horse in front of the tavern's door. Only the windows to his own room were open, just as he'd left them. Fox sometimes slept there when he was gone. He'd spent the whole journey lining up the words he wanted to say to her. But there was no version that made the truth sound any better.

Chanute's new cook was behind the counter, washing the previous night's dirty glasses. Chanute had hired the former soldier after too many tavern guests had complained about the food the owner cooked himself. Tobias Wenzel had lost his left leg in one of the battles with the Goyl, and he drank too much, but he was a very good cook.

"He's upstairs," he said as Jacob approached the bar. "Careful, though. He's got a toothache, and the Goyl just raised the taxes."

The Goyl had been ruling Austry for half a year, and nobody in Schwanstein suspected that the Reckless brothers had not been entirely blameless in this. Not that it would have interested anyone much, anyway. The men were back from the war (those who had survived it), and the Goyl were building new factories and roads, which was good for trade. Even the mayor was still the same. There were bombings and organized resistance in the capital, but most of the country had learned to live with the new masters. And the Empress's throne now belonged to her daughter, who was pregnant by her stone-skinned husband.

Chanute barked a grouchy "What?" when Jacob knocked

on his door. His chamber was crammed with even more memorabilia than The Ogre's taproom.

"Well, I never!" he growled. His hand was pressed to a swollen cheek. "This time I really thought you wouldn't come back." A toothache. Not something you wanted to have on this side of the mirror. Jacob had once had an infected tooth extracted in Vena. Fighting an Ogre took less courage.

"And?" Chanute scrutinized him through squinting eyes. "Did you find the bottle?"

"Yes."

"See? I told you it wouldn't be a problem." Chanute wiped a quill on his wooden hand and stared at the paper in front of him. He'd been writing his memoirs ever since some drunk patron told him he could make a fortune from them.

"Yes, I found it." Jacob went to the window. "But the blood didn't help."

Chanute put down his quill. He tried very hard not to look concerned, but he'd never been a good actor. "Damn," he muttered. "Never mind, though. You'll think of something else. What about the apple? The one in that sultan's cursed garden? You know the one!"

Jacob already had the answer on his tongue, but the old man looked worried, so he quickly swallowed the truth. Chanute probably would have ridden off himself to find a cure. Chanute had grown old. He wore his prosthetic arm less often now because it caused him too much pain. And his hearing had grown so weak that twice already he'd nearly run into a carriage in the market square. No. Jacob still felt those calloused hands on his skin from all the beatings the old man had given him, but he owed everything he'd achieved in this world to Albert Chanute and to what the old treasure hunter had taught him. He owed him a lie.

"Sure," Jacob said. "The apple. How could I forget?"

Chanute's ugly face stretched into a relieved smile. "There you go. You'll sort it out. And there's also always that well."

Jacob turned his back to him. He couldn't let Chanute see the truth on his face.

"Damn! I wish that Ogre had chewed off my head instead of my arm." Chanute held his hand to his cheek again. "You don't have any moor-root on you?" Eating moor-root numbed any pain, but it also made you feel for days as if you were being swarmed by will-o'-the-wisps. Jacob pulled the tin that contained his first-aid kit from his rucksack: moor-root, fever-haulm, a wound-dressing salve Alma had concocted for him, iodine, aspirin, and some antibiotics from the other world. Jacob fished out one of the roots and offered it to Chanute. The roots looked like shriveled grubs, and they tasted hideous.

"Where is Fox? Is she here?"

She'd been sensing for a while that something was wrong. But as long as there'd been hope, he'd found it easy to convince himself that it was best for her not to know the truth. He couldn't wait to see her.

Chanute shook his head as he put the root into his mouth. "She's been gone for weeks. The Dwarf wanted to hire you to get him a Man-Swan feather, and since you weren't around, Fox offered to get it for him. Don't look at me like that! She's more careful than you, and smarter than the two of us together. She got the feather, but the swan got her on the arm. Nothing to worry about. She's staying at the Dwarf's until it's fully healed. He bought himself some ramshackle castle with all the gold your tree's giving him. Fox left you the address."

He lifted the Ogre's jaw, which he used as a paperweight, and held out an envelope to Jacob. The crest on it was embossed in real gold. The tree that Jacob had paid to buy a way into the Goyl fortress had made Evenaugh Valiant a very rich Dwarf.

"Take her this if you're going to see her." Chanute pushed a package toward him. It was wrapped in silk. "Tell Fox it's from Ludovik Rensman. His father has the law offices behind the church. Ludovik is a good catch. You should have seen his face when I told him she was gone." He rolled his eyes. The last woman Chanute had been involved with was a rich widow from Schwanstein, but she hadn't been able to tolerate the wolf heads he'd hung in her parlor.

"Ahhh!" Relieved, Chanute dropped on his bed. "It tastes worse than a Witch's backside, but you can always count on moor-root!" He still slept on the same old tattered blanket he'd always snored on in the wilderness. Maybe it made him dream of his old adventures.

Gold leaf stuck to Jacob's fingers as he opened the envelope with Fox's letter. Her handwriting was much better than his, even though he had taught her to write in the first place. The letter contained nothing more than a brief greeting and directions.

He'd been gone a long time.

"Gallberg," he muttered. "That's more than ten days' ride from here. What does the Dwarf want with a castle in those godforsaken mountains?"

"How would I know?" Chanute's eyes were already glazing over. "Maybe he's trying to commune with Mother Nature? You know how sentimental those Dwarfs get with old age."

Maybe, but that was definitely not true for Evenaugh Valiant. The Dwarf must have discovered a ream of silver beneath the castle. Jacob tucked Fox's letter into his backpack. A Man-Swan feather...a dangerous assignment. But Chanute was right: Fox already knew just about as much about treasure hunting as he did.

"Why aren't you getting drunk?" Chanute began to babble as his hand swatted at imaginary will-o'-the-wisps. "That apple isn't going nowhere." He giggled at his own joke like a child. "And if that doesn't help, you can still work your way through my list."

Chanute's list. It hung in the taproom, under his old jagged saber: the list of those magical objects he'd sought and never found. Jacob knew it by heart, and there was nothing on it that would save him.

"Sure," he said. He put another moor-root next to Chanute's pillow. "Now sleep."

Ten days. The damn Dwarf. Jacob could only hope Alma was right and he had a little time left. If death managed to catch up with him before he saw Fox, he couldn't even wring Valiant's short neck for it.

9. GODFORSAKEN MOUNTAINS

Ten days' ride. After studying the route on Chanute's grimy map, Jacob decided to take the train. Valiant's castle was so inaccessible that any horse would have broken its legs on the way up there, but luckily the Dwarfs had spent the past years blasting tunnels with such abandon that there was actually a railroad station nearby.

The train took four days and nights. A long journey with death as your luggage. Every tunnel made breathing harder, as though someone were already shoveling dirt onto his chest. He tried to distract himself with the memoirs of a treasure hunter who'd scoured Varangia for firebirds and emerald nuts for his prince. Yet while Jacob's eyes were trying to hold on to the printed letters, his mind saw other images: the blood on his shirt after the Goyl shot through his heart; Valiant standing by a freshly dug grave; and, over and over again, the Red Fairy whispering the name of her sister. Four days...

A cable car took him from the sleepy railroad station where he'd stepped off the train up to the rocky peak on which Valiant's castle stood. Its high walls rose from the deep snow, and Jacob only cursed the Dwarf even more after having to pay a farmer one gold coin for the use of his snappish donkey.

The castle didn't make a very impressive sight. The left tower was collapsed, and the others were also nearly shot to pieces, yet when Valiant greeted Jacob by the decayed gates, the Dwarf wore as proud a grin as if he'd acquired the Empress's palace itself.

"Not bad, is it?" Valiant called out toward Jacob while a grouchy Dwarf servant took his bag. "I'm the lord of my castle! Yes, I know, the renovations are stagnating a little," he added as Jacob's eyes went over the hole-riddled towers. "Not easy getting materials up here. And also"—he shot a quick glance at the servant and lowered his voice—"the tree is giving me some trouble. It's taken to shedding nothing but slimy pollen."

"Really?" Jacob had to try hard not to show his pleasure. He'd never had much luck with the tree himself.

Valiant stroked the mustache he'd been growing. It sat on his upper lip like a caterpillar, but a Dwarf with any more beard than that would have been considered hopelessly old-fashioned. "And how are you? Hunting for something?" He leered at Jacob. "You're looking pale."

Great. *Pull yourself together, Jacob.* The last thing he needed was the Dwarf guessing how bad things stood with him.

"No. Feeling fine," Jacob answered. "I was looking for something, but I didn't find it." The best lie was always the one closest to the truth.

The servant who opened the castle door for them was a human. No Dwarf could have reached the handle, and of course nothing showed off Valiant's wealth better than a human servant. While the man took Jacob's snow-encrusted coat, Valiant named the price of every piece of furniture in the drafty entrance hall. They were, without exception, made for humans. Dwarfs were prone to ignoring their own size. But Jacob had no time for Mauretanian vases or tapestries depicting the enthronement of the last Dwarf King.

"She's upstairs," Valiant said as he finally noticed Jacob's impatience. "I had a doctor look at her yesterday, even though she would have none of it. You two spend too much time together. She's already just as bullheaded as you. Mind you, she did bring me a gorgeous feather. You couldn't have gotten me a better one yourself."

⁂

Valiant had put up Fox in the best-preserved tower of his castle. She was asleep when Jacob entered her room—on a bed that would have been big for a Dwarf but that was barely long enough for her. She'd been lucky. The swan had only given her a flesh wound. Jacob picked up a bloody shirt from the floor next to the bed. It had once been his. Fox had learned from Clara that men's clothes could be much more practical.

Jacob pulled the blanket over her bandaged shoulder. She'd changed so much in the past months. There wasn't much left of the girl who'd first shown him her human form nearly five years ago. The vixen made her age so fast that he had to keep warning her not to shift too often. One day soon she was going to have to choose between the fur and the chance of a long human life. He'd always believed he'd be there when she made that decision, but now it didn't look as though he would.

He brushed the red hair from her forehead. A feather lay on the nightstand next to the bed. Jacob picked it up and smiled. She'd kept one for herself. Just as Chanute had taught him: "Whatever you find for a client, always make sure you keep some of it for yourself." It was a flawless specimen. Jacob had never seen a more beautiful Man-Swan feather. The easiest way to get one was to steal it from the nest, but even that was dangerous. Man-Swans were very combative. Unbearable sorrow had turned them into swans, and only a blood relative could release them and give them back their human form. Jacob had once nearly paid with his life for finding the feathered son of a baker's wife. Anything a Man-Swan feather touched disappeared immediately and reappeared only when the feather was put down again. Chanute had transported many treasures that way. It didn't always work, though. Some things got lost along the way.

"Don't even think about it. That feather's mine." Sleep was clinging to Fox's eyes. She flinched as she propped herself up on her injured arm.

Jacob returned the feather to the nightstand. "Since when do you go treasure hunting without me?" *I missed you*, he wanted to add, but her eyes were cold, as they always were when he'd been gone too long.

"It wasn't a difficult job. And I was tired of waiting."

She'd become a woman without his really noticing. In his eyes she'd always been beautiful, even when she was the scrawny little thing that only reluctantly picked the burrs from her hair. Beautiful like all wild and free things. But now she wore the vixen's beauty on her human skin.

"You're still shifting too much," he said. "If you don't watch it, you'll soon end up older than I."

She pushed the blanket off her. "And?" She was wearing her fur dress. She always wore it in her sleep, for fear someone might steal it off her. "Stop worrying about me all the time. You never used to do that." *Yes, Jacob, what are you doing? You'll see; she'll get along just fine without you.* Only that he wouldn't see.

From his backpack he pulled the package Chanute had given him. "You never told me you had a rich suitor in Schwanstein."

Fox opened the paper and smiled. It was a shawl. She stroked the green velvet and put it next to the feather.

"What about you?" She gave him an inquiring look. "Did you find what you were looking for?"

"Yes and no."

"What does that mean?" She pulled the sleeve over her bandaged shoulder. "Will you now finally tell me what you're looking for?"

Spit it out, Jacob. You want to tell her. She's the only one you want to tell. He'd missed her so much. And he was tired of hiding his fear.

He unbuttoned his shirt.

"I was looking for a cure."

The moth's red outline looked as though someone had traced it with fresh blood.

Fox took a deep breath. "What does it mean?" Her voice sounded even more gravelly than usual.

She read the answer on his face.

"So that was the price." She was trying to sound composed. "I knew your brother didn't just get his skin back for free." Her eyes filled with tears. The vixen's eyes. Brown, like tarnished gold. She couldn't remember whether they were the color she'd been born with or whether they'd come with the fur. "Which Fairy was it?"

Tell her something, Jacob. Something to console her. But what?

He stepped closer and wiped the tears from her cheeks. "You always have to pay with your life for crossing one of them. And I managed to get on the wrong side of two of them."

Fox wrapped her arms around him.

"How long?" she whispered.

"I don't know. I don't know anything anymore." It was only half a lie. Jacob buried his face in her hair. He didn't want to think anymore. What he wanted were the times when he'd go searching for lost magic with her, when he'd lived believing he was immortal, that he could own a whole world. He wanted to dream of what he'd do when he became as old as Chanute, of buying a castle in Etruria, of fishing for pirate gold in the White Sea. Childish dreams. He'd hoped he'd still be dreaming them on his hundredth birthday. Instead, he was going to have to think about which world he wanted to be buried in.

There was a knock on the door.

Valiant didn't wait for a reply. Fox quickly stepped out of Jacob's embrace as the Dwarf came through the door. That probably just fired up Valiant's imagination even more, but Jacob wasn't planning on telling him the real reason for her tears.

"How about some dinner?" Valiant gave them a sleazy smile. "We're having mountain goat. I know it doesn't sound like much, but I have a cook from Vena who can turn even a donkey into a feast." He nodded at Fox. "Ask her if you don't believe me."

Fox forced a smile on her lips. "You really should try the mountain goat," she said.

10. DIGGING DEEP

Valiant's dining hall was as drafty as the rest of his castle, and Fox was grateful for the jacket Jacob put over her shoulders. Of course, it didn't help against the fear, and neither did the fireplace, which Valiant's servants kept feeding with damp wood.

The table, the chairs, the plates, the glasses, even the cutlery was human-sized, but the chairs had been fitted with steps so that the Dwarf could get on them without the embarrassment of having to be lifted up by a servant. Valiant was in a formidable mood and, luckily for Jacob, he assumed that Jacob's silence was merely a result of his being tired after days of traveling.

You're going to lose him, Fox.

The thought clamped around her heart like an iron ring.

She was ashamed for thinking he'd stayed away so long because of Clara. She should have known him better. But she'd been so tired—all that helpless love, the longing for him. It had felt good to turn her back on Schwanstein, to be by herself for a while, to feel her own strength. To be happy without Jacob. That much love was not good, especially if it was for someone who thought that emotion was nothing but a short-lived rush that was best slept off or forgotten. Several times she'd toyed with the idea of never returning to Schwanstein. But now everything had changed. How could she leave him now?

Valiant asked how she liked the mountain goat.

Yes, how? Even the meat on her plate made her think of death. Fox poked her fork into the meat and looked at Jacob. His face looked so young even when he was scared. And so vulnerable.

You promised to protect him, her heart whispered over and over. *Back when he freed you from that trap.* And? Promises were nothing when measured against death, which was like a hungry wolf in the forest. Death had claimed her father so soon after her birth that she couldn't even remember his face. And three years later, her only sister had also become its prey.

But not Jacob!

Please, not Jacob.

Valiant filled his plate for the third time, challenging Jacob to a bet that the Goyl would attack Lotharaine next, and not Albion. Who cared about that, or whether the

Empress's daughter was really going to give the Goyl King a child? Outside, the wind was howling like a ravenous creature, and the night was as cold as her fear.

"Yes, I know. I myself voted against it in the Dwarf council!" Valiant had drunk too much, which only made him more talkative. And of course the toothpick he was using to pry the goat meat from his teeth was made of gold-plated wood. "Digging that deep was greedy, but these days there's nothing more profitable than iron ore." The Dwarf waited until the servants had cleared the plates, then he leaned over the table toward Jacob. "They never intended to dig all the way under the Dead City. Those idiots only realized it once they hit that door."

"Really?" Jacob mumbled.

He'd barely eaten anything.

Fox threw the bones from her plate to the two mastiffs lounging in front of the fireplace. The vixen in her knew how good they tasted. Valiant didn't like the hounds. They were so big that he topped them only by a hand's breadth, but they had come with the castle.

"They should have dumped a lorry full of rubble in front of it and forgotten about it." Valiant dropped the toothpick into a servant's hand. "You know I will always get behind a good deal, but who are they ever going to sell the thing to? Provided they ever manage to get inside."

Jacob poured himself what dismal rest Valiant had left of the wine. "Inside what?"

He'd obviously been paying as little attention as Fox.

"Inside the tomb! What do you think I've been talking about all this time? Didn't she tell you anything?" Valiant shot a dismayed look at Fox. He'd probably told the story a dozen times. But she'd been preoccupied and had soon grown tired of listening to endless lectures on Dwarf history and Dwarf politics. One of the dogs came trotting over and sniffed her hand. Maybe he smelled the vixen beneath the human skin.

Valiant lowered his voice. "It's the tomb of that King with the unpronounceable name. Kissmount or something. You know... the Witch Slayer."

Jacob emptied his glass. "Guismond?"

"Yes. Whatever. All tip-top secret." Valiant waved at one of his servants and pointed at the empty wine bottle. "What do you think this is?" the Dwarf barked at him. "Bring a new one.

"A lot of winemakers now spike their red wine with elven dust!" he whispered to Jacob while the servant rushed off. "I wonder why they didn't come up with that earlier. They keep Elves in cages. Hundreds of cages. Phenomenal!" He raised his glass toward Jacob. "To modern times!"

Jacob stared into his glass as though he could see the captured Elves swimming in it.

"Has the tomb been looted?" His voice sounded as casual as though he was inquiring about Valiant's tailor.

The Dwarf shrugged. "You know the Dwarf council. Always penny-pinching in the wrong places. Of all the treasure hunters they sent in there, not one has come out. And I say: just as well! Who'd want a weapon that can put an end to every war with one single shot? How's that good business?"

The Dwarf babbled on, and Fox could feel Jacob's eyes seeking hers. She wasn't sure what she saw in them: hope, or the fear of it. The Witch Slayer. She tried to recall what treasure hunters associated with that name, but all she could remember was that at least one headstone in every Witches' graveyard cursed his name.

"Can you take me to the tomb?"

Valiant was still raving about the excellent profits to be made in a war, but Jacob's question immediately shut him up. The Dwarf's mouth twisted into a smirk that exposed the gold teeth beneath his ridiculous mustache. "I knew it! You nearly had me convinced that you actually have a conscience. But you're all about business, too, aren't you?"

Jacob took the glass from Valiant's hand. "Can you take me there? I need an answer before you drink yourself out of this chair."

Valiant wrestled the glass back from him. "Who're you going to sell it to? The Goyl? Or will you grace a human potentate with your help, for a change? To make up for what you did for the stone-skins in the cathedral? Jacob Reckless, the treasure hunter who decides who gets to rule the world."

Jacob's face turned a little paler. He didn't like to remember the Blood Wedding and the role he'd played in it. His voice was hoarse with anger as he answered the Dwarf.

"I wasn't helping the Goyl; I was helping my brother."

Valiant rolled his eyes. "Sure. I know. You're a saint! Still, you should be glad the Goyl are keeping mum about who saved their stone skins at the Blood Wedding. They're more despised than ever. Those attacks in Vena are nothing compared to the trouble they're having in their northern provinces. There are daily attacks in Prussia and Holstein, and Albion is supplying the rebels with weapons. The world is a powder keg. Business with explosives and munitions has never been better. Fairy lilies, Witch needles..." The Dwarf grunted disdainfully. "Those are yesterday's commodities. Weapons—that's the future. And Dwarf hands build very handy bombs." His smile was rapturous, as though he were looking straight into paradise.

"What is in that tomb?" Fox looked at Jacob.

Valiant rubbed his napkin over his wine-soaked mustache. "The deadliest crossbow ever built." His tongue was getting heavier by the minute. Fox was having trouble understanding his slurred words. "One bolt into the chest of a general reduces his entire army to a pile of corpses. Not bad... not even the Goyl have anything like it."

Fox gave Jacob a puzzled look. What was this about? Was he going to squander what time he had left hunting for treasure?

"My share's fifty percent," said Valiant. "No—sixty. Or you can forget about it."

"I'll give you sixty-five," Jacob replied. "If we leave tomorrow morning."

11. TOGETHER

Elven dust and red wine. When Jacob took Fox to her room, Valiant was sitting in his oversize chair, his feet on his oversize table in his ridiculously oversize and crumbling castle, and he was talking to the paintings on the walls. They were all chasing their childhood dreams.

Fox's shoulder was aching, though she tried to hide it. Jacob found a sleepy servant down in the kitchen who heated a bowl of water for him. A Man-Swan's beak was not the cleanest of weapons, and so he also dressed the wound with some of the salve Alma had mixed for him.

Bites, knife wounds, burnt fingers... like him, Fox had probably lost count of how often they'd patched each other up over the years. To Jacob, her body was as familiar as his own, but as he touched her now he caught himself feeling self-conscious. She belonged to him like his own shadow. Younger sister, best friend. Jacob loved her so much that the other kind of love seemed like something he had to protect her from: the hungry game that was best ended before it got too serious. He wished he'd observed that rule himself with the Fairy.

Fox didn't say a word while he put a fresh bandage on her shoulder. Her silence used to be an expression of the wordless familiarity that connected them. But not this time. Jacob opened the window and poured the bloody water into the night. A few snowflakes drifted in.

Fox stepped to his side and caught them with her hand.

"What's your plan? Are you going to trade the Dark Fairy the crossbow for your life?" She leaned out the window and inhaled the cold air as though it might drive away her fear.

"A few hundred thousand dead, for my own skin? Since when do you think so little of me?"

She looked at him. "You would have done it for your brother. For him you would have done anything. Why not for yourself?"

Yes, why not, Jacob? Because he'd grown up with the certainty that Will's life was more precious than his own? Did it matter?

"I'm not planning to trade or sell the crossbow," he said. "The Witch Slayer used it three times. The first bolt killed an Albian general who took fifty thousand men with him to his death. The second killed the commanding general of Lotharaine and seventy thousand soldiers.

A few weeks later, Guismond had himself crowned King of both kingdoms."

Fox held out her hand into the falling snow.

"I think I know the rest. I'd forgotten that story. It always frightened me." The flakes planted crystal flowers on her skin. "One day"—she spoke the words into the night as though snatching them from the darkness—"Guismond's youngest son was dying. Gahrumet. I think that was his name. A Witch had poisoned him to take revenge on his father for killing hundreds of her sisters. His son was in such terrible pain that Guismond couldn't bear it anymore. He shot a bolt from the crossbow into his son's heart, but Gahrumet didn't die; he was healed. They say he hated his father later on, but he lived for many years." She closed the window and turned around. "It's nothing but a fairy tale, Jacob."

"And? Everything in this world sounds like a fairy tale. I'm dying for having uttered the name of a Fairy!" He stepped toward her and brushed the snowflakes from her hair. "Why shouldn't there be a weapon that brings death when it's yielded in hatred but gives life when it's used out of love?"

Fox shook her head. "No."

They both knew who was going to have to shoot the bolt.

Jacob took her hands. "You heard Valiant: Nobody came out of the tomb alive. You know we can make it. Or shall we just wait together for death to catch up with me?"

What could she say to that?

12. LIVING SHADOWS

Looking at the valley where the Dwarfs had found the tomb, no one would have guessed that it had once been famous for its flowering slopes. Mirror-blossoms could make even the ugliest face irresistible for a few hours. But the sale of iron ore made riches faster.

The valley lay in the steep mountains of Helvetia, a little under a day's ride from Valiant's castle. The country was so small that it spent a lot of effort and gold on appeasing its mighty neighbors. It had once been part of Lotharaine but had won its independence with the help of an army of mercenary Giants. And since a Stilt had stolen the last King's only heir, a parliament had been ruling the tiny country, keeping peace with the Goyl by allowing them to move troops through its mountains. When Jacob had asked what price the Dwarfs had paid for the permission to scour iron ore from Helvetia's blooming valleys, Valiant merely replied with an indulgent smile. The country needed tunnels if it wanted to keep up with its neighbors' railroads and fast highways. And nobody could blast holes through mountains the way the Dwarfs could.

Jacob's boots sank into deep snow as he climbed out of Valiant's carriage. The cowering huts around the mine's buildings did not show any of the wealth that was being scraped out of the earth, and the smoke rising from the chimneys scribbled a dirty future into the sky.

A crowd of Dwarf children were waiting by the cages that would take them down into the belly of the earth. They could crawl deeper into the tunnels than any human could, and they weren't afraid of the mine-gnomes that made mining behind the mirror even more dangerous than in the other world.

"Is that what you call good business these days?" Jacob asked the Dwarf as they passed the pale urchins. "Children scraping for ore?"

"And? They'd be doing it without me," Valiant retorted blankly. "Life's an ugly affair."

Fox eyed the women who were unloading the tenders as they came up from the tunnels loaded with ore. She whispered to the Dwarf: "Did you hear about the mine owner in Austry whose workers sold him to mine-gnomes?"

Valiant gave Jacob an alarmed look. "You should keep a close eye on her," he hissed. He disgustedly shoved back one of the children who'd been stretching a little hand toward his wolf-fur coat. "She already sounds like one of those anarchists who smear their slogans on every factory wall."

"I liked you better when you were less of an honorable businessman," Jacob said. He helped the little tyke back to his feet. "Go on, show us the tomb before this cold drives someone to kill you for your coat."

❧

A rusty chain-link fence, surrounding three buildings with copper roofs to keep out the mountain wraiths... rail tracks, smokestacks, a drainage ditch...nothing here gave away that the Dwarfs had found anything else but ore.

Fox looked around. "Can we see the Dead City from here?"

Valiant shook his head and pointed westward. "Unless you can see through that mountain there."

The Witch Slayer had built his city after Albion, Austry, and Lotharaine had been united by the crossbow, and Helvetia had become the center of his gigantic empire. Silberthur was what he named it, but now it was only known as the Dead City, for all its people had disappeared the day Guismond died. There were stories that their faces still looked out from the crumbling walls like fossils. Jacob had never seen the ruins with his own eyes, for even Chanute had always steered clear of the Dead City. Even after four centuries, it was still considered unhealthy to walk its deserted streets.

Valiant opened the gate in the rusty fence. The chain was loose, and there were footprints leading through the gray snow toward the mine elevator.

"I thought you closed the mine," Fox said.

Valiant shrugged. "A foreman comes by here every now and then to check on things. They sent in the last treasure hunter about a week ago." His face showed a satisfied grin. "And I've got three ounces of gold on the idiot never coming out again."

Jacob pushed open the gate. "Three ounces of gold? Not bad. And what did you bet on me?"

Valiant's smile turned as sweet as elven honey. "How stupid do you think I am?"

Fox shone one of the mine lamps into the pit with the elevator cages hanging above. Valiant looked around furtively, but none of the men who guarded the workers on the other side of the fence had taken any notice of them. "Right. Once more, just to avoid any trouble," the Dwarf whispered. "I only brought you here to consult with Jacob."

Fox climbed into the swaying cage. "You've told us so often, your dogs can probably repeat it by now. But I forgot the next part. We steal the crossbow, and you get dragged off by mine-gnomes before you can stop us, right? Or is it we who drag you off after we steal the crossbow?"

"Very funny!" Valiant growled. "You obviously have no idea of the risk I am taking here! The Dwarf council will have me shot should they ever suspect anything. And nobody outside the council knows of this tomb."

"Nobody except the council members, their secretaries, their wives, the mine workers who found the tomb..." Jacob lifted the Dwarf into the cage. "I wouldn't count on your secret being safe. And about you getting shot? Nonsense! You'd talk your way out of anything. I should know. I wanted to shoot you a dozen times already."

❦

The cage descended endlessly into the deep. When it touched firm ground, the light of their lamps exposed the roughly hewn walls of a chamber with a number of tunnels branching from it into the darkness. Wooden beams supported the low ceiling. Pickaxes and shovels leaned against piles of rubble. Laid out on a flat stone were the usual offerings for the mine-gnomes: coffee powder, scraps of leather, coins. If the mine-gnomes disappeared, the miners could breathe easy. If they stayed, one had to expect sharp cries in the dark, rock falls, and spindly fingers stabbing into ears and eyes.

Valiant picked a tunnel leading west, toward where, high above them, the Dead City lay nestled among the mountains. At some point, they reached a crude drill that in Jacob's world would have stood in a museum but that Valiant proudly pointed out as the pinnacle of Dwarf engineering. The drill had exposed an arched entrance in the rock face and, beyond it, a broad staircase leading steeply down, lined with burnt-out torches. The metal clamps were covered with soot. At the bottom, the steps opened into a wide chamber. A few forlorn gas lamps created a pale pool of light on the stone floor, and in the middle of it lay a sleeping Giantling. He wore the uniform of the Dwarf army and lumbered to his feet only after Valiant kicked him hard in the side.

"You call this standing guard?" the Dwarf yelled at him. "Why are we paying you thrice what we'd pay any human guard?"

The Giantling picked up his helmet and anxiously snapped to attention, even though Valiant barely reached his kneecaps.

"No incidents to report!" he mumbled with a sleepy tongue. "I have orders not to—"

"Yes, yes, I know!" Valiant interrupted him impatiently. "But I have brought an expert who traveled here from afar. This is his certificate of authority."

He pulled out an envelope so small that the Giantling's gross fingers could barely take hold of it. Valiant gave Jacob a wink while the guard looked helplessly at the tiny thing.

"What?" Valiant barked at him. "Look at me! I know to you all Dwarfs look alike, but you should at least try to remember my face. I'm the owner of this mine."

The Giantling suppressed a yawn and adjusted his helmet. Then he pushed the tiny envelope into his uniform and stepped aside.

His huge body revealed a door, framed by a frieze of

skulls. The slits above the noses clearly identified them all as the skulls of Witches.

Guismond the Witch Slayer. Chanute had once told his story to Jacob in some filthy tavern. He'd been so drunk, he'd barely managed to pronounce the name. "Guismond, yes, there's no man ever knew more about witchcraft. You know what they called him?" Jacob thought he could hear his own voice answer, the high voice of a boy: "The Witch Slayer." That name resonated with everything that had made him follow the old treasure hunter in the first place: danger, mystery, the promise of enchanted treasure to gild his life. His life, which on the other side of the mirror had tasted only of boredom and yearning.

Already Chanute didn't have to explain to Jacob how Guismond had earned his byname. No human on either side of the mirror was ever born with magical powers, but in this world there was a way to acquire them. It was a sinister way, and Guismond had not been the first one to follow it: One had to drink the blood of a Witch when it was still warm. "How many Witches did he kill?" Chanute had refilled his glass with the acrid liquor that had cost him one arm and almost his mind. "How would I know? Hundreds, thousands. Nobody counted them. He's supposed to have drunk a cup of blood every week."

Jacob examined what was left of the crest on the gold-plated door: a crowned wolf, a cup of blood, and there was the crossbow....

Behind them, the Giantling was leaning against the wall.

Fox eyed him pensively. "Your guard's suspiciously sleepy," she said to Valiant.

"Elven dust," the Dwarf replied. "These big idiots always have some in their pockets. Can't get them off that stuff."

Jacob listened, but all he could hear was the Giantling's heavy breathing. Elven dust? Maybe. He pulled a pair of gloves from his bag. Fox had given them to him after a tomb's protective spell had nearly cost him his fingers. Like all shape-shifters, she was immune to such spells.

Valiant looked uneasily at Jacob. "Why the gloves?"

"You don't need them, as long as you don't touch anything. Are you sure you want to come with us?"

"Sure." The Dwarf didn't sound too convinced, but there was serious loot to be had, and that outweighed even his fear of a dead Warlock.

Jacob exchanged a quick glance with Fox, then he put his hand against the crowned wolf. It didn't take much force to open the door. He could feel that others had already done it before him.

The scent wafting toward them was barely noticeable. Tomb-cloves were a simple method to protect the dead from the greed of the living. Their poisonous pollen could survive over centuries. Jacob held Valiant back. Fox took a pouch from her belt. The seeds she offered were barely bigger than the pips of an apple.

"Eat!" she told Valiant, who eyed her suspiciously.

"Unless you want to look like a moldy loaf of bread after a few steps."

"Watch your step!" Jacob whispered. "Don't touch anything and keep your mouth shut, especially if something asks you a question."

"A question? Something?" Valiant popped the seeds into his mouth. His wide eyes stared into the dark tunnel in front of them.

The walls were lined with burial niches. Fox grabbed the Dwarf just before he stumbled into one of the mummified corpses.

"Why do you think they were buried here?" she hissed at him while Jacob pushed the mummy back into its niche. "This is the tomb of a Warlock. I'm sure they are easily woken."

The man they found a few steps in had been dead only a few days. The tomb-cloves had covered him with a carpet of deadly green blossoms. The whispers began as soon as Fox stepped over his corpse.

"Who are you?" The voices came from the burial niches.

Valiant froze, but Jacob pushed him along. "Don't answer!" he breathed. "They are harmless as long as you don't reply."

The mummies wore weapons belts and armored breastplates over their rotting clothes. Most of Guismond's knights had followed him to his death, though if historic records were to be believed, few of them had done so voluntarily.

They found five more fresh corpses: the treasure hunters who hadn't returned. In addition to being covered in tomb-cloves, some of them also showed sword wounds. And the dead whispered all around them. Jacob had never seen so much fear on Valiant's cunning face. Even Chanute used to grow a little paler in tombs than in other places. Jacob was usually not affected. In his experience, the places of the living were much more dangerous. Yet as he walked past the burial niches, he could feel the moth like a cold hand on his chest. *Look at them, Jacob. Soon you'll look like them. The leatherlike skin, teeth exposed, and spiders nesting where your eyes used to be.* His breathing grew labored, and Fox noticed. She silently pushed past him and walked ahead, as though that could draw death's attention from him. The tunnel took a bend. The scent of the tomb-cloves was now so heavy that it clung to their skin like perfume, and then they came upon the curtain of corpses. Twelve mummified knights hanging from the ceiling, blocking their path, but one of the bodies ended beneath the rib cage. Someone had hacked off the rest with a saber. Not the most elegant way to get through a corpse curtain, but it did the trick. Maybe the Dwarfs hadn't hired only amateurs after all.

Valiant cursed disgustedly, though he was the only one who could walk upright under the mutilated corpse. The reward came just beyond the curtain: another door, inlaid with the golden likeness of a man.

The crown identified him as a King, and the cat-fur coat showed him to be a Warlock. On his shoulder sat a Gold-

Raven, the symbol of limitless wealth, and his feet stood in seven-league boots to symbolize the vastness of his empire. He was holding the crossbow in his right hand. Supposedly, the Witch Slayer had sold his soul to the Devil to get it. Stories. However, Jacob had already seen too many of them proved true on this side of the mirror to dismiss this one.

The door with Guismond's portrait stood open a crack. The treasure hunter whose corpse they found just inside had probably thought himself at the goal of his quest, and he had obviously forgotten that traps were usually left invitingly open. His body was uninjured, as far as Jacob could make out, but the horror on the pallid face spoke clearly. Fox peered over Jacob's shoulder.

"A shadow-spell?" she whispered.

Yes, probably. Jacob put his lamp on the floor and drew his knife. The resin he rubbed on the blade brought the smell of tree bark into the stale air. Behind him, Fox was shifting shape. Sometimes the vixen's senses were more useful than an additional pistol. *Forget this is about your life, Jacob. Enjoy the hunt.* There it was again, the familiar thrill mixed with fear and the desire to conquer it. Irresistible. He'd never had to explain that to Fox. She slipped through the door ahead of him.

The tomb was enormous.

The frescoes on the walls still glowed in vibrant color, thanks to the centuries of darkness that had cocooned them since their creation. They were depictions of hell, rendered so masterfully they made one feel the fire on the skin. One of the walls showed Guismond himself riding through the flames in the armor of a knight. The Devil he was riding toward didn't have much in common with the Devil Jacob knew from the other side of the mirror. Except for the horns, he looked like an ordinary human dressed in the clothes of a wealthy merchant of the time. The frescoes on the ceiling showed a battlefield, the spirits of the dead departing from their lifeless bodies. The columns that supported the ceiling were hewn from the same black marble as the sarcophagus standing in the center of the tomb. Four knights knelt around it, each leaning on a sword as black as its wings.

Jacob heard Valiant behind him, muttering a disappointed curse.

The sarcophagus was open.

They were too late.

Jacob looked at Fox. It wasn't easy to tell what she was feeling when she was wearing her fur, but through the years he'd learned to read her. The despair he saw in her eyes was even worse than his own. The hope that he might yet save himself hadn't lasted very long.

The pieces of the sarcophagus's smashed lid were scattered among the kneeling knights. Between them lay the guard against whom Jacob had prepared his knife: Guismond's shadow, faceless, and as tall as though it had been cast onto the flagstones by the evening sun. The pool of blood around it indicated that the shadow had been brought to life by a spell only Witches could perform—or those who drank their blood. A shadow like that would kill for his master as silently as he had followed him through life. Jacob leaned over the black corpse. A knife stuck out of the shadow's neck. It smelled of resin. The mistake of pulling it out would immediately bring the shadow back to life. Whoever had killed him knew that. Jacob stood up. For an instant he thought he could hear steps between the columns, but when he spun around, he saw only the vixen behind him.

"Elven dust?" She gave Valiant a scornful look.

Jacob leaned down to her. "Is he still here?"

She lifted her nose to sniff, and shook her head.

Damn! Jacob tucked his knife back into his belt. Not many treasure hunters knew how to get past a Giantling, or what resin to use to defeat a dead man's shadow. They usually avoided each other on the hunt, but Jacob knew them all, at least by name and reputation. Which one had done this?

"Damned bastard!" Valiant was standing on the debris of the lid, staring down into the open sarcophagus. "He even took the crown!" he clamored. "And who told him to cut out the heart? Are those graybeards in the council now trading with Dark Witches?"

The corpse in the sarcophagus had not decayed at all, but it was missing the right hand and the head, and there was a hole in the chest where the heart had once beaten. The wound, like the ones on the arm and neck, had been sealed with gold. This meant that the body had been buried like this. Valiant reached for the scepter next to the body, but Jacob pulled him back. "You see those leaves he's lying on? They're hexed. Why else do you think he looks so fresh?"

He looked around. The tomb's floor was laid with green marble, and strips of alabaster ran like the dial of a compass from each of the four columns to the sarcophagus. Jacob picked up the mine lamp Valiant had put down next to the sarcophagus, and walked along one of the alabaster strips. It was inlaid with letters cast in white gold. They were barely visible in the white stone.

HOUBIT WESTARHALP

Every treasure hunter knew that language. Fox watched Jacob as he paced off the second and third strips.

HANDU SUNDARHALP

HERZE OSTARHALP

The inscriptions were easy to translate.

THE HEAD IN THE WEST

THE HAND IN THE SOUTH

THE HEART IN THE EAST

Maybe the hunt wasn't over yet.

Jacob went to the fourth strip. Its inscription was much longer than the others:

NIUWAN ZISAMANE BESIZZANT HWAZ
THERO EINAR BIEGEROT.

FIBORGAN HWAR SI ALLIU BIGANNUN.

"What've you got those gloves for? Take that scepter off him!" Valiant clamored. "And he's still got his signet ring on the other hand."

Jacob ignored the Dwarf. He was staring at the letters.

ONLY TOGETHER MAY THEY POSSESS
WHAT EACH DESIRES.

CONCEALED WHERE THEY ALL BEGAN.

No. The other one hadn't found the crossbow. Not yet.

"Jacob?" Fox was still wearing her fur.

Steps...

Barely audible.

Jacob lifted the lantern. He thought he could make out a shape between the columns, dark like the stone it was trying to hide behind. Before Jacob could stop her, Fox was dashing toward it. The vixen's compulsion to hunt made her careless. Jacob ran after her, cursing himself for not having given the tomb a thorough search. He heard Fox yelp, and nearly stumbled over her. She was lying between the columns, already shifting shape as she struggled to her feet. That instant, the Dwarf cried out for help behind them.

The man who shoved Valiant out of his way was wearing clothes of lizard skin over his own, which was as black as onyx. A Goyl. Just as Jacob took aim, Valiant staggered into his line of sight. The Goyl gave him a little taunting wave before pulling the tomb's door shut behind him. Valiant screamed, stumbling toward the door. He clawed his fingers into the frieze of skulls and yanked at the door so hard that the bones cracked under his hands.

"Why didn't you shoot him?" he yelled. "Perishing inside a tomb! Is that your idea of a good death?"

Fox's forehead was bleeding. Jacob brushed away her hair, but luckily the gash wasn't deep.

"Why didn't you smell him?"

"He didn't have a scent." She was angry. Angry with herself and with the stranger who'd gotten the better of her.

No scent. Jacob looked toward the shadow and the resin-covered knife stuck in its neck. The Goyl knew his trade.

"We're going to starve!" Valiant looked around like a rat caught in a trap.

Jacob went back to the alabaster strips and looked at the letters. "Suffocation is more likely."

Fox came to his side. "I'll find his trail," she whispered. "I promise."

But Jacob shook his head. "Forget about the Goyl. He doesn't have the crossbow." He was still looking at the letters. The words were the trail they'd have to follow. *A dead man*... not yet.

"What the devil are you two doing there?" Valiant's voice filled the tomb with Dwarf panic. "Do something! This can't be the first tomb you've gotten trapped in!"

The Dwarf was right about that. Jacob returned to the sarcophagus and, with his gloved hand, reached for the scepter. The architects of royal tombs often believed that their master was only sleeping and that he would wake up again one day. So they always left him with a key, even though it seemed even more unlikely than usual that a headless King would awaken and need it.

The door swung open as soon as Jacob wrote Guismond's name in the air with the scepter. Relieved, Valiant immediately stumbled through the door, but Jacob carefully stepped over the dead treasure hunter in front of it and listened. The hanging knights were swaying gently, and he thought he could hear steps in the distance.

Valiant growled, "How did the Goyl know about the tomb? If the Dwarf council hired him behind my back, then—"

Jacob interrupted him: "Nonsense. If he was hired by the council, then why would he have gone through the trouble to drug the Giantling? No." He took the jacket off the corpse by the door. "They call him the Bastard, and he's the only Goyl who's any good at treasure hunting."

"The Bastard... of course!" Valiant rubbed his face. The cold sweat of fear still clung to his forehead. "He likes to cut off his competitors' fingers."

"Fingers, tongues, noses . . . he's got quite a reputation." Jacob wrapped the scepter in the dead hunter's jacket.

"Don't you think it's only right to let me have that?" Valiant purred, smiling his most innocent smile. "For all the hospitality and my invaluable assistance?"

"Really?" Fox took the bundle with the scepter from Jacob's hand. "You still owe me half my fee for the feather, but we'll give you a little discount if you get us horses and provisions."

"Provisions? What for?" The innocence disappeared immediately. It had looked as out of place on Valiant's face as a rash, anyway.

"Go back to the tomb if you really want to know. I'm sure the Bastard was not as blind as you."

Jacob stepped to the tomb's door and inspected Guismond's golden portrait. He could only hope the Goyl wouldn't beat him at solving the Witch Slayer's riddle.

Perfect. As if having to race against death wasn't enough.

13. THE OTHER ONE

The hall where Crookback received them was so dark that Nerron could barely see his own hands. Any light from the high windows was swallowed by dark blue brocade curtains, and the candles burning next to the throne were low enough so as not to hurt a Goyl's eyes. The King of Lotharaine was a very smart man. He'd done much to ensure the comfort of his stone-skinned visitors, for a guest who is comfortable is also less vigilant.

Charles de Lotharaine had fixed his crooked spine years ago with a corset of hexed fish bones, yet the moniker had stuck, very much to Crookback's vexation, for he was a vain man. There were rumors that he had the gray in his beard refined with powdered silver and that he was very unhappy about the furrows in his face, which, thanks to his love for tobacco and good wine, grew ever deeper into his skin.

The onyx lord kept his head bowed as he approached the King. The court of Lotharaine had shunned the old-fashioned ceremonial the onyx loved so much. No kneeling, no uniforms, except on official occasions. Crookback had put the ermine robes and brocade jackets of his ancestors in mothballs. He loved suits of black silk, tailored in the newest fashion, and he was very partial to the slender tobacco sticks the Albian ambassador had brought to the Lotharainian court. He was holding one between his fingers even now. Cigarettes. To Nerron's ears, the name sounded like a stinging insect. Rumor had it that Crookback liked to hide behind the smoke so nobody could read his face. Charles de Lotharaine was a crowned cat pretending to be vegetarian while the tail of a mouse hung from its mouth.

The gray haze surrounding the King was so thick that the onyx lord suppressed a cough before he stopped an adequate distance from the throne.

"Your Majesty." The old onyx's voice betrayed none of the disgust he felt toward humans. His dark face hid his hatred as effortlessly as it concealed his insatiable hunger for power. Nia'sny. His name meant "darkness" in their language, and it described his appearance as adequately as his heart. He'd given Nerron strict instructions to remain invisible until called upon. Nothing easier than that. A bastard was practiced at being a shadow.

"Your treasure hunter was unsuccessful, just like the men the Dwarfs hired. I am very disappointed." Crookback waved at a servant, who was standing behind the throne with an ashtray. "You were obviously exaggerating when you praised his skills."

Nerron wanted to stub the tobacco stick out on Crookback's forehead. *Calm, Bastard. He is a King.* But he'd never been good at controlling his emotions, and he wasn't sure whether that was a skill he ever wanted to acquire.

"He managed to open the tomb, just as I promised. And he will find the crossbow! May I remind you that if it hadn't been for our spies, you never would have learned about the tomb? The Dwarfs like to think they are, like us, at home in the deep, yet the womb of the earth has no secrets a Goyl won't discover."

No. The old lord could not mask the arrogance in his voice. He was onyx. The most noble skin a Goyl could have—until a carnelian Goyl had declared himself King. The onyx hated Kami'en with a passion that nearly melted their stone skins. In order to depose him, they had revealed the positions of Goyl fortresses, and they had filled Crookback's wishing sack, into which he made his enemies disappear, with so many of Kami'en's spies that it had finally refused to take any more. It was a miracle that the King of the Goyl was still alive. Nerron knew of a dozen assassins the onyx had sent out, but Kami'en's bodyguards were the best in their trade, even now that the Jade Goyl was gone. And he also still had the Dark Fairy on his side.

The old onyx turned around.

Finally.

The Bastard's cue.

Nerron moved out from where he'd been standing behind the pillar, and stepped toward the throne. The armrest was supposedly carved from the jaw of a Giant. No matter... stories like that were just another attempt to prove that humans had always been the rulers of this world. The history books of the Goyl knew better. In contrast to Elves, Fairies, and Witches, humans were infants. A salamander had more history than they did.

Crookback eyed him so disparagingly that Nerron imagined ramming the bones of the Lotharainian King's hexed corset between his ribs. Not that the Goyl wasn't used to such looks. He did not possess what would have shielded him from them—neither beauty nor a noble heritage. When he was a child, he told himself that a Fairy had cut him from the marble of the night and that the green speckles in his skin were the traces of the leaves she'd used for it.

The malachite that dappled his skin came from his mother. Officially, onyx only ever paired with onyx, but many of them had a strong appetite for anything that wasn't theirs. They had different expectations for their bastards than for their legitimate sons, and Nerron had caught on to that very early. A bastard had to be like the snake, crawling and wriggling in order to survive. But he had also mastered the other virtues of the snake: the art of invisibility, deception, the ability to strike from the shadows. Nerron bowed his head as low as the old onyx had done. To the left and right of Crookback stood two of his bodyguards. Their eyes were as cold as the ponds from which they had come. The King of Lotharaine entrusted his protection to Watermen. Their skin was nearly as impenetrable as Goyl skin, and their six eyes were perfect for the task.

"So?" The look Crookback gave Nerron was not much warmer than that of his Watermen. "If you really did make it into the tomb, then why are you not handing me the crossbow right now?"

The powerful were all the same, whether their skin was as soft as a human's or made of stone. They thrived on power, and they always wanted more, more, more.

"It never was there." Nerron's voice did not sound like velvet, like Crookback's or the onyx lord's. His was like the rough garments of a servant.

"Is that so? And where is it?"

"In Guismond's palace, in the Dead City."

Crookback flicked a speck of ash from his black trousers. "Don't talk nonsense. There is no more palace. It disappeared on the day of his death, together with ten thousand of his subjects. My nannies told me this story already. After all, he's one of my ancestors. And you have nothing else than this treasure-hunter yarn for me?"

Oh, the rage of the Goyl. Nerron felt it like oil broiling in his veins. In Lotharaine, they used to feed their Kings to the Dragons if they couldn't get the winter to end. *They'd probably like your smoked flesh, Your Crooked Majesty.*

Nerron!

He forced a smile. "Guismond's corpse was missing the heart, the head, and a hand. Which means he used an old Witch spell. You take three parts of the body and hide them in far-apart places, and whatever you wish to conceal will disappear. It has to be hiding his vanished palace. The clues in the tomb were clear. Could there be a safer hiding place? It will reappear as soon as the corpse is put together again."

There. The eyes behind those heavy lids now showed a little more respect.

"And? Do you know where to look for the three missing pieces?"

"It's my business to find things that were lost."

And he would find them. Unless Jacob Reckless beat him to it. Of all the treasure hunters of this world, it had to be Jacob Reckless who'd appeared in the tomb! And Nerron had even taken care of Guismond's shadow for him. If Reckless had shown up just a couple of hours later, the inscriptions on the floor would have been illegible. He'd already had the bottle of acid in his hand. Annoying. Very annoying.

Their paths had nearly crossed a few times before. Reckless had beaten Nerron to the glass slipper. Back then his face had been on the front page of every newspaper. Nerron had cut the pictures out and burnt them, in the hope of putting some bad luck on his rival. But Jacob Reckless had only grown more famous, and if you asked anyone the name of the world's best treasure hunter, his was the name you'd hear.

For now, Nerron.

This time he was going to beat Jacob Reckless.

Crookback's eyes were as dark as peacock jasper. The world was a mouse hole, and he was the cat sitting in front of it, waiting for his prey. *Let him believe you're nothing but another mouse, Nerron.* It was the only way the powerful would let you go on the hunt by yourself.

Crookback whispered something into the ear of one of his Watermen. It was always stunning to see how nimble they were on dry land.

A shaft of light fell into the dark room as the Waterman exited through one of the high doors. Charles de Lotharaine inspected his fingernails as though he was comparing them to the claws of a Goyl. "That crossbow," he said, "would give Lotharaine the weapon with which we could finally check the warmongering of your species. So I am sure you will understand that I can't leave the search for it to a Goyl alone."

Goyl. He pronounced the word as they all did with their soft lips: as though they had something rotten on their tongues, something that needed to be retched up and spat out.

Nia'sny's face turned into a mask of black stone. There was nothing for which the onyx hated Kami'en more than for forcing them to ally themselves to the Doughskins.

The mere scent of a human made Nia'sny nauseous. Yet his voice gave none of that away.

"Certainly, Your Majesty," he said with perfectly pitched reverence. "And whom do you have in mind to support his quest?"

The Waterman returned. He whispered something to his master before resuming his position next to the throne. Charles de Lotharaine's soft forehead creased into a frown. Human skin was as defenseless as a worm wriggling in the sun. It was a wonder they didn't dry out.

"I am told that my son Louis is out hunting." The King's voice betrayed his anger as well as his reluctant love. "But we shall have everything ready for him to depart as soon as he returns. This quest shall be an excellent training for his future responsibilities as my successor."

Louis of Lotharaine. Nerron bowed his head. What was he hunting? His mother's maids? Nerron had heard a lot of things about this crown prince, none of them very good.

"I cannot possibly guarantee his safety." Nerron's voice barely concealed his anger. He worked alone. Always alone. And this was the most important hunt of his life.

The old onyx shot him a warning glance.

What? Whoever found the crossbow would be the best—forever. Power. Land. Gold.... There were many things for which the onyx and Crookback would have sold their wives and children. The Bastard wanted only one thing: to be the best in his trade. There was nothing on or below the earth he desired more. He was never going to find the Lost Palace, or the crossbow, if he had to babysit a prince along the way. Especially with the competition he was facing. Nerron hadn't told the onyx about Reckless. It was far too personal. They would learn about him when the hunt was over and Reckless had lost.

Crookback's eyes had turned as cold as the skin of his Watermen. Kings assumed that the company of their sons was nothing if not an undeserved honor, even if they didn't think much of their offspring themselves.

"You will guarantee his safety. I once had my best huntsman shot because he returned Louis to me from a hunt with a graze to his arm." The crowned cat was showing its claws. "I will send my best bodyguard along with Louis."

Perfect.

Maybe the prince could also bring his tailor. Or the servant who procured his elven dust. Louis was known to have a weakness for the stuff.

Nerron bowed his head and pictured the tomb-cloves from Guismond's grave spreading green mold on Crookback's skin.

And he would still beat Jacob Reckless.

14. JUST A CARD

He ran and ran. He had no feet anymore, but he stumbled on, on bloody stumps, through a forest that was darker than the one in which he'd faced the Tailor. Always following the man who he knew was his father, even though that man never turned around. Sometimes he just wanted to catch up with him; sometimes he wanted to kill him. It was a dark forest.

"Jacob! Wake up!"

He shot up. His shirt was so wet with sweat that he shivered in the cold night air. At first he had no idea where he was. He wasn't even sure which world he was in, until he saw the two moons through the branches above and Fox kneeling next to him.

Flanders, Jacob. Soggy meadows, windmills. Broad rivers. The bedbugs had eaten them alive at the last inn, so they'd decided to sleep outside. They were on their way to the coast to catch a ferry to Albion.

"Everything all right?" Fox looked worried.

"Yes. Just a bad dream." An owl screeched in the oak above them. Fox was still looking anxious. *Of course, Jacob. Now that she knows the truth, every sneeze sounds like dying.* He took her hand and placed it over his heart. "Feel it? Strong and regular. Maybe Fairy curses only work on those who were born in this world."

Fox attempted a smile, but it wasn't very convincing. They both knew what she was thinking: His brother had also not been born into this world, and yet he'd grown a skin of jade.

They'd left the mine four days earlier and had not rested since. Jacob was quite certain he knew what the inscriptions on the tomb floor meant, but the only proof would be holding the crossbow in his hands. They'd both seen the mutilated corpse and had immediately realized that head, hand, and heart were missing to make something disappear. It was a common enough spell. But it was the alabaster words that had revealed to them that it wasn't merely the crossbow that Guismond had made vanish. Fox and Jacob had turned and twisted the words every which way, until they were convinced it could mean only one thing.

The Witch Slayer had three children. His eldest son, Feirefis (or Firefist, as he later called himself), had claimed the crown of Albion while his father lay on his deathbed.

Albion lay to the west. His younger brother, Gahrumet, the one who'd supposedly been saved by the crossbow, was made King of Lotharaine, the southern part of Guismond's empire. Guismond's only daughter, Orgeluse, had founded the dynasty of Austrian emperors by marrying one of her father's knights and bearing him two sons. Austry lay to the east.

THE HEAD IN THE WEST

THE HAND IN THE SOUTH

THE HEART IN THE EAST

Feirefis had received his father's head. Gahrumet the hand. Orgeluse his heart.

ONLY TOGETHER MAY THEY POSSESS
WHAT EACH DESIRES.

It wasn't hard to guess that this was the crossbow.

CONCEALED WHERE THEY ALL BEGAN.

Guismond's children had all been born in the palace above the Dead City, which he'd built and which had been nothing but an empty plain since the day of his death. To conceal the crossbow, the Witch Slayer had made an entire palace disappear, and he'd left macabre clues as a riddle to his children. If the madness to which he'd succumbed in the final years of his life had convinced him this would sow peace among his offspring, then that wish was not to be granted. They'd hated one another as strongly as they'd hated their father. Some stories claimed that their mother was a Witch and that she was the reason for Guismond's deep hatred of all Witches. Others claimed the Witch had been his second wife and that she had revealed to him the path by which he became a Warlock. Whichever was true, Guismond's children had warred with one another without ever solving their father's riddle, and it was quite likely that they'd never even read the inscriptions in his tomb. But the Bastard had, and Jacob had no illusions about whether the Goyl had also deciphered them. The only question left now was who'd be faster finding the three macabre keys.

Head, hand, heart. West, south, east.

Fox had suggested they make the longest journey first. That meant Albion. With any luck, they would be there in two days, provided the ferries were running. This early in the year, storms often kept them in port. *Two, three months. Maybe less.* It was going to be tight, even if the Bastard didn't manage to find any of Guismond's gruesome parting gifts before they did.

Fox pulled the fur dress from her saddlebag.

"Whom do you think the Bastard's working for?"

She still shifted nearly every night, even though she realized herself how quickly the fur stole her years. But he couldn't presume to say anything about it. He'd never stopped going through the mirror—not for his mother's sake, nor for Will's—and he definitely wouldn't have done it in exchange for a less perilous and potentially longer life. When the heart craved something so forcefully, then reason became nothing but helpless observer. The heart, the soul, whatever it was...

"He usually works for the onyx, as far as I know," Jacob said. He pulled the tin plate that had saved him from many hungry nights from his saddlebag. "His father is one of their highest lords. If the Bastard finds the crossbow, then I guess the Goyl will soon have a new King."

Jacob rubbed his sleeve over the plate, and immediately it filled with bread and cheese. He wasn't really hungry, but he was afraid of falling back asleep and finding himself in that forest again, stumbling endlessly after his father. He never really acknowledged the thought, but it was always present, like an annoying whisper: *You'll actually die without ever having seen him again, Jacob.*

Fox had swapped her human clothes for the fur dress. It kept growing with her, like a second skin, and it still had the same silky sheen as on the day Jacob had seen it the first time.

"Jacob..."

"What?" He could barely keep his eyes open.

"Lie down. We've not had a rest in days. There won't be a ferry until the morning, anyway."

She was right. He reached for his backpack. He still had some sleeping pills from the other world somewhere. If he remembered right, they were from his mother's nightstand. For years she hadn't been able to fall asleep without them. A card dropped out of the backpack onto the frost-covered grass, and he picked it up. NOREBO JOHANN EARLKING. The odd stranger who'd vouched for him at the auction and been so interested in his family's heirlooms.

Fox shifted shape and licked her fur, as though she had to clean the human scent off. She quickly snuggled up to him the way she used to when there was still a child hiding under that fur. They were both children when he'd found her in the trap. Jacob stroked her pointy ears. So beautiful. In both bodies.

"Be careful. The hunters are already out stalking." As if he really needed to remind her.

She snapped at his hand—the vixen's way of showing her love—and then she disappeared between the trees, as silently as if her paws weren't carrying any weight at all.

Jacob stared at the card he was still holding in his hand. He'd meant to ask Will to find out more about his strange benefactor. Where was his head? *Yes, Jacob, where? Death is breathing down your neck. Norebo Johann Earlking will have to wait, no matter how much you disliked the color of his eyes.*

He threw the card back into the grass. *Two, three*

months...Two days on the ferry, and who knew how long it would take them to find the head in Albion. Then back to Lotharaine and Austry for the hand and the heart. Hundreds of miles, with death hard on his heels. Maybe his last chance really had come along too late.

The wind blew through his sweat-soaked shirt and brought the stench of a nearby swamp. The two moons disappeared behind a dark cloud, and for an instant the world around him became so dark and strange that it seemed to want to remind him it wasn't his home. *Where would you like to die, Jacob? Here or there?*

A few wilted leaves blew into the fire—and Earlking's card went with them.

It didn't burn.

The leaves it had landed on crumbled to ashes, but the card was as unblemished as when Earlking had first put it into his hand. Jacob drew his saber and used its blade to flick the card out of the flames. The paper was lily-white.

A magical object.

How had it come to the other world? *Stupid question, Jacob. How did the Djinn get there?* But who had brought the card through the mirror, and had Earlking been aware of what he was putting in his hand? Too many questions, and Jacob had the nasty feeling that he wouldn't like the answers.

He turned the card around. The back side had filled up with words, and when he brushed his finger over them, it came away with a trace of ink on it.

Good evening, Jacob,

I regret that we met only so briefly, but I hope we shall have more opportunities in the future. Maybe I can be helpful sometime with the task you're facing. Not for purely unselfish reasons, of course, but I promise you my price will be affordable.

The writing disappeared as soon as Jacob had read the last word, and the card again showed nothing but Earl-king's printed name.

Grass-green eyes.

A Leprechaun? Or one of the Gilches that the Witches up in Suoma molded from clay and awakened with their laughter? But in Chicago? No. This had to be some cheap trick, the prank of an old man who'd happened upon a magical object. Jacob was tempted to throw the card away, but then he wrapped it in his gold handkerchief and tucked it into his pocket. Fox was right. He needed sleep. But as soon as he lay down next to the dying fire, he heard shots, and then he could only lie there and listen to the darkness until, hours later, he heard the vixen's paws and Fox a little later as she spread her blanket next to his.

She was soon breathing deeply and steadily, in a sound sleep. And as he felt her warmth next to him, Jacob forgot the dreams awaiting him and the card that brought him words from the other world, and he finally fell asleep.

15. A SPIDER'S REPORT

Carriages and racehorses. Charles, King of Lotharaine, collected both, just as he collected the portraits of actresses. Nerron was sitting in a carriage painted in the national colors of Lotharaine with diamond-studded doors. Crookback clearly had better taste when it came to selecting his suits. Nerron had spent a lot of time searching for a place that was watched neither by the King's spies nor by those of the onyx—for what he was trying to find out was neither of their business.

Where was Jacob Reckless? That little trick with the door couldn't have kept him in the tomb for long. The golden rule of treasure hunting (and of life in general) was never to underestimate the skills of your competition.

So—where was he?

The medallion Nerron pulled out from under his lizard

shirt was one of his most prized possessions. Out of it crawled a spider he'd stolen when he was five—an act that had then saved his life. The onyx invited all bastard children between their fifth and seventh birthdays to a palace on the shores of an underground lake. The lake was so deep that the moray eels in it supposedly grew three hundred feet long. At the time, Nerron couldn't understand why his mother wasn't happy about the honor of the invitation. She had barely spoken a word while he'd admired, open-mouthed, all the wonders of that underground palace. Until then, home had been a hole in a wall, with a niche for him to sleep in and a table on which his mother cut the malachite that resembled her skin. But Nerron was neither tall nor beautiful, both of which the onyx valued very much, and his mother had been very aware what that meant: The onyx lords were miserly with their blood, and bastards who didn't pass muster were drowned in the lake. A five-year-old, however, who managed to steal a valuable reconnaissance tool while he awaited his sentence in the library, definitely showed promise.

The spider was sleepy, but she began to dance as soon as Nerron poked his claw into her pale belly.

Twin spiders.

Rare and very valuable.

It had taken him months to comprehend what the eight legs wrote on his palm. Their silent dance was not unlike that of bees pointing their kin toward the best flowers. The spider, however, didn't report what she had seen but what her twin sister was seeing right then. And that twin sister had crept into Jacob Reckless's clothes in Guismond's tomb.

The head. The hand. The heart. What was he going to search for first?

The spider wrote what appeared to be fragments of a conversation: . . . *an old friend . . . no idea . . . long time ago . . . two, three hours from the ferry . . .*

The ferry. That could only mean Albion, and hence the west. Perfect. The mere thought of the Great Channel made Nerron nauseous. The Goyl's wet fear. If the head was in Albion, then Reckless was doing him a favor by finding it and bringing it back to the mainland.

The spider danced on, but her twin sister was awfully chatty and babbled whatever she picked up. Who the hell cared what color sky Reckless was looking at, or whether he was sleeping outside or in a hotel? *Come on!* Where exactly was Reckless headed? Did he already know where he was going to look for the hand and the heart? But all the spider danced was the menu of some Flandrian tavern. Damn. If only those beasts were a little smarter.

"Are you the Goyl who'll be accompanying the prince?"

The voice was barely more than a damp whisper.

A Waterman was standing outside the carriage window. He was as scaly as the lizards that had given their skin for Nerron's clothes. His six eyes were colorless, like the water the stable hands had left out for Crookback's horses.

"The Goyl accompanying the prince." Wonderful . . .

"The prince is waiting." Every word from a Waterman's mouth sounded like a threat.

Fine. The prince could wait until he had moss growing from his royal armpits. Nerron let the spider slip back into the medallion.

Little waves rippled across the Waterman's uniform as he walked ahead of Nerron across the courtyard—as though his body was protesting against the clothes. Back in their slimy native ponds, they wore only a covering of algae and mud, and they didn't keep very clean on land, either. There were few creatures more repulsive to a Goyl than a Waterman.

The prince and a Waterman. "Lizard-crap!" Nerron spat out, which immediately earned him a reproving look from the colorless eyes. At least Watermen were known for not being very talkative, and as royal bodyguards they hopefully also refrained from dragging every halfway-decent-looking human girl into the nearest pond.

The prince is waiting.

Nerron cursed Crookback with every step that brought him closer to the King's offspring. Louis of Lotharaine was waiting for them in front of the stables where his father kept his racing horses. His traveling clothes were going to attract every highwayman within a hundred miles. It was all Nerron could do to hope that they'd soon get filthy and that Thumblings would pick off all the diamond buttons. The crown prince of Lotharaine ate too well, that much was obvious, and his unkempt white-blond curls hung into his pudgy face as though his servants had only just dragged him out of bed. Louis had even brought one of them with him: The man barely reached up to his master's chest, and his stiff black frock coat made him look like a bug. He scrutinized Nerron with a look full of surprise, as though he'd never seen a Goyl before. Nerron stared back at him. *Whatever you heard about us, Bug Man—it's all true.*

A Waterman, a prince, and a bug... Jacob Reckless would be rubbing his hands in glee.

"So, what exactly are we looking for?" Louis sounded grouchy, just as one would expect from a spoiled royal brat. He had only just celebrated his seventeenth birthday, but his innocent face was deceptive. Apparently not much was safe from him—not his mother's maids nor her silver, which he regularly fenced to pay his gambling debts and his tailors.

"Your father has informed me that this is about Guismond the Witch Slayer, Your Highness." The Bug sounded as though his metal spectacles were pinching his nose. "You may remember our lessons on your ancestry. Guismond's youngest son is your ancestor. Not in direct line"—the direct line had their heads chopped off by the people of Lotharaine—"but through an illegitimate cousin." The Bug closed his mouth and brushed back his thin hair, no doubt congratulating himself on the extent of his learning.

A teacher. The Crookback was sending a teacher along with his son on a treasure hunt. Nerron wished himself far, far away. Even hell sounded attractive right now.

Louis gave a bored shrug. He was staring at a scullery maid crossing the yard. Hopefully, he was just as stupid as he looked. It would make keeping secrets from him easier. "Could we at least take a carriage?" he asked. "The one that doesn't need horses? My father had it brought over from Albion."

Ignore him, Nerron. Otherwise you'll have killed him by the second day.

"We depart in an hour," he said to the Waterman. "On horseback," he added with a glance at Louis. "But first I have to take a closer look at your tutor." He grabbed the Bug by his lapels and pulled him away, which, just as he'd expected, did not interest his pupil in the slightest.

"Arsene Lelou. I will not solely be traveling in my capacity as Louis's tutor!" the Bug stammered. "His father charged me with recording his son's adventures for posterity. We have interest from some newspapers...."

Nerron silenced him with one click of his tongue. The onyx were excellent teachers when it came to intimidating subordinates.

"I assume you know a few things about the Witch Slayer's youngest son?"

The Bug's beardless mouth showed a hint of a condescending smile. "I know everything about him. But of course I shall not share my knowledge about the royal family with any..."

"Any what? Listen to me, Arsene Lelou!" Nerron whispered to him. "Killing you would be easier than breaking a Thumbling's neck, and I think we both know your pupil wouldn't raise a finger to save you. Maybe you'd like to reconsider sharing your knowledge with me?" Nerron gave him a smile any wolf would have envied.

Arsene Lelou went so red, he looked as if he were turning into carnelian.

"What would you like to know?" he said with a twang. He was trying to be a brave Bug. "I can give you the dates and places of his most important victories. I have memorized large portions of his correspondence with his sister, Orgeluse, concerning the Austrian line of succession. Then there are the armistice treaties with his brother, which Feirefis breached several times. And his—"

Nerron impatiently waved all that aside. "Do you know anything about a severed hand the Witch Slayer left to Gahrumet?"

Make my day, Bug. Say yes.

But Lelou just pursed his lips disgustedly. "Pardon me, but I never heard about such a grotesque heirloom. Would that be all?"

His receding chin trembled—whether from fear or indignation wasn't clear. He gave a stiff bow and made to return to the others. But after two steps, he suddenly stopped.

"Mind you, there was an incident"—Lelou adjusted his spectacles with such a haughty face that Nerron nearly swiped them off his nose—"involving the favorite servant of Gahrumet's grandson. He was choked to death by a severed hand."

Bull's-eye.

"What happened to that hand?"

Lelou brushed down his waistcoat. It was embroidered all over with tiny royal Lotharainian crests. "Gahrumet's grandson had it sentenced to death. In a regular trial."

"Meaning?"

"It was delivered to the executioner, quartered, and then buried at its victim's feet."

"Where?"

"In the graveyard of the abbey of Fontevaud."

Fontevaud. A six-day ride—if the princeling didn't have to take too many breaks. Reckless was going to be in Albion at least that long.

The head in the west. The hand in the south.

Nerron smiled. He was certain he'd have the hand before Reckless could even as much as find out where the head was. This was easier than expected. Maybe having an educated Bug along for the hunt wasn't such a bad thing. Nerron was no friend of books, unlike Reckless, who he'd heard knew every library between the White Sea and Iceland and who spent weeks poring over old manuscripts before embarking on a treasure hunt. No, that was not Nerron's style. He preferred to pick up his trails in prisons, in taverns, or by the side of the road. Yet a smart Bug like this... Nerron slapped Lelou's delicate shoulders.

"Not bad, Arsene," he said. "You just considerably increased your chances of making it through this whole venture alive."

Lelou looked unsure whether this statement made him feel more at ease. Louis was still standing by the stables, arguing with the Waterman over how many horses they'd need to transport his travel gear.

"Not a word about our little conversation!" Nerron whispered to Lelou as they walked back to them. "And you should forget about the newspapers. No matter how much Louis loves to see his face on the front pages. I want to see every syllable you write about his adventures. And I will, of course, expect my own role to be recounted in the most flattering terms."

16. THE HEAD IN THE WEST

Most of the ships that anchored in the harbor of Dunkerk still used wind to navigate the oceans of the Mirrorworld. The wind blowing through their riggings flavored the air with what they'd brought back from the remote corners of this world: silverpepper, whisperwood, exotic creatures for the royal zoos of Lotharaine and Flanders... the list was endless. The ferries that crossed over to Albion, however, already had smokestacks instead of masts, and they proudly blew their dirty steam at the wind. Even so, the ferry Jacob and Fox boarded still needed more than three days to cross the Grand Channel that separated Albion from the mainland. The sea was rough, and the captain repeatedly ordered the engines throttled back to watch out for a giant squid that had pulled another ferry into the deep a few weeks earlier.

Jacob felt time was trickling through his fingers like sand. Fox stood by the railing and stared across the frothy waves as though she could will the coast to appear. Jacob's dislike for ships was almost as big as the Goyl's, but Fox was standing on the swaying planks as if she'd been born on them. She was the daughter of a fisherman; she'd told Jacob at least that much about her roots. Fox was even more reluctant to speak about the past than he was. All he knew was that she'd been born in a village in northern Lotharaine, that her father had died shortly after her birth, that her mother had married again, and that she had three stepbrothers.

The chalk cliffs that finally emerged from the gray waves on the fourth day were the exact equivalent of those in Jacob's world, except that there were seven Kings and one Queen looking out from Albion's white cliffs. Each of the effigies was big enough to be seen for miles on a clear day. The salty air gnawed at the faces as relentlessly as exhaust fumes attacked statues in the other world. The face of the current King was covered by scaffolds, on which a dozen stonemasons were busily freshening up the mustache that had earned him his nickname: the Walrus.

Fox eyed Albion's coast like enemy territory. In theaters there, shape-shifters were forced onstage to shift into donkeys or dogs while audiences howled along. And in its green hills, foxes were hunted with such abandon that Jacob had made her promise not to wear her fur on the island.

Albion. Chanute claimed there used to be more magical creatures there than in Austry and Lotharaine combined. Now, however, factories were shooting up from Albion's soggy meadows even faster than in Schwanstein. As Jacob steered his horse past the waiting carts on the ferry docks, he looked up at the surrounding hills and imagined he could already see the cities that were sprouting all over them on the other side of the mirror. For now, however, those hills were still covered with the enchanted forests that had always explained his own heart to him so much better than the streets and parks where he and Will had grown up. Jacob had often wondered whether his father had felt the same—whether it was the wildness of this world that had beguiled him, or just the fact that here he could pass off the inventions of another world as his own.

They took one of the less traveled roads leading northwest. It wound past fields and meadows that let you forget that Thumblings and Stilts were now as rare in Albion as Hobs, the Albian version of Heinzel, or the scaly-skinned waterhorses that only a few years earlier could still be seen grazing on the banks of every river. Albion's last Gold-Raven now stared out of a glass cabinet in a museum; the only Unicorns left were the ones on the regal crest; and in Londra, the ancient capital, Albion was now building palaces to celebrate the new magic: science and engineering. But Jacob was headed for another town.

Pendragon lay less than forty miles inland. It had nearly as many towers as Londra and was so old that its age was the subject of endless debates. Pendragon was also home to Albion's most famous university. The town's center was marked by a big stone, polished to a sheen by the touch of countless hands. Even Fox briefly reined in her horse to touch it before riding on. This was the stone from which Arthur Pendragon supposedly had pulled a magic sword and had—long before Guismond's time—made himself King of Albion. In this world, there was no King shrouded in a web of truth and myth so thick as Arthur was. The story went that he'd been born to a Fairy and that his father had been an Alderelf, one of the legendary immortals who later made enemies of the Fairies and were destroyed by them so thoroughly that there was no trace of them to be found. Arthur had not just named the town Pendragon; he'd also endowed the famous university himself and had imbued its foundations with so much magic that the old walls still glowed bright enough to render any street lighting unnecessary.

The buildings stood behind the same wrought-iron fence that had surrounded them for centuries, like the remnants of an enchanted city. The gate was closed at sunset. Fox listened into the night before she swung herself over. The guards patrolling the grounds had been performing this duty so long, they should have been granted honorable retirement years before. All they were guarding, anyway, were a myriad of old books and the scent of the past, which mingled reluctantly with the perfume of progress.

Towers and gables of pale gray stone. Dark windows reflecting the light of the two moons. Jacob loved Pendragon's labyrinth of learning. He'd spent endless hours in the Great Library, listening to lectures about Leprechauns or the dialects of Lothian Witches in the old auditoriums; practiced a few new (and surprisingly dirty) feints in the fencing hall; and realized time and time again how much more eagerly he wanted to understand this world than the one he'd been born into. All the years he'd spent finding lost magical treasures made him feel like the guardian of a past the people of this world no longer valued.

Most windows in the history department were dark, like those of the other buildings. Only one, on the second floor, was still illuminated. Robert Lewis Dunbar loved working late into the night.

He didn't even lift his head when Jacob walked into his office. Dunbar's desk was so littered with books that it was difficult to spot him behind them all, and Jacob wondered what century he'd lost himself in this time.

Being a talented historian as well as the son of a purebred Fir Darrig was not easy. It meant he'd had to be more brilliant than any human colleague, but that had never been a problem for Dunbar, in spite of the rat's tail and the very hairy skin his father had passed on to him. Dunbar had not inherited the pointy snout, luckily—his mother's beauty had given him a halfway-decent face. Most Fir Darrigs came from Eire, Albion's belligerent neighbor island. They were able to make themselves invisible, and they had—although few people knew this about them—photographic memories.

"Jacob!" Dunbar still hadn't lifted his head. He turned the page he'd been reading and scratched his hairy cheek. "'Tis one of the mysteries of this universe why the regents of our university employ night guards who are as blind as they are deaf. Luckily, your pirate's gait is unmistakable. And I of course did not hear you, Fox!" He looked up and gave her a smile. "By Pendragon's sword, the vixen is all grown up! And you still endure his company?" He closed the book and gave Jacob a taunting look. "What are we looking for this time? A Habitrot shirt? A gryphon hoof? You should consider a change of career. Lightbulbs, batteries, aspirin—those are the words that bring magic to these times."

Jacob approached the desk and scanned the books Dunbar disappeared into every night, like a paper landscape. "*The History of Mauretania*... *Flying Carpets*... *The Realm of the Magic Lamp*. Are you going on a trip?"

"Maybe." Dunbar caught a fly and popped it into his mouth. A Fir Darrig could never resist a passing insect. "What's a historian to do in a country that only believes in the future? What good will come of it if we allow our lives to be run by cogwheels and pistons?"

Jacob opened one of the books and looked at the illustration of a flying carpet carrying two horses and their riders. "Believe me, this is just the beginning."

Dunbar gave Fox a wink. "He so loves playing prophet, doesn't he? But whenever I ask him exactly what he sees in the future, he evades the question."

"One day I may tell you." There was nobody whom Jacob would have more liked to tell about the other world than Dunbar. Whenever he saw his friend, Jacob pictured his myopic eyes going wide at the sight of a skyscraper or a jet plane. Although Dunbar was critical of progress in this world, Jacob didn't know anyone who had as much knowledge and wisdom and still possessed the insatiable curiosity of a child.

"You still haven't answered me." Dunbar took a pile of books and carried them to the dark bookshelves that lined every wall of his study with printed knowledge. "What are you looking for?"

Jacob put the book on flying carpets back on the desk. He wished he were on the hunt for some harmless magical object like that.

"I am looking for the head of Guismond the Witch Slayer."

Dunbar stopped so abruptly that one of the books slipped from his arms. He bent down and picked it up.

"You'd have to find his tomb first." His voice sounded unusually cold.

"I found it. Guismond's corpse is missing its head, its heart, and its right hand. I believe he had his head sent to Albion. To his eldest son."

Dunbar pushed the books into the shelf, one after

another, without saying a word. Then he turned around and leaned back against their leather spines. Jacob had never seen such hostility in Dunbar's face. He was wearing his usual long coat, which hid his rat's tail. Only its bright red color gave away the Fir Darrig. They never wore any other color.

"This is about the crossbow, isn't it? I know I'm in your debt, but I will not help you with this."

A few years back, Jacob had rescued Dunbar from a bunch of drunken soldiers who'd thought it amusing to set his fur on fire. "I'm not here to call in a debt. But I have to find the crossbow."

"For whom?" Dunbar's fur stood on end, like that of an angry dog. "Farmers are still plowing up bones from the old battlefields. Have you traded your conscience for a sack of gold? Do you, at least every now and then, think about what you're doing? You treasure hunters turn the magic of this world into a commodity only the powerful can afford."

"Jacob is not going to sell the crossbow!"

Dunbar ignored Fox's protest. He returned to his desk and leafed absentmindedly through his notes. "I know nothing about the head," he said without looking at Jacob. "And I don't want to know anything. I'm sure you'll ask others, but I am hopeful nobody can give you the answer you're looking for. Luckily, this country has lost its interest in black magic. There's at least that to be said for progress. And now you must excuse me. I have to give a lecture tomorrow on Albion's role in the slave trade. Another sad chapter."

He sat down behind his desk and opened one of the books in front of him.

Fox shot Jacob a helpless look.

He took her arm and pulled her toward the door.

"Forgive me," he said to Dunbar. "I shouldn't have come."

Dunbar didn't look up from his book. "Some things are best never found, Jacob," he said. "You're not the only one who likes to forget that."

Fox wanted to say something, but Jacob pushed her through the door.

"I forget less often than you think, Dunbar," he said before pulling the door shut behind him.

What now?

He looked down the dark corridor.

Fox's face held the same question. And the same fear.

A swaying lantern appeared at the end of the corridor. The night watchman carrying it was nearly as old as the building. Jacob ignored his puzzled look and simply walked past him without a word.

It was a clear night, and the two moons speckled the roofs with rust and silver. Fox spoke only once they'd reached the iron gate.

"You always have a second plan. What is it?"

Yes, she knew him well.

"I'll get some blood shards." He started to swing himself

over the gate, but Fox grabbed his arm and pulled him back. "No."

"No what?" He didn't mean to sound that irritated. But he was dog-tired, and he was thoroughly sick of running away from death. *You're forgetting something, Jacob. Fear. You're scared.*

"I have to find the head, and I have no idea where to look, not to mention the heart and the hand. The only man I thought could help me thinks I'm a ruthless thug now, and the way things stand, I myself will be lying in a coffin in less than two months."

"What?" Fox's voice broke, as though the truth lodged in her throat like a splinter.

Damn it, Jacob!

She shoved him into the iron gate. "You said you didn't know!"

"I'm sorry!" Reluctantly, she let him embrace her. Her heart was beating fast, nearly as fast as when he had freed the vixen's leg from the trap.

"Knowing it doesn't change anything, does it?"

She struggled free.

"Together," she said. "Wasn't that the plan? Don't ever lie to me again. I'm sick of it."

17. THE FIRST BITE

Some things need to be sought in the filth. Sinister things, found by following the scent of poverty to the dark streets beyond the gaslights and the stuccoed houses, to backyards stinking of refuse and bad food. Jacob asked for directions from a man sitting on his front steps and squeezing silver dust from a captured Elf. Elven dust. A dangerous path to escape the world.

There was nothing ominous about the windows of the shop the man sent them to. It was way past midnight, but what Jacob was after was best purchased under the cover of night anyway. In Albion, trade in magical objects and substances was strictly regulated. Still, nearly anything that was available on the mainland could also be found here, if only one looked in the right places.

The screams of a Hob sounded through the door when

Jacob knocked against the frosted glass. The Albian variant of the Heinzel had carrot hair and much longer legs than its Austrian kin. The woman who opened the door was trying hard to look like a Witch, but she had the round black pupils of a human, and the herbal perfume she'd sprinkled deep into her décolletage didn't smell anything like Alma's forest scent. The Hob was sitting in a cage above the door. Hobs were good guards as long they were fed regularly, and their mood was barely worse in a cage than when they were free. The creature's red eyes clung to Fox as she stepped into the shop. The Hob could smell the shape-shifter.

The fake Witch locked the door while she appraised Jacob's clothes. The cut and fabric seemed to whisper "money" to her, and she gave him a smile as fake as her perfume. The shop reeked of dried moor lilies, which wasn't a good sign. They were often passed off as Fairy lilies, and the fungus-sponges that hung from the ceiling were sold as an aphrodisiac, even though the only effects they had were lifelong hallucinations. But among the items on the shelves, Jacob did spot a few things that had real magical properties.

"And what can Goldilocks do for you two darlin's?" Her hoarse voice gave her away as a lentil-chewer. The Cinderella addiction... for a few hours of princess dreams. Goldilocks gave Fox a sleazy smile. "Need something to fan the old flames? Or is there someone in your way?"

Jacob would have loved nothing more than to give her

an infusion of her own deadliest potion. Her locks were indeed golden—the kind of sticky gold that fake Witches liked to concoct to color their hair and lips.

"I need a blood shard." Jacob dropped two talers on the grimy counter. His handkerchief was becoming quite unreliable at producing them. It was so thin in places that he would soon have to start looking for a new one.

Goldilocks rubbed the coins between her fingers. "There's five years' hard labor for selling blood shards."

Jacob put another coin in her hand.

She dropped the money into her apron pocket and disappeared behind a threadbare curtain. Fox's eyes followed her. Her face was pale.

"They don't always work," she said without looking at Jacob. Her voice sounded as rough as the lentil-chewer's.

"I know."

"You'll lose blood for weeks."

Her look was so desperate, he wanted to take her into his arms and kiss away the fear on her face. *What are you doing, Jacob?* Was the garbage on the shelves fogging his senses? All the love potions and cheap amulets, the finger bones that were supposed to bestow lust and love? Or was this another effect of his fear of death?

Goldilocks returned with a paper bag. The glass shard Jacob took out of it was colorless and a little bigger than the bottom of a bottle.

"How do I know it's real?"

Fox took the shard from him and ran her fingers over

the glass. Then she looked at the fake Witch. "If he's harmed in any way, I will find you," she said. "No matter where you hide."

Goldilocks sneered. "It's a blood shard, honey. Of course it'll harm him." She took a vial from her apron and put it in Jacob's hand. "Rub this on the wound. It'll slow the bleeding."

The Hob stared through the doorway before his mistress shut and locked it behind them. A rat scampered down the dark alley, and in the distance Jacob and Fox could hear the wheels of a cab rattling over the cobblestones.

Jacob stepped into the nearest doorway and pushed up his sleeve. Blood shards. He'd never used one himself, but Chanute acquired one once, when they'd been hunting for the wand of a Warlock. To use the blood shard, one had to picture the item one was looking for as exactly as possible and then cut the shard deep into the flesh until the object appeared in the glass, hopefully also showing its location. Blood shards only revealed objects that had been touched by dark magic, but the Witch Slayer's head definitely had enough of that.

"Did you ever find the wand?" Fox turned away in disgust as Jacob pressed the shard against his skin.

"Yes." What he didn't tell her was that Chanute had nearly bled out. It was the worst kind of magic.

Just as he was about to cut into his skin, a pain pierced his chest, unlike any Jacob had felt before. Something was digging its teeth into his heart. The shard dropped from his hand, and the scream that crossed his lips was so loud that a window opened on the other side of the street.

"Jacob?" Fox grabbed him by the shoulders.

He wanted to say something, anything reassuring, but all he could utter was a wheeze, and he could only manage to stay on his feet because Fox held him up. His old self wanted to hide himself from her, too proud to be seen in such a vulnerable state, so helpless. But the pain just wouldn't go away.

Breathe, Jacob. Breathe. It'll pass.

The Dark Fairy's name had six letters, but he could recall only five of them.

He leaned against the door and pressed his hand to his chest, certain that he'd see his own blood seep through his fingers. The pain subsided, but the memory of it still quickened his breath.

"It's not going to be pleasant." The understatement of the year, Alma.

Fox picked up the shard. It was broken, but there was no blood on it. Fox stared in disbelief at the clean glass. Then she pulled Jacob's hand off his chest. The moth above his heart had a spot on its left wing now. It was shaped like a tiny skull.

"The Fairy is claiming her name back." He could barely speak. He could still feel the scream in his throat.

Pull yourself together, Jacob. Oh, his damned pride. He

held out his hand, even though it was trembling. "Give me the shard." Fox dropped it into her pocket and pulled his sleeve over his bare arm.

"No," she said. "And I don't think you have enough strength to take it off me."

18. THE HAND IN THE SOUTH

The Waterman turned out to tax Nerron's nerves the least. Eaumbre—when his name crossed his scaly lips, you felt as though you had the mud of his pond in your ears. Even Louis was bearable, though he was constantly asking about their next meal or riding after every peasant girl. But Lelou! The Bug was talking all the time, at least whenever he wasn't scribbling in his notebook. Every castle above the winter-bare vineyards, every collapsed church, every town name on a weathered signpost—each triggered a flood of commentary. Names, dates, royal gossip. His chatter was like the hum of a bumblebee in Nerron's ear.

"Lelou!" he interrupted at some point as the Bug was explaining why the village they were riding through was certainly not the birthplace of Puss in Boots. "See this?"

Arsene Lelou fell silent as he cast a confused look at the three objects Nerron had poured into his hand from a leather pouch. It took him a few moments to realize what they were.

"You're seeing right!" Nerron said. "A finger, an eye, a tongue. They all annoyed me. What do you think I'll cut out of you?"

Silence. Delicious silence.

Nerron had picked up the Three Souvenirs, as he lovingly called them, in one of the onyx's torture chambers. The objects never failed to work. Maintaining a bad reputation was hard work, especially if, like Nerron, you didn't actually find pleasure in cutting off fingers or scooping out eyes.

Lelou's silence held until they saw the walls of the abbey of Fontevaud appear ahead of them. One glance at the rotten wooden gate and they knew that the abbey was deserted. The cloisters were overgrown with nettles, and the sparse cells housed no more than mice. The only cemetery they could find consisted of merely eight crosses with the names and dates of deceased monks. None of the graves were older than sixty years, but yet, if the Bug was right, the hand would have been buried here more than three hundred years ago.

Nerron felt the urge to cut Lelou into thin, moonstone-pale slices. The Bug saw it in his eyes and quickly hid behind Eaumbre. Lelou had not forgotten the Three Souvenirs.

"The farmer," he stammered, pointing a trembling finger at an old man who was digging up potatoes from a fallow field behind the abbey. "Maybe he knows something."

The old man dropped his meager harvest as soon as he saw Nerron coming toward him. He stared as though the devil himself had emerged from the damp earth. Goyl were still a rare sight in Lotharaine. Kami'en would change that soon enough.

"Is there another graveyard?" Nerron barked at the old man.

The farmer crossed himself and spat in front of Nerron's feet. Touching. People believed that kept demons at bay. But it didn't help against Goyl. Nerron was just about to grab the old man by his scrawny neck to shake some sense into him, when he dropped to his knees.

Louis was coming toward them, with Lelou and the Waterman in tow.

The princely garments had grown a little scruffy, but they still looked a thousand times better than anything the old man had ever worn. He probably had no idea that he was looking at the crown prince of Lotharaine—the old peasant didn't look like he read a newspaper—but the vassals always knew what masters look like, and that it was better to do as they were told.

"Ask him about the cemetery!" Nerron whispered to Louis.

All he got was an irritated look in return—sons of

Kings were not used to receiving orders. But Lelou came to his aid.

"The Goyl is right, my prince!" he warbled into Louis's perfumed ear. "He's sure to answer you."

Louis cast a disgusted look at the peasant's filthy clothes. "Is there another cemetery?" he asked with a jaded voice.

The old man ducked his head between his lank shoulders. His bony finger pointed at the pine trees beyond the fields. "They built a church from them."

"From what?" Nerron asked.

The man still held his head bowed. "The whole ground was full of them!" he mumbled. He quickly dropped a couple of potatoes into his baggy pockets. "What else could they have done with them?"

He took them to the church, which, at first sight, looked no different from the other churches of the region. The same gray stone, a stout tower with a low roof, a few weathered battlements. But the peasant made a quick getaway as soon as Nerron pushed the brittle door open.

Even the crest that was set into the wall behind the altar was made of human remains. The pillars were encrusted with skulls, and the fenced-off alcoves were piled to the ceiling with bones. There were hands as well, of course. They served as candleholders or were splayed across the walls as ornaments. Frustrated, Nerron kicked in one of the skulls. How, by his mother's green skin, was he supposed to find the right hand here? He was going to be stuck neck-deep in brittle bones while Reckless easily picked up the head and the heart.

"What are we looking for again?" Louis poked his fingers into a skull's eye socket.

"Your ancestor's crossbow." The empty church made the Waterman's damp whisper sound even more ominous.

"A crossbow?" Louis's mouth tightened into a contemptuous smile. "What's my father hoping for—that the Goyl will laugh themselves to death when they attack?"

"This is a very unusual crossbow, my prince..." Lelou began. "And it's a little more complicated, if I understand the Goyl right." He pursed his mouth like a toad about to spit venom. "First, we have to find a hand, and then—"

"You can explain that later," Nerron interrupted gruffly. He went to one of the alcoves and stared through the metal trellis at the piled-up bones. "If Lelou is right, then the hand was quartered. Also, it probably isn't decomposed, and it has golden fingernails."

All Warlocks gilded their nails to hide that the Witches' blood made them rot.

"Yuck!" Louis muttered, fiddling with his diamond buttons. He still wasn't missing a single one. You couldn't even rely on the Thumblings anymore. *Pretend he's not here, Nerron. Neither he, nor the Waterman, nor the prattling Bug.*

He pried open the gate with his saber and immediately stood to his knees in bones. Great. A forearm splintered under his boots. Goyl bones turned to stone after death, just like their flesh. Much more appetizing than human putrefaction.

"This is ridiculous. I'm going to a tavern." The boredom on Louis's face had given way to anger. He had a hot temper, when he didn't numb it with elven dust or wine.

A hand-sized gnome crawled out from one of the skulls on the pillar next to the prince. Eaumbre grabbed it before it could bite Louis. "A yellow follet!" Lelou quickly pulled his charge away. "Easily confused with house follets, but..." One glance from Nerron ended the lecture.

Crack.

The Waterman hung the follet's corpse from the cobwebs, which were catching flies and dust between the pillars. "If you break the neck of one, it'll be a warning to the others," he whispered.

Lelou threw up on the bones, but Louis stared in fascination at the small corpse. Nerron thought he could make out a trace of cruelty in the pudgy face. Not an entirely unsuitable character trait for a future King.

"Right, then. Enjoy the search." Louis threw a skull at Lelou's chest and laughed as the Bug stumbled back. "You're staying as well!" he ordered the Waterman. "I don't need a guard dog to get myself drunk. And your ugly mug scares away the girls."

He turned around, but Eaumbre stepped into his path. "I'm under orders from your father," he whispered.

"But he's not here!" Louis hissed at him. "So just haul

your fishy body out of my way, or I shall telegraph him that I caught you dragging a screaming peasant girl into the village pond." He flicked back his curly hair and gave the Waterman a princely smile. "We can all have our fun." Then he marched regally through the church door and slammed it behind him so hard that the brittle wood shed a few more splinters.

"Go after him," Nerron said to the Waterman.

"Yes, go after him, Eaumbre!" Lelou echoed. His voice sounded panicky.

But the Waterman just stood there and stared with his six eyes at the door Louis had disappeared through.

"Eaumbre! Go!" Lelou repeated shrilly.

The Waterman didn't move.

As proud as a Waterman. Even the Goyl knew that saying.

"Never mind. He'll be back," Nerron said. "Our princeling is right. He doesn't need us to get himself drunk."

Lelou moaned. "But his fa—"

Nerron cut him off: "Didn't you hear me? He'll be back! We have to find a hand with gilded fingernails. So start looking, Lelou."

The Bug wanted to reply, but then he ducked his head and began sifting through the bones that had poured out of the alcove.

Eaumbre gave Nerron a nod.

Six-eyed gratitude.

Who knew when that might come in handy.

19. MAYBE

The hotel where Fox brought Jacob was just as run-down as the fake Witch's shop, but the pain had weakened him more than he would admit, and the streets were deserted, so she couldn't find a cab that would have taken them to a better hotel.

Jacob closed his eyes as soon as he stretched out on the bed. Fox stayed by his side until she was sure he was fast asleep. His breathing was too rapid, and she could still see the shadows the pain had left on his face.

She gently stroked his forehead, as though her fingers could wipe away the shadows. *Careful, Fox.* But what could she do? Protect her heart and leave him alone with his death?

She felt love stirring inside her like an animal roused from sleep. *Sleep!* she wanted to whisper to it. *Go back to sleep. Or, better still, be what you once were: friendship. Nothing else. Without the craving for his touch.*

In his sleep, Jacob reached for his chest, as though his fingers needed to soothe the moth that was gnawing away at his heart.

Eat my heart instead! Fox thought. *What good is it to me, anyway?*

Her heart felt so different when she wore her fur. To the vixen, even love tasted of freedom, and desire came and went like hunger, without the craving that came with being human.

It was hard to leave Jacob behind. She was worried the pain would return. But what she was about to do, she did for him. Fox locked the dingy room behind her and carried the blood shard with her.

Dunbar had probably left his desk by now. Morning was not far off. Fox had visited his home with Jacob only once, but the vixen never forgot a way.

It was a little difficult to explain to the cabdriver that she didn't have an address, that she would give him directions using trees and smells, but in the end he dropped her off in front of the high hedge surrounding Dunbar's house. Fox rang the bell by the door half a dozen times before she heard an angry voice inside. Dunbar had probably not been in bed long.

He opened the door a crack and pushed the barrel of a rifle through it, but he immediately lowered the weapon when he realized who was standing there. He waved Fox into his living room without saying a word. His late mother's portrait hung above the fireplace, and on the piano, next to a photograph of his father, was one of him and Jacob.

"What are you doing here? I thought I made myself clear." Dunbar leaned the rifle against the wall. He listened into the dark hallway before closing the door. His father lived with him. Jacob had told her that the old Fir Darrig hardly left the house. Anyone would have eventually grown tired of being stared at all the time. There were still a few hundred Fir Darrigs in Eire, but here in Albion they were as rare as a warm summer.

Fox ran her fingers over the spines of the books, which surrounded Dunbar at home just as they did at the university. There had never been a single book in the house where she grew up. It was Jacob who'd taught her to love them.

"So you now need a rifle if you've got a Fir Darrig in your house and in your blood?"

"Let's just say it's better to be safe than sorry. But I've never had to use it. I'm still not sure whether rifles were a good invention or not. I guess that's the question with any invention, but I do feel it's a question one has to ask too often these days." He looked at Fox. "We're both stuck between the times, aren't we? We're wearing the past on our skins, but the future is too loud to be ignored.

What has been and what will be. What is being lost and what is being gained…"

Dunbar was a wise man—wiser than any man Fox knew—and on any other night, Fox would have loved nothing more than listening to him explain the world to her. But not on this night.

"I am here so Jacob won't be lost, Dunbar."

"Jacob?" Dunbar laughed out loud. "Even if the whole world were lost, he'd just find himself another one."

"That wouldn't help him. He'll be dead in a few months if we don't find the crossbow."

Dunbar had his father's cat-eyes. Like foxes, Fir Darrigs were creatures of the night. Fox could only hope those eyes could see she wasn't lying.

"Please, Dunbar. Tell me where the head is."

The living room filled with thick silence. Tears might have helped, but she could never cry when she was afraid.

"Of course. The third shot…Guismond's youngest son." Dunbar went to the piano and touched the keys. "Is he that desperate, that he puts his hope into some half-forgotten legend?"

"He's tried everything else."

Dunbar struck a key, and in that single note Fox heard all the sadness of the world. This was not a good night.

"So the Red Fairy found him?"

"He went back to her himself."

Dunbar shook his head. "Then he doesn't deserve better."

"He did it for his brother." *Talk, Fox.* Dunbar believed in words. He lived among them. But the Fairy's moth was eating Jacob's heart, and there were no words to stop it.

"Please!" For a brief moment, Fox was tempted to point the rifle at Dunbar's chest. The things fear made you do. And love.

Dunbar looked at the rifle as though he'd guessed her thoughts. "I nearly forgot I'm talking to a vixen. Your human form is so misleading, though it suits you very well."

Fox felt herself blush.

Dunbar smiled, but his face quickly turned serious again. "I don't know where the head is."

"Yes, you do."

"Really? And who says so?"

"The vixen."

"Then let's put it this way. I don't know exactly, but I have a hunch." He picked up the rifle and stroked its long barrel. "The crossbow is worth a hundred thousand rifles like this. One single shot will turn the man who wields it into a mass murderer. I'm sure they'll come up with machines that can do the same soon enough. The new magic is the old magic. The same goals, the same greed . . ."

Dunbar took aim at Fox—then he lowered the rifle.

"I need your word. By the fur you're wearing. By Jacob's life. By all that's holy to you, that he will not sell the crossbow."

"I'll leave you my fur as a bond." No words had ever been more difficult to say.

Dunbar shook his head. "No. I won't ask that much."

A head poked around the living-room door. The rat-snout was gray, and the cat-eyes were clouded by age.

Dunbar turned around with a sigh. "Father! Why aren't you sleeping?" He led the old man to the sofa where Fox was sitting.

"The two of you should have a lot you can talk about," Dunbar said. The old Fir Darrig was eyeing Fox warily. "Trust me, he knows everything about the blessings and the curse of wearing fur."

He went to the door. "It's an old tradition from a distant land," he said as he stepped out into the corridor, "but for the past two hundred years, Albion has believed in the miraculous properties of tea leaves. Even at five in the morning. Maybe they'll make it easier for my tongue to say what you've come to hear."

His father looked confused. But then he turned to Fox and looked at her with his milky eyes. "A vixen, if I'm not mistaken," he said. "Since birth?"

Fox shook her head. "I was seven. The fur was a gift."

The Fir Darrig heaved a compassionate sigh. "Oh, that's not easy," he mumbled. "Two souls in one heart. I hope the human in you won't prove to be stronger in the end. They find it so much harder to make peace with the world."

20. THE SAME BLOOD

More nothing. Nerron threw another hand onto the pile of bones they'd already sifted through. Lelou had all but disappeared behind the pile. Eaumbre had smashed up one of the pews and stuck its wood into all the chandeliers, burning as torches, but the night smothered what little light they gave, and thousands of bones were still hidden in the dark, even from Goyl eyes.

What if the hand wasn't in the damned church? What if it was still somewhere out there in the damp earth? They can't possibly have dug up all the bones!

Nerron had run out of curses. He'd wished himself to a hundred different places, and he must have asked himself more than a thousand times whether Reckless had found the head yet. Still, all he could do was sift through another pale pile of human remains and hope for a miracle.

Lelou and the Waterman were helping him with moderate enthusiasm, but at least there were extra hands to sort the legs, skulls, and ribs from the bony fingers. *The good ones to your pot, the bad ones to your crop*—he felt like Cinderella. *Wrong thought, Nerron.* That only reminded him that Reckless had found the glass slipper before him.

The Waterman lifted his head and reached for his pistol.

Someone was coming through the church door.

Louis stumbled over the first skull in his path. He reached for a hold on the nearest pillar. "The wine around here is even more sour than my mother's lemonade," he babbled. "And the girls are even uglier than you, Eaumbre."

And of course he had to throw up over the bones they hadn't searched yet.

"How much longer are you going to be doing this?" He wiped his tailored sleeve over his mouth and tottered toward Nerron. "And anyway . . . all that treasure hunting . . . the magical crossbow . . . My father should be looking for engineers that are as good as Albion's instead."

He stopped abruptly and stared at a pile of skulls to his left. Something was moving beneath them. Eaumbre drew his saber, but Louis waved him away impatiently.

"I'll break his neck myself," he shouted drunkenly. "Can't be that hard. Nasty little . . ."

Lelou shot Nerron an alarmed look. A yellow follet's bite was nearly as dangerous as that of a viper. But what came crawling out from between the bones had neither a yellow skin nor legs or arms.

"Don't!" Nerron yelled as the Waterman lifted his saber.

Three fingers, pale as wax.

They moved as fast as locust legs. Nerron tried to grab them—and immediately let go with a curse. His arm was numb all the way up to the shoulder. *The hand of a Warlock—what were you thinking, Nerron?*

The fingers scurried toward Louis. He stumbled back, but something was crawling down the pillar behind him. Thumb and forefinger. The second piece. Eaumbre hacked at them with his sabre, but the fingers skillfully dodged the blade. Louis tugged at his dagger, but he was too drunk to get it out of the scabbard.

"Damn it!" he screeched. "Do something!"

A piece of the hand was crawling up his boot.

"Grab it!" Nerron barked at him. "Do it now!"

There wasn't much of Guismond's blood flowing through Louis's veins. Still, maybe it would give him enough protection. If not... but Louis was already leaning down. The fingers kept twitching like the legs of an unappetizingly large beetle, but they didn't give Louis a jolt. So the princeling was useful after all! Things were now crawling from all directions toward him. The two halves of the carpus slithered like turtles across the flagstones.

Louis put the pieces together like a child playing with a grisly model kit. The dead flesh stuck together like warm wax. There was still gold on the stump and the fingernails. Nerron smiled. Yes, this was the right hand.

The swindlesack he pulled from his jacket was from the mountains of Anatolia, a place from which one didn't easily return alive. Still, every treasure hunter had to own at least one of these sacks. Whatever was put inside disappeared and would reemerge only when one reached for it deep within the sack.

Nerron held out the sack to Louis.

The prince flinched away from him, and he hid the hand behind his back like a spoiled child.

"No," he said, yanking the swindlesack from Nerron's fingers. "Why should you have it? The hand came to me!"

Lelou couldn't hide his gleeful grin. The Waterman, however, exchanged a look with Nerron, and floating in that look like pebbles in a pond was the memory of every one of Louis's insults.

Good.

One day that might save him the trouble of having to snap the princeling's neck himself.

21. IMPOSSIBLE

What would you do without her, Jacob? Fox was looking out the train window, but he wasn't sure whether she was gazing at the fields drifting past outside or at the reflection of her face in the glass. Jacob often caught her staring at her human form as if she were staring at a stranger.

Fox noticed his look, and she smiled at him with that mix of confidence and bashfulness only her human self knew. The vixen was never bashful.

The steam of the locomotive drifted past the windows, and a coattailed waiter balanced cups and plates through the swaying dining car. Jacob felt as though the previous night's pain had sharpened his senses. The world around him seemed just as wondrous and strange as when he'd seen it the first time he came through the mirror. He touched the teacup the waiter brought him. The white porcelain was painted with Elves, the kind that were still found on many flowers in Albion. At the next table, two men were arguing over the use of Giantlings in the Albian navy, and nearby a woman's neck glistened with Selkie-tears, which were found all along the island's southern shores, like unshelled pearls. He still loved this world, even though it was trying to take his life.

The tea was bitter, despite the elven cup. So bitter that he barely managed to get it down, but it helped against the fatigue the moth's bite had left inside him.

Fox reached for his hand. "How are you feeling? We'll be there soon."

Beyond the hills they could see the roofs of Goldsmouth, the home port of the Albian navy. Beyond that was the sea, gray and vast. It seemed calmer than on their crossing. *Good.* Jacob couldn't believe he had to get on a ship again.

Fox whispered across the table: "Do you still have money? Or did you spend it all on the blood shard?"

Jacob knew a ship's outfitter who sold genuine navy uniforms, but they weren't cheap, and his handkerchief was becoming less and less reliable. It had produced the last coin so reluctantly, they'd nearly been unable to pay for their train tickets. Jacob put his hand in his pocket, and his fingers touched Earlking's card. He couldn't resist. He pulled it out.

That hurt, didn't it? And it will get worse with every bite.
Fairies love the pain they can cause to mortals.

By the way, I visited your brother today.

Fox looked at him.

"Who's the card from?" She tried to make the question sound casual, but Jacob knew who she was thinking of. She hadn't forgotten the Larks' Water. And he could remember the pain in her eyes even more clearly than Clara's kisses. *Maybe you should have told her, Jacob.*

He pushed the card across the table. The words were already fading as she reached for it.

"It's a magical thing!" Fox turned the card around. "Norebo Johann Earlking?"

The conductor came through the carriage to announce the next stop.

"Yes. And he didn't give me the card in this world." Jacob got up. The other world suddenly felt so close that the clothes everyone around him wore seemed like costumes. Top hats, buttoned boots, laced hems... He felt lost between the two worlds, neither here nor there.

"What has he got to do with Will?"

Yes, what? It didn't sound as though this was just about

a few heirlooms. Jacob didn't like it at all, but the mirror was far, and it might be weeks before he got to see Will again. If he got to see him again.

Oh, to hell with it.... He would see his brother again.

Fox lifted the card to her nose. Always the vixen, even in her human skin. "Silver. And there's a scent I don't recognize." She returned the card to him and reached for her coat. Jacob had been with her when she bought it. The fabric was nearly the same color as her fur. "I don't like that smell. Be careful."

The other travelers started pushing them toward the door. Though the platform was lost in the steam of the locomotive, the wind brought the smell of salt and tar from the port. Porters. Cabdrivers. There were two porters with wooden seats on their backs; they were waiting for the two Dwarfs who'd been sitting behind them in the dining car. Being barely three feet tall and trying to push one's way through a train station was no fun.

They took one of the cabs waiting in front of the station. Fox got off at the square where the ships' outfitters had their shops, but Jacob instructed the driver to take him to the port. They could only hope Dunbar was right with his theory about the Witch Slayer's head. But to be certain, they had to find a way to get on board the royal flagship first.

22. IRON FLANKS

There they lay, hull by hull. The creaking of wet rope mingled with the screeching gulls and the voices of men readying their ships for departure. Albion's navy was matched by no other on this side of the mirror. And that confidence was stamped on the faces of every one of the sailors carrying ditty bags up the swaying gangways, and of the officers leaning on the railing. The flag with the crowned Dragon flapped above them all. Albion wasn't even keeping the fleet's mission a secret.

Jacob picked up a newspaper from the wet cobblestones. Every letter of the headline on the front page sprouted curlicues yet was as clear as the headlines in his world.

Regal Fleet to Deliver Arms to Flanders

From Albion's Factories Springs Hope in the Fight Against the Goyl

They felt very safe. Everybody knew about the Goyl's fear of the sea. Albion didn't supply weapons to just Flanders, either. Her ships also took arms to the north, where an alliance was forming against the Goyl. Almost the entire fleet sailed under both steam and wind these days, and its cannons' firepower was legendary. But that still didn't seem to be enough for Wilfred the Walrus.

Jacob stared at the sketch printed on the next page. Though he could barely make it out on the wet paper, his heart began to beat at a ridiculous pace, just as it did when he'd seen the airplanes in the Goyl fortress. The quest he'd abandoned so long ago. The trail that had always disappeared into nothing. And he'd stumbled onto it again, in a place where he never would have thought to look.

The Vulcan in Its Berth in Goldsmouth

Our Tempered Terror of the Seas Embarks on Third Mission to Escort Arms Delivery

Masterpiece of Albian Engineering Sets Goyl Atremble

Jacob put down the newspaper and scanned the row of ships.

To his left lay the ship he'd come to Goldsmouth for: the *Titania*, flagship of the Albian fleet, named after the King's mother. Three hundred seventy-six crew. Forty-five cannons. The grimy waters of the harbor reflected the figurehead, but Jacob only gave her a cursory glance. His eyes were searching for the ship from the front page.

Where was it?

His glance wandered past wooden hulls and masts until it found pale sunlight reflected on metal.

There she was. At the last berth. Gray, ugly, like a steel shark in a school of wooden mackerel. The low hull rose just a few feet above the water and was clad, like the funnels, in iron all the way down to the waterline. In Jacob's world, the first iron ships had been instrumental in deciding the American Civil War. This, however, was already a much more modern version.

Jacob! Forget it! But reason didn't stand a chance. His heart beat in his throat as he picked his way past crates and duffel bags, through groups of seamen hauling munitions and provisions, women saying farewell to their husbands, and children pressing teary faces into their fathers' uniforms. It was like stumbling through one of his dreams, only this forest was made up of ships' masts.

Up close the iron ship looked even more impressive. It was enormous, even though most of the hull was hidden beneath the waterline. Four men stood by the gangway that led from the pier up to the deck. Three of them were officers of the Regal Navy, but the fourth was wearing civilian clothes. That man had his back to Jacob. His hair was gray, and he wore it short, just as Jacob did.

What if it was him? After all these years. *Turn back, Jacob. It's over; it's in the past.* But he was twelve again. The moth on his chest was forgotten. Forgotten, too, was what he'd come here for. He just stood there and stared at the iron ship and at the back of a stranger.

Jacob!

A cabin boy ran past him, two boxes of cigars under his scrawny arms. A final errand for the officers. He looked up in alarm as Jacob grabbed hold of him. "Do you know who that man is? The one standing with the officers?"

The boy gave him a look as though Jacob had asked him to name the sun. "That's Brunel. He built the *Vulcan*, and he's already planning a new ship."

Jacob let the boy go.

One of the officers looked around, but the civilian still had his back to Jacob.

Brunel. Not a very common name. Isambard Kingdom Brunel was one of his father's heroes. Jacob had barely been seven when John Reckless had tried to explain Brunel's iron-bridge blueprints to him.

All those years, and now there were just a few steps left.

"Mister Brunel?" How timid his voice sounded. As though he really was twelve again.

Brunel turned around, and Jacob found himself looking into the eyes of a stranger. Only the eyes were as gray as his father's.

Jacob wasn't sure what he felt. Disappointment? Relief? Both?

Say something, Jacob. Go on.

"Brunel. That's an unusual name."

"My father was from Lotharaine." Brunel smiled. "May I ask who..."

"Why, that's Jacob Reckless." The officer standing next to Brunel gave Jacob a nod. "Quite a different kind of trade, John. Hunting for old magic. And this man here happens to be very good at it." He offered his hand to Jacob. "Cunningham. Not nearly as interesting a name. Lieutenant in the Regal Navy. Pleased to make your acquaintance. Thankfully, our newspapers still like to publish reports about treasure hunters, even if they mostly poke fun at the artifacts these days. A medal from the Austrian Empress for a glass slipper. The Iron Cross of Bavaria for a pair of seven-league boots. I admit to harboring some envy for your trade. As a child I was determined to pursue your profession and no other."

"Congratulations." Brunel gave Jacob an appreciative nod. His accent didn't at all sound Lotharainian.

Behind them, torpedoes were being loaded on board. They'd shred any wooden hull like paper.

Cunningham's eyes followed Jacob as he bade the men farewell. Brunel, however, had already turned his attention to the ship again. Albion's new magician.

Relief and disappointment. An old hope, all but forgotten. Jacob barely saw where he was walking. Barrels, ropes, crates...everything around him was blurred like his face on the dark glass of the mirror. *"Look at that, Jacob. This bridge is weightless and as perfect as a spider's web—but it's made of iron."* Did he even remember what his father looked like? He remembered his voice, the hands that had lifted him onto the desk so he could touch the model planes that hung above it.

"Jacob!"

Someone grabbed his arm. Fox.

"The outfitter wanted a fortune." She shot a furtive glance at the sailors hauling sacks of coal to the *Titania*'s cargo hatch. "I only had enough for one uniform. Have you found a way to get us on board?"

Damn. He'd found out nothing. He'd so lost himself in memories that he had nearly forgotten he soon would have no future.

"What's with you?" Fox looked worried. "Did something happen?"

"No. Nothing." And that was the truth. Nothing had happened. He'd seen a ghost, the same ghost he kept stumbling after in his dreams. It was high time he buried not just his mother but also his father. He'd thought he'd done so already.

He took the bundled uniform off Fox. A few sailors

were staring so openly at her that Jacob gave them a sharp look. "How will you get on board?"

Fox shrugged. "I'll let the vixen find a way."

"That's too dangerous."

"Mister Reckless?"

Jacob turned around. He'd expected Brunel's slender face, but it was Cunningham who was standing behind him.

The officer bowed stiffly to Fox and gave Jacob a slightly awkward smile. "We . . . eh . . . only set to sea in an hour. I would like to introduce you to our captain. I'm sure he'd find some of your adventures very interesting."

Jacob quickly had a polite refusal on the tip of his tongue, but Fox interceded. "Which ship do you serve on, Mr. Cunningham?"

Cunningham pointed behind him. "The *Titania.* We're escorting a shipment of arms to Flanders. We sail at sunset."

Fox gave Cunningham her most seductive smile. "It will be our pleasure," she said, taking the bundle with the uniform from Jacob's arms and quickly hiding it behind her back.

Cunningham's bearded face beamed with delight, and Jacob sent a silent apology to all the reporters he'd ever cursed for the lies and exaggerations they had published about him.

"Certainly," he said. "We're in no rush. I wouldn't even mind coming along for the whole journey. I love going on voyages." A more brazen lie had never left his lips.

Cunningham looked as though he couldn't believe his luck.

The captain of the *Titania* shared his first officer's passion for treasure hunting. He put them up in the cabin the King himself used whenever he paid a visit to his flagship. When Cunningham introduced them as Jacob Reckless and wife, Jacob had to explain that Fox was only blushing because they hadn't been married long. It was just one of the many lies he'd have to come up with over the next hours.

The captain served them a dinner opulent enough for a journey of three hundred days instead of three. As the *Titania* weighed anchor, the ship's cook was serving dessert, and Jacob found it increasingly difficult to ignore the movements of the ship while Cunningham quizzed him about adventures that had been completely made up by some newspaper. When the captain, whose mustache was just as dreadful as his King's, began quizzing Jacob about the butchering techniques of Ogres, Fox used the bloody subject as a pretext to excuse herself. Jacob would have loved to follow her, but Cunningham wouldn't let him go. Jacob had to console himself with the fact that by the time he'd be able to get away, Fox would have checked all the guards and escape routes on board. Through the stern windows of the captain's cabin, Jacob could see lanterns of other frigates, and ahead were the moonlit iron flanks of Brunel's ship.

"Would Mr. Brunel be on board the *Vulcan* on a voyage like this?" Jacob was proud of the nonchalance with which he asked the question.

The captain shook his head with disdain. "To my knowledge he's never even left Albion. Isn't that right, Cunningham?"

His first officer nodded as he poured himself another glass of port. "Brunel's not too fond of the sea."

"And his ship shows it." The captain downed his glass as though he could wash away the iron ship with it. "Sadly, our King has been smitten with Brunel ever since he built that horseless carriage. You see them everywhere now. Ridiculous. Absolutely ridiculous. That iron monstrosity out there is making us the laughingstock of the world. Our metal babysitter."

Jacob's eyes were glued to the *Vulcan* while Cunningham and the captain waxed lyrical about past military engagements at sea and the beauty of wooden ships on fire. When the two officers began to discuss the penetration power of modern cannons and the annoyance of smashed-up limbs, Jacob quickly made his excuses—though they would have certainly loved the story about Chanute's missing arm.

The silver moon, which resembled the one in the other world so much, was standing between the black clouds. Its red twin stained the waves like rusty metal. Fox was waiting at the bow. Below her, the figurehead stretched over the frothy waters.

"How's your stomach?" Nobody except her knew about

his dislike of sea travel. Not even Chanute. "You're lucky the sea is calm."

And lucky that an officer of the Regal Navy had recognized him after he mistook Albion's leading engineer for his father. Maybe his luck had returned. About time...

"Three guards on the prow," Fox whispered. "I'll distract them while you climb over the railing."

One of the guards was leaning just a few yards away between the lifeboats, looking in their direction. What did he see? Lovers in the moonlight? *And what if that were true, Jacob?* What if he allowed himself to forget what Fox had been to him all these years? Even the guard wanted to kiss her. It was written all over his face.

You'd break her heart, Jacob. Or Fox, his.

"What are you waiting for?" She put the backpack in his hand.

"Don't give him too much hope. He's nearly two heads taller than you."

Fox smiled. "I think you have the more dangerous task."

She sauntered toward the guard in a straight line, just as the vixen approached her prey.

Jacob leaned over the railing. The figurehead had the body of a Dragon but the head of a man. Dunbar had first noticed how much the gilded face resembled statues of the Witch Slayer during his research for a lecture on the history of the Regal Navy. Jacob still thought it was a rather far-fetched theory, but the figure supposedly came alive whenever the fleet was attacked. The head of a Warlock to protect Albion's fleet. Some black magic was always useful, even in these modern times. Dunbar claimed that Feirefis's great-great-grandson had begun the tradition of fitting the flagship's figurehead with the miraculous head, not knowing that it was that of his wizarding ancestor.

Jacob looked around.

Robert Lewis Dunbar, I hope you're not wrong about this!

He couldn't see the guard anymore. Where had Fox lured him? *Forget about it, Jacob.* She's a grown-up. He took the Rapunzel-hair from the snuff tin where he kept it. The golden hair was one of the few items he hadn't lost in the Goyl fortress—thanks to Valiant. Jacob rubbed it between his fingers, and the hair grew fiber on fiber until it was stronger than any hemp rope. Jacob tied one end to the railing. The other end he dropped down, and it immediately wrapped itself around the neck of the figurehead. He jumped over the railing and rappelled down the glistening rope until he could clamber onto the Dragon's back.

Don't look down, Jacob.

He could stand on any precipice without the slightest reaction from his stomach, but the sight of the water beneath nearly made him vomit all over Guismond's golden head. The Dragon's wings, which were pressed against its body, were also covered with golden scales, but its body and neck were made of scarlet-painted wood.

Jacob loosened the Rapunzel-rope from the bulky neck and tied it around his waist. Then he pulled a fishing net from his backpack and wrapped it around the head and neck so that the head, once he cut it off, wouldn't just drop into the ocean. His fingers were damp from the spray, and the high waves made him slip twice, but the Rapunzel-rope saved him from falling into the water.

The head was attached to the Dragon's neck with a broad metal band, but the knife Jacob pulled from his belt could even cut through steel. He'd stolen it from the kitchen of Valiant's castle. There was nothing better than a Dwarf knife, and Valiant owed Jacob much more than a knife, anyway, for the scars he bore on his back.

On the horizon, the first light of morning was eating into the night like mold. *Hurry, Jacob.* Of course, he expected that Guismond had secured his three bequests with a spell that would allow only his children to touch them without harm. So before Jacob slipped the knife through the net, he pulled on the gloves that had protected him in the tomb. The knife cut through the metal band like fresh bread, and as he touched the head, he felt nothing—the gloves worked. Good. Jacob was halfway through when he heard a sound from above. Fox was standing by the railing. He motioned her to wait up there; the figurehead's mounting didn't look strong enough to support them both. Suddenly, the wooden body beneath him bucked. Even though it was only connected by a few inches of metal, the golden head opened its mouth and let out a scream that resounded far across the water.

Jacob heard the engines even before the planes appeared out of the dawn light. A squadron of double-deckers was headed toward them across the black waves. The sailors were so dumbfounded that the planes managed to reach the ships before a single gun was aimed at them. They bore down on the Albian fleet like an aerie of eagles swooping down on a swarm of defenseless fish. Their red fuselages were painted with the black outline of a salamander—which had replaced the Fairy's moth on the Goyl crest ever since their King had taken a human wife.

The figurehead flapped its wings, and Guismond's head screamed through the net that Jacob had pulled over its gilded skin. He held on tight to the Dragon's neck as the first bombs exploded between the ships. Screams and shots joined the noise of the howling engines. Explosions tore through the wooden hulls, and men dropped from the riggings like birds. Fire rained from the sky, setting even the sea itself aflame. *The head, Jacob! Or you'll soon be as dead as those already being eaten by the fish down there—even if you manage to survive today.*

Above him Fox was trying desperately to steady the rope. Jacob clawed his fingers into the net; he ducked just before one of the wings could slice its barbed shoulder through his back. Fox was screaming something at him, but Jacob couldn't hear her through the noise. And he could hardly see anything, either. His eyes were burning from the biting smoke gathering between the ships. Even the wind reeked of powder and burning wood, but the planes kept up their attacks. The howl of their engines nearly burst Jacob's ear-drums, and the *Titania* groaned like a wounded animal.

Jacob! The head! He pulled the knife through the last bit of metal, and finally the head dropped into the net. The gilded face stared up at him, its mouth still wide open in midscream. He pulled a swindlesack from beneath his wet shirt. It clung to his trembling fingers. Jacob tugged it over his loot and then looked up at the railing. Fox held on to the ship with one hand, steadying the Rapunzel-rope with the other. They could barely see each other through the thickening smoke that was enveloping the ship. The deck was on fire, but he had to get up there. Fox was up there, and maybe not all the lifeboats had been put out to water yet.

She started to haul in the rope, though she could barely hold on. The *Titania* was swaying too wildly, and Jacob was heavy. The flagship was sinking, together with the entire Albian fleet. Drifting among the burning frigates was the iron ship, its armored flanks torn open and planes swarming over it like scarlet wasps.

Jacob tucked the swindlesack back under his shirt and began to climb, his feet pushing against the hull to make Fox's work easier. Underneath, the figurehead still flapped its wings like a beheaded chicken. The warning Fox screamed over the railing came too late. Jacob tried to dodge the wings, but their barbs were as sharp as blades. The black magic inside them cut through the Rapunzel-rope barely a hand's breadth above Jacob's head—and he dropped like a stone toward the blazing water.

23. MAL DE MER

Jacob wasn't sure whether his ears were filled with his own scream or the calls of the drowning men floating all around him. The sea was frigid, despite the burning ships. He grabbed hold of a drifting plank while he desperately tried to spot Fox on the flagship above. But the smoke was too thick. Jacob hoped she'd jumped, because the big ship was going to take everything with it when it sank. He yelled her name, but he could hardly even hear his own voice. The screams and moans were too loud, as though the waves were suddenly roaring through a thousand human throats. An explosion tore up one of the sinking ships, and the *Titania* started listing dangerously, yet Jacob kept searching for Fox among the floating bodies and debris.

Where was she?

He yanked the head of every passing corpse out of the water. Their pale faces floated like wax blossoms between the charred sails and the empty powder kegs. He could barely feel his limbs anymore in the icy water, and the smoke made every breath an ordeal, but he had to find her.

"Jacob." Wet arms wrapped around his neck. A cold cheek pressed against his. Fox's red hair, which stuck to her face, was so wet that it looked almost black. Jacob squeezed her tight and could feel her heartbeat through their wet clothes. He didn't dare let her go, afraid the waves would wash her away again.

"You have the head?"

"Yes."

"We have to get away from here."

Away to where? Jacob looked around. What was Dunbar going to think when he opened his paper in the morning? Iron ships, airplanes, bombs falling from the skies... would he wonder whether they'd drowned with the head? Would he finally begin to fear the new magic of technology as much as he feared that of the Witch Slayer?

"The coast can't be far. We were sailing southeast for hours."

Whatever she said. The planes were gone, but there would definitely not be any rescue mission.

"Come." Fox pulled him with her. She seemed certain in what direction the coast lay.

Swim, Jacob.

The smoke followed them for a long time. The smoke. The debris. The cries for help. But finally there was nothing around them but the sea, heaving like a giant animal digesting all the bodies it had just drowned. Fox looked at him with concern. She was a good swimmer, but Jacob's arms were getting heavy, and every wave left him gasping for air. Fox came to swim by his side, but he only got slower and slower. *Don't hold on to her, Jacob!* He would pull her down with him. His skin was numb, and he felt himself losing consciousness.

"Jacob!" Fox wrapped her arms around him and pulled his head out of the water. "You won't make it to the shore. Let yourself sink. Do you hear?"

Sink? What was she talking about? He tried to breathe, but even the air seemed to be made of salt water.

"It's your only chance. They don't come to the surface."

They? Fox pulled him down before he could understand what she meant. Water rushed into his mouth and nose. He tried to resist, but Fox wouldn't let go. She pulled him deeper and deeper, no matter how much he struggled. Jacob tried to push her away—he wanted to breathe, only breathe—but then suddenly he felt other hands. Warm and slender, like the hands of children. They pushed one of their scales into his mouth, and his lungs began to breathe the water as though they'd never done anything else. The bodies floating around him and Fox were transparent, like frosted glass. Fish or human—they were both. The Lotharainians called them Mal de Mer, but they had a different name on every coast. It was said that they capsized boats to take the souls of the dead to their cities at the bottom of the sea. The Empress had a specimen of a Mal de Mer in her Chambers of Miracles, but death had turned its crystalline beauty into dull wax.

They swarmed around Fox as though she were one of them, weaving flowers into her hair, stroking her face, but she would not let go of Jacob, and when they tried to pull him deeper, she pushed the naiads away. It was like a dance between her and them, until at some point Jacob felt a wave wash him onto firm ground. He felt damp sand, shells crushing between his fingers. His eyes burnt from the salty water, but he managed to open them to see clouds and a gray sky above. Fox was crouched next to him. She was also too weak to get to her feet, but they dragged each other along, away from the water's hissing waves that still sounded so hungry, until, exhausted, they finally dropped side by side onto the sand.

Jacob spat out the scale the Mal de Mer had pushed between his lips, and he greedily gulped the damp air into his burning lungs. It was salty and cold and more delicious than anything he'd ever tasted.

Breathing. Just to be breathing.

Fox reached for the blossoms the Mal de Mer had put into her hair. Underwater they'd shone in all the colors of the rainbow, but now they were wilted and dull. Fox threw them into the waves as if trying to give them back their life. Then she knelt down again next to Jacob and dug her hands deep into the gray sand.

"That was close." Her voice sounded as though she couldn't believe that they were still alive.

Alive. Jacob reached under his wet shirt, but all his fingers found was the moth.

The swindlesack with the head was gone.

Fox smiled as she put her hand up her sleeve. She pulled out the sack and threw it onto his chest.

The gloves, like his backpack, had been claimed by the sea. Still, as Jacob put his hand into the sack and touched the golden hair, all he felt was a slight tingling. Swindlesacks could have a dampening effect on black magic, though Jacob had never seen such a strong effect. It didn't matter...he had the head. He could only hope that the Goyl had been less successful in the meantime. Jacob tied up the sack and looked at the sky, where a few hungry gulls circled among the clouds. In his mind's eye, he could still see the red airplanes diving at the burning ships.

"Why did the Mal de Mer help us?"

Fox was wiping the sand from her bare arms. She'd pulled her dress off in the water, and now she was just wearing the one of fur. She wore it beneath her clothes whenever things might get dangerous, but this time it wasn't the vixen who had saved them, but her human self.

"They usually only help women," she said. "When I was a child they saved my mother's sister. Normally, they take the men with them, and I wasn't sure if I'd be able to protect you from them, but without their help, you would have drowned." Fox smiled. "Luckily, they realized I wasn't going to let them have you without a fight."

Yes, luckily. She was so fearless, it sometimes scared him. Jacob sat up. He could only hope the hand and the heart would be easier to find. Not that he really expected they would be. He looked around. Steep sandy cliffs and a pebbly beach. A lighthouse in the distance.

"Do you know where we are?"

Fox nodded. "I grew up not far from here. I asked the Mal de Mer to take us here. We're in Lotharaine, just a few miles from the Flandrian border." She got to her feet. "We'd better see that we move on, though. The fishermen here are not very friendly toward strangers. You still have the gold handkerchief? We'll need money for horses and new clothes."

Jacob reached into his pocket. The handkerchief was soaking wet, but Earlking's card dropped from his pocket as dry and untouched as though it had just snuck into his hand. Fox gave the card a nervous look, but it was blank except for Earlking's name. The card was pearly white, as though the sea had washed away the ink. Jacob shooed away a little spider that had crawled from his pocket, then he tucked the card away again. He still wanted to throw it out, but ever since he'd seen Will's name on it, the card felt like a connection to his brother—even though Jacob knew the notion was irrational.

The handkerchief usually worked even when it was wet, but Jacob had to rub it for what seemed an eternity before it finally released one paper-thin coin. Yes, he really needed a new one, but these handkerchiefs weren't easy to find.

Jacob poured out the water from his boots. "How many times has it been now?" He got to his feet.

"How many times has what been?" Fox could also barely stand. They were both shivering in their wet clothes.

"That you saved my skin."

Fox smiled as she brushed the sand off his back. "I think we're nearly even."

24. A BOOT PRINT

Coast...his hand...almost crushed. The spider danced haltingly, as though she'd swallowed as much water as her sister.

Albion had lost its fleet, and Nerron had almost lost his eight-legged spy. Luckily, twin spiders were made of hardier stuff than ships of wood or iron. And Reckless had also done quite well, if the spider's report was true. *Fire from the sky...water...smoke...death.* Nerron had some trouble figuring out exactly what had happened, but in the end all he needed to know were two things: The Goyl attack had made the crossbow even more attractive to all their enemies, and Reckless had made it back to the mainland—with the head.

Oh, this race was fun. Even if the princeling had the hand for now. And speak of the devil...the knocks on

Nerron's door sounded like someone who wasn't used to standing in front of closed doors. Nerron nudged the spider back into the medallion and opened the door.

"Look at this!" Louis shoved a discolored shirtsleeve into Nerron's face. "They can't even wash clothes in this dump! And what do you think my father will say when I telegraph him that Lelou had to pick lice from my hair this morning?"

Nerron pictured the chandelier he wanted to build from Louis's bones. Imagination was such a wonderful gift!

"What are we looking for next?" Ah. He'd tasted blood. The hunger for the hunt. Louis had far too many royal robbers in his ancestry to be immune to it.

"Get the others and meet me behind the stables."

Nerron wanted to slam the door shut, but Louis put his expensive boot in the jamb. "You're not really the chatty kind, Goyl. I think you're not telling us everything you know about this search."

And why should I, my princeling? So you or your dad might get the idea to search for the crossbow yourselves?

"Ask Lelou. He'll know more than I," Nerron replied. "And about those lice: Why don't you just have the landlord waive your wine bill?"

Louis picked a particularly fat specimen from his forehead and crushed it with disgust between his fingers.

"Fine," he said, pulling his boot out of the door. "Behind the stables. But remember, I don't like waiting."

Of course, it was Nerron who ended up waiting. Maybe they found some more lice. Quite astonishing that Louis's eau de toilette didn't kill them all on the spot. Eaumbre trudged silently behind his royal charge, but Lelou was talking at Louis in his usual breathless way. He only quieted when he saw Nerron beside the saddled horses.

"Lelou says you told him we have to also find a heart and a head before we get the crossbow?" Louis had the swindlesack with the hand hanging from his gold-studded belt. He ran his fingers over it, as if to remind them that so far he was the more successful treasure hunter, not Nerron.

Blue-blooded idiot.

Nerron gave him his most innocent smile.

"Yes, that is correct," he said. Best to let Lelou think he had every detail about this hunt. It would keep the Bug from asking too many questions. But now it was time to deviate a little from the truth.

He put on a concerned face. "Sadly, I just had news that a spy from Albion has gotten hold of the head. And he may get the heart before we catch up with him by coach or train. So I suggest we use magic to stop him."

A deep frown furrowed Louis's deceptively high forehead.

"Albion. Always Albion," he growled. "My father's too nice to them."

Lelou rubbed his pointy nose. "I traveled with magic once. It's very unhealthy. My own shadow started talking to me afterward."

Nerron pulled a leather pouch from his saddlebag. "Not to worry. We Goyl use magic that has no side effects." He didn't actually know if that applied to humans, but of course he didn't mention that little detail.

The pouch contained soil Nerron had collected from a boot print near the elevators at the mine where Guismond's tomb was discovered. He was certain it belonged to Reckless. Lelou watched warily as Nerron spread the soil on a flat stone. What an opportunity to get rid of them all! He could barely resist the temptation, but Louis still had the hand, and Lelou's knowledge might prove useful in the search for the heart. *What about the Waterman, Nerron?* He shot a quick look at Eaumbre. Nerron's instinct told him that even Eaumbre might yet prove useful, even if only to kill the other two.

"There . . . it's quite simple. As long as you do exactly as I say." Nerron waved them to his side impatiently. "Hold the reins in your left hand and put your right hand on the shoulder of the man in front of you."

Lelou had to stand on his tiptoes to reach Louis's shoulders, and the princeling pulled on his calf-leather gloves before he touched the Waterman. Eaumbre, however, clawed his fingers into Nerron's shoulder as if he wanted to remind him how much damage they could do.

Nerron pressed his boot into the soil Jacob Reckless had stood on a few days earlier. He smelled salt in the air.

Water.

He shuddered.

Hopefully, they weren't about to land up to their necks in it.

25. THE SECOND TIME

They had the head. Jacob caught himself feeling ridiculously confident as he and Fox checked in to an inn. After all that cold water, they wanted to spend at least one night in a warm bed. They were in Saint-Riquet, a small town with narrow alleys that spoke of a time long forgotten even on this side of the mirror. The market square was lined by timber-framed houses whose roofs were tiled by Giants, and the church bell always chimed right before death claimed one of its people.

That evening Fox set out to find a livery stable and organize some horses for the journey, and Jacob telegraphed Dunbar and Chanute, hopeful they might have leads in the search for the hand and the heart. He wasn't sure how Dunbar would react to the news that his theory had been right and that they had found the head. Maybe he'd at least be glad they were still alive. Jacob also sent a telegram to Valiant just to keep the Dwarf happy, but he didn't tell Valiant about the head, nor where they were at the moment. Jacob did not trust Valiant's discretion, and the Dwarf would find out soon enough that Jacob had no intention of selling the crossbow to the highest bidder.

It was the first warm day of spring, but the barefoot flower girl selling primroses on the corner was probably still freezing. She was redheaded and as scrawny as a young bird. Fox had barely been much older when Jacob had first seen her human form. He bought a posy off the girl because he knew how much Fox loved primroses. He was just taking the flowers from her small hand when the pain shot into his chest again.

It was even worse than the first time. Jacob stumbled against the nearest wall and pressed his forehead against the cold stone, desperately fighting for air. The pain was so horrendous that he nearly dropped to his knees to beg the Fairies for mercy. Nearly.

The child looked frightened. She picked up the flowers he'd dropped and held them out to him. Jacob could barely grip them.

"Thanks," he stammered.

He somehow managed a smile as he put a copper sou into the girl's hand. The child smiled back with relief.

The inn was only a few alleys away, and yet he could barely manage to get back. The pain lasted until he unlocked the door to his room. He locked it before unbuttoning his shirt. The moth had another spot on its wing, and he could remember only four letters of the Fairy's name.

Start counting, Jacob.

He took some of Alma's powder, but his hands were shaking so badly that he spilled most of it.

Damn, damn, damn...

Where was Fox? Getting a couple of horses shouldn't take that long. When there finally was a knock on the door, it was only the landlady's youngest daughter.

"Monsieur?" She had mended his waistcoat. Her hands reverently brushed over the brocade before she handed it to him. The waistcoat had been a gift from the Empress, and the girl's dress had probably been worn by her older sisters before her. Cinderella. Except in this case, the girl's own mother played the role of the evil stepmother. Jacob had seen how she ordered her youngest about. And here Jacob himself had sold Cinderella's real glass slipper to the Empress. Maybe Dunbar was right. Jacob could still hear the Fir Darrig's angry voice in his ear: *"You treasure hunters turn the magic of this world into a commodity only the powerful can afford!"*

The girl had done her job well, and Jacob put his hand on his gold handkerchief to pay her. The coin that came from it was even thinner than the previous one, but the girl stared at the golden piece as though he had brought her a glass slipper after all. Her hand was rough from cleaning and sewing, but it was as slender as a Fairy's hand, and she looked at him with such longing, as if he were the prince she'd been waiting for. *And why not, Jacob? A little tenderness to fend off death? You're still alive now.* But all he could think of was when Fox would return.

As he opened the door for her, the girl stopped and turned around. "Oh, and I found this in your waistcoat, Monsieur."

Earlking's card was still spotless white. Except for the words on the back:

Forget the hand, Jacob.

Jacob was still standing there, staring at the card, long after the girl had left. He warmed it between his hands (no, it was not Fairy magic), soaked it in gun oil (the simplest way to detect Stilt or Leprechaun spells), and rubbed it with soot to rule out witchcraft. The card stayed perfectly white and kept displaying just those four words: FORGET THE HAND, JACOB. What the hell was that supposed to mean? That the Goyl already had it?

Jacob had seen many writing spells behind the mirror: threats that suddenly appeared on your skin, paper that filled with curses after a wind dropped it in front of your boots, prophecies that carved themselves into the bark of a tree. Gnome, Stilt, or Leprechaun hexes... magical pranks filled the air of this world like pollen.

FORGET THE HAND. And then what?

When Fox returned, the landlady was explaining to Jacob how to get to Gargantua. The city had a library that collected everything about the Kings of Lotharaine, and Jacob hoped to find some clues about the hand there—or maybe get news that the Goyl had already been there....

He decided not to tell Fox about the moth's second bite. She looked tired and was strangely absentminded. When he asked her about it, she claimed it was because of the horses—they weren't really very good. Saint-Riquet was more the place to buy good sheep. Still, Jacob sensed there was something else on her mind. He knew her as well as she knew him.

"Come on, tell me. What's the matter?"

She avoided his eyes.

"My mother lives not far from here. I was wondering how she's doing."

That wasn't all, but Jacob didn't press her any further. There'd always been a tacit understanding between them to respect each other's secrets, an agreement that the past was a land they both didn't care to visit.

"It's not a big detour. I could meet you in Gargantua tonight."

For a split second, he wanted to ask her to stay with him. *What's the matter with you, Jacob?* And of course he didn't. It was bad enough that he himself had never gone to see his mother until it was too late. It had been all too easy to pretend she'd always be there, just like the old house and the apartment full of old ghosts.

"Sure," he said. "I'll be in the hotel right by the library. Or do you want me to come with you?"

Fox shook her head. She only ever spoke very reluctantly about why she'd left her home. All Jacob knew was that the fur was not the only reason.

"Thank you," she said. "But I'd better do this alone."

Yes. There was more, but her face did not invite Jacob to ask.

"How are you feeling?" She put her hand over his heart.

"Good!" Jacob hid the lie behind his brightest smile. Fooling her wasn't easy, but luckily there were plenty of reasons for the tiredness in his voice.

He kissed her on the cheek. "I'll see you in Gargantua." Her skin still smelled of the Mal de Mer.

26. THE BEST

They didn't land in the sea but on a beach as gray as powdered granite. The Waterman complained that his scales were itching, and Lelou swore the magic had made his fingernails grow, but the tracks they found in the sand were so fresh that even the prince managed to follow them. Nerron let him have his fun until they reached the first crossing, where, to the untrained eye, the trail disappeared among the tracks of cart wheels and farmers' feet. For Nerron they were still easier to read than the signposts by the roadside. Reckless and the vixen had taken the road to Saint-Riquet, a provincial town where the inhabitants once used to get regularly trampled by Giants. Their huge teeth could still be found in the surrounding fields. The ivory fetched a good price.

Finding the inn where Reckless and the vixen were

staying wasn't hard. The Bug, with his innocent face, even got the landlady to give him the room number.

"What are we waiting for?" Louis asked while the Waterman eyed the curtained windows with a blank face. "Let's get that spy."

"So he can destroy the head as soon as we come through the door?" Nerron quickly waved them behind a coach that was parked by the curb. "We have to lure him out!" he hissed. "We need a bait."

Lelou shot him a reproachful look.

Oh, this is going to be difficult, Nerron. But he had to get rid of the three for a few hours. Reckless was his. And he wasn't going to see the head dangling from Louis's tacky belt as well.

"We need a girl," he whispered to them. "But I heard he only goes for virgins. Golden-haired. Eighteen years at the most."

Lelou adjusted his glasses. That was usually a warning signal. "Virgins? Isn't that the bait for Unicorns?" he twanged.

"Are you now going to teach me treasure hunting?" Nerron hissed at him. "I'm sure you're as good at dealing with Albian spies as you are at teaching Louis his ancestral history."

The Bug wanted to retort something, but Louis found his new task as irresistible as Nerron had hoped.

"I'll find a virgin for the Goyl." His smile was smug, as befitted a prince. "But then that head is mine."

Lelou pressed his thin lips together, and Eaumbre shot Nerron a knowing glance before he followed Louis, but all three disappeared into the narrow alleys, and Jacob Reckless was less than a stone's throw away.

Nerron hid in an archway opposite the inn, but he had to change his position several times because some upright burgher stopped to stare at him. He was just beginning to pray for a mounted Goyl squadron to sweep through this sleepy street when he saw Reckless step out of the inn with a woman. The color of her hair left little room for doubt—it was the vixen. Nerron usually didn't find human women attractive, but she was as beautiful as everybody said. He wondered whether she and Reckless were a pair. What other reason could there be for taking a woman on a treasure hunt, even if she was a shape-shifter? Women were either unfathomable, like the Fairy Kami'en had fallen for, or they were weak, like his own mother, who'd gotten involved with an Onyx and had made her son a bastard. Sometimes you convinced yourself that you loved them, but they could never be trusted, and in the end all one really desired was their amethyst skin. Never mind.... The vixen turned her horse westward, while Reckless took the road south. Excellent. Things would be much easier with him on his own.

The horse Nerron had hired found the sight of him just

as disturbing as the good people of Saint-Riquet had. And by the time it finally allowed him to climb into the saddle, Reckless was out of sight. Nerron caught up with him just as he entered the forest that soon replaced the fields and meadows to the south of the town. Nerron was grateful for the shade under the trees, not only because it made him almost invisible. Sunlight no longer hurt his eyes since he'd had them hexed by a child-eater. It did, however, still crack his skin, even though he oiled it every day.

The forest was one of the former royal woods that had for a long time been the exclusive hunting grounds of the Lotharainian nobility. In the meantime they also provided wood for the factories and the railroads. This one, however, was still nearly as dense as it had been in the old days, and it reminded Nerron of the stone forests beneath the earth, which filled enormous caves with branches of garnet and leaves of the same malachite that ran through his skin.

He only pulled out his blowpipe once Reckless had ridden far between the trees. The plant shoot Nerron pushed into the narrow steel pipe was covered with thorns so sharp that only a Goyl could touch them without tearing his skin. It landed on the clearing Reckless was headed toward, and it began to grow as soon as it touched the ground. Choke vines grew fast. Faster than any prey could run.

Reckless reined in his horse as soon as he realized what was creeping toward him. He wanted to turn about, but the vines were already growing around his horse's hooves. The vines clawed into Reckless's clothes and wrapped themselves around his arms while his horse reared up in panic. Reckless was nearly trampled to death when the vines pulled him from the saddle. *Careful!* Nerron wanted him alive.

The Goyl tethered his horse to a tree. The stupid nag still shied from him. Reckless's horse had managed to free itself. It trotted toward him, bleeding and trembling, as soon as he stepped out into the path. Nerron caught the animal and reached into the backpack hanging from the saddle. The head was still in a swindlesack. Of course. Only amateurs carried their quarry in plain sight.

Reckless had already all but disappeared. The vines had enveloped him in a spiky cocoon. Nerron pulled them apart until he could see the face of his rival. Reckless was unconscious—choke vines quickly suffocated their victims—but he opened his eyes when Nerron punched him in the face.

Nerron held up the swindlesack. "Thank you! I'm very glad I didn't have to go on a boat. Where do you think I should look for the heart?"

Reckless tried to sit up, though the vines were driving their thorns into his soft flesh. The wolves would soon catch the scent of his blood. These woods were home to an infamous pack that had been accustomed to human flesh by a local nobleman who used to feed his enemies to them.

"Even if I knew, why should I tell you?" The gray eyes were alert, and there wasn't much fear in them. It was exactly as everybody said: *Reckless fears nothing. He thinks he's immortal.*

Nerron tied the swindlesack to his belt.

"If you tell me, I will kill you before the wolves eat you."

Oh yes, he was afraid, though he hid it well. And he didn't care. Enviable. Nerron despised fear. Fear of water. Fear of others. Fear of himself. He fought it with rage, but that only made it grow, like a well-fed creature.

"I already have the hand." He couldn't resist a little bragging. Too often had he been forced to listen to the tales of Jacob Reckless's glorious deeds.

"Perfect." His adversary's face turned white with pain as he tried to sit up once more. "Then I can take it off you when I get my head back."

"Really?" Nerron was wearing the gloves that had already protected him from many spells, yet the pain shot all the way to his shoulder as he pulled the head from the sack. The eyes were closed, but the lips were slightly parted. Nerron quickly shoved the head back into the sack before it could utter something. Even a dead Warlock might still have a spell waiting on his lips.

Nerron put the swindlesack in his coat pocket. His lizard-leather coat would have given Reckless's human skin much more protection than the fabric his coat was made from. As soft as his skin, and just as tearable. "Now, before all your wisdom gets ingested by a wolf...how did you manage to steal the red riding hood from the child-eater in Moulin? I heard she already had you in her oven."

"I'll tell you if you tell me how you found that white blackbird. I searched for it for months." Reckless tried to free one of his hands, but choke vines were very reliable fetters. "Does its song really make you young again?"

"Yes, but the effect barely lasts a week. My client had already paid me before he found out." Nerron rubbed his cracked skin. It ached, even in the shade of the forest. Once this hunt was over, he urgently needed a few months underground. But there was one more question he wanted to ask.

He pulled his knife.

"Just out of curiosity...and I promise you'll take the answer with you to your grave—or should I say, into a wolf's intestines? Where are you hiding your jade-skinned brother?"

Ah. So there was a way to get through that smug mask.

"Will. Wasn't that his name?" Nerron leaned over his prisoner and cut a fresh shoot from the vine that had wrapped around Reckless's soft neck. There'd always be another opportunity to use choke vines. "Did you know the onyx have tasked five of their best spies to find him?"

Reckless's eyes followed every move Nerron made. He had himself under control again, but human eyes were still much more treacherous than a Goyl's. Their alertness betrayed what his silence was trying to conceal. Yes, the rumors were true: the Jade Goyl, who had saved Kami'en's stone skin, was indeed Jacob Reckless's brother.

"Where is he?" Nerron wrapped the fresh shoot in the cloth that still had a few thorns of the old one stuck in. "You could both buy a palace in Lutis with all the silver the onyx have spent searching for him, and they still haven't found even the faintest trail. That must be quite a remarkable hiding place."

Reckless smiled. "Maybe I'll tell you if you get these thorns off me."

Oh, Nerron liked him—as much as he was capable of liking anyone. It was just as well that feeling overcame him so rarely. His mother was the only person he'd ever given his unquestioning affection to. Love was a luxury you paid for with far too much pain.

"No," he said. "I'd better not. The onyx are already unbearable. Doesn't bear thinking about what will happen if the Jade Goyl helps one of them grab Kami'en's crown."

"Yes?" Reckless swallowed a groan. His skin was probably well larded with thorns by now. "What do you think will happen when you get them the crossbow?"

Nice try.

Nerron tucked the cloth with the shoot into his pocket. "Our clients are our professional secret, aren't they?" He could already hear the wolves between the trees. "I'm not asking you whom you're seeking the crossbow for."

He gave his rival one last smile.

"I really am glad our paths crossed this way. I was getting sick of constantly hearing that you are the best in our trade. Good luck with the wolves. Maybe you'll think of something. Surprise me! They don't leave much behind, and it would be such a pity if the vixen has to spend the rest of her life searching for you."

Nerron jumped onto his horse just as the first wolf came slinking toward Reckless. The others would soon follow. Unlike the onyx lords, however, Nerron didn't find the screams of a dying man very entertaining.

And Louis had probably found a virgin by now.

27. A HOUSE AT THE EDGE OF THE VILLAGE

The house looked even more shabby than she'd remembered. Mold sprouting in the stone walls. The stench of rotting straw and pig manure. Fishing had made some men along this coast rich, but her father had always taken his money to the tavern rather than bring it home. *Father. Why do you still call him that, Fox?* Her mother had married him when Fox was three. Two years and two months after the death of her actual father.

A stump was all that was left of the apple tree by the gate, which she had climbed so often as a child because the world always seemed much less frightening when viewed from above. The sight nearly made her turn her horse about, but her mother had planted primroses in front of the house, just as she used to every spring. The pale yellow blossoms reminded Fox of all the good times she'd had because of her behind those shabby walls. As a child she'd wondered that something as fragile as a flower could withstand the wind and the world. Maybe her mother had always planted those primroses to teach her and her brothers just that.

Fox touched the posy she'd tucked into her saddle. The blossoms had withered, but that didn't make them any less beautiful. Jacob had given them to her. For a brief moment, those dried flowers made her feel as though he was by her side. Their two lives, connected through a flower.

The gate stood open, just as it had on the day they chased her away. Her two older brothers and her stepfather. They'd tried to take the fur dress away from her. Fox had torn it from their hands, and she'd started to run. She had felt the bruises from the stones they'd thrown at her for weeks, even under the vixen's fur. Her youngest brother had stayed hidden in the house, together with her mother, who'd stared through the window as though trying to hold her back with her eyes. But she hadn't protected her daughter; how should she have? She could never even protect herself.

As Fox walked toward the door, she could see her younger self running across the yard. Her red hair braided into pigtails, her knees covered in scabs and bruises. *Celeste, where have you been this time?*

She'd been in Ogre caves with Jacob, and in the oven

rooms of Black Witches, yet she'd never wanted to leave a place as badly as she had this one. Not even her love for her mother had been able to bring her back. Now it was her love for Jacob that led her here again.

Knock, Celeste. They won't be here. Not at this time.

As soon as her hand touched the wood of the door, Fox was assaulted by the past. It gulped up whatever strength and confidence she'd been given by the fur and the many years away from this place. Jacob! Fox pictured his face so it would remind her of the present and of the Fox she'd become.

"Who's there?" Her mother's voice. What a mighty animal the past is. The hushed songs her mother used to sing to her at bedtime...her mother's fingers in her hair as she braided it...Who is there? Yes, who?

"It's me, Celeste."

The name tasted of the honey Fox used to steal from the wild bees when she was a child, and of the nettles that used to sting her bare legs.

Silence. Was her mother standing behind the door, once more hearing the impact of the stones on the ground and on her child's skin? It felt like an eternity before she pushed back the latch.

She'd grown old. The long black hair was now gray, and her beauty had all but faded, washed, little by little, from her face by each passing year.

"Celeste..." She spoke the name as though it'd been waiting on her lips all these years, like a butterfly she'd never shooed away. She took her daughter's hands before Fox could pull them away. Stroked Fox's hair and kissed her face. Again and again. She held Fox tight, as though she wanted to get back all the years when she hadn't held her child. Then she pulled the girl into the house. She latched the door. They both knew why.

The house still smelled of fish and damp winters. The same table. The same chairs. The same bench by the oven. And behind the windows, nothing but meadows and piebald cows. As though time had stopped. But on her way here, Fox had passed many abandoned houses. It was a hard life, having to rely on sea and land to feed you. The machines' noisy promises were so alluring: Everything could be made by human hands, and wind and winter no longer had to be feared. Yet it was the wind and the winter that had shaped these people.

Fox reached for the bowl of soup her mother had pushed toward her.

"You're doing well." It wasn't a question. There was relief in her voice. Relief. Guilt. And so much helpless love. But that wasn't enough.

"I need the ring."

Her mother put down the milk jug from which she was filling her cup.

"You still have it?"

Her mother didn't answer.

"Please. I need it!"

"He wouldn't have wanted me to give it to you." She

pushed the milk toward her daughter. "You can't know how many years you still have."

"I'm young."

"So was he."

"But you're alive, and that's all he ever wanted."

Her mother sat down on one of the chairs on which she'd spent so many hours of her life, mending clothes, rocking babies....

"So you're in love with someone. What is his name?"

But Fox didn't want to say Jacob's name. Not in this house. "I owe him my life. That's all." It wasn't all, but her mother would understand.

She brushed the gray hair from her face. "Ask me for anything else."

"No. And you know you owe me this." The words were out before Fox could hold them back.

The pain on the tired face made Fox forget all the anger she felt. Her mother got up.

"I never should have told you that story." She smoothed the tablecloth. "I just wanted you to know what kind of a man your father was."

She brushed her hand across the tablecloth again, as though she could brush away everything that had made her life so hard. Then she slowly walked to the chest where she kept the few things she called her own. From it she took a wooden box that was covered in black lace. It was lace from the dress she'd worn in mourning for two years.

"Maybe I'd have survived the fever even if he hadn't put it on my finger," she said as she opened the box.

Inside it was a ring of glass.

"What I need it for is worse than fever," Fox said. "But I promise you, I'll use it only if there is no other way."

Her mother shook her head and firmly closed her fingers around the box. But then she heard some noises outside.

Steps and voices. Sometimes, when the sea was too rough, the men returned early from their boats.

Her mother looked toward the door. Fox took the box from her hand. She felt ashamed of the fear she saw on her mother's face. Yet it wasn't just fear; there was also love. There was always love, even for the man who struck her children.

He knocked on the door, and Fox pushed back the latch. She longed for the vixen's teeth, but she wanted to look her stepfather in the eyes. She'd barely reached up to his shoulders when he drove her out of the house.

He wasn't as big as she'd remembered him. *Because you were smaller then, Celeste.* So small. He'd been the Giant and she the Dwarf. The Giant who smashed everything in his path. But now she was as tall as he, and he'd grown old. His face was red, as always—red from the wine, the sun, and the rage. Rage against anything that moved.

It took him a moment before he realized who was standing in front of him.

He flinched, as if from a snake, and his hand closed around the stick he was leaning on. He'd always had sticks or belts. He used to throw boots and wooden logs at his sons and Fox, as though they were rats hiding behind his oven.

"What are you doing here?" he barked. "Get out!"

He wanted to grab her as he used to, but Fox shoved him back and slapped the stick out of his hand.

"Let her go." Her mother's voice was trembling, but at least this time she said something.

"Get out of my way," Fox said to the man she once had to call Father, even though he'd taught her to despise the word itself.

He lifted his fists. How often had her eyes been glued to those hands, full of fear of the tanned skin on the knuckles tightening, turning white. She saw him in her dreams sometimes, and he always had the mouth of a wolf.

She pushed past him without saying another word. She wanted to forget he existed, to imagine that he'd just disappeared one day, like Jacob's father, or that her mother had never married again.

"I will be back," Fox said to her.

Her mother stood by the window as Fox walked toward the gate. Just like the last time. And just like then, the three of them blocked her path, her stepfather and his two sons. He'd gotten his stick back, and his eldest was holding the pitchfork. Gustave and René. Gustave looked even more dense than he used to. René was smarter, but he did whatever Gustave told him. It was René who'd thrown the first stone.

Shape-shifter. Nobody had understood better what Jacob's brother had felt as he grew a skin of jade. Yet unlike Will, Fox had always been able to choose to wear the fur.

"Go on! Find a stone!" she hissed at René. "Or are you waiting for your brother's orders?"

He ducked his head and looked uneasily at the pistol on her belt.

"Get the hell out of here!" Her stepfather squinted his myopic eyes.

She was no longer afraid of him. It was an exhilarating feeling. "Where is Thierry?" she asked. There was one more brother.

Gustave just gave her a hostile stare. His shirt was speckled with fish blood.

"He went to the city," said René.

"Shut your mouth!" his father yelled.

Being his stepdaughter hadn't been easy, but his youngest had it just as bad. Thierry had envied Fox her fur, and she was glad that he'd managed to get away.

"You know what they say about shape-shifters." She held up her hand. "Everybody we touch will grow a fur as well. Who wants to go first?"

She shoved her hand into her stepfather's chest, so hard he would be checking his skin for red hairs for days. Gustave stumbled back with a curse, and Fox was out of the gate before the three could regain their courage. As she mounted her horse, she remembered how she'd stumbled across the meadows, sobbing and bleeding, pressing the fur dress to her chest. This time she took the road. She looked around once more at the window where her mother had been standing, but all she saw was the reflection of the sky on the glass, and the primroses growing next to the door.

❦

She made one more stop before continuing on to Gargantua. The house was dilapidated, and the grave by the crumbled garden wall was overgrown, its headstone poking out from a thick nest of grass and roots. A hazel bush had sprung up in front of it. The branches were covered in catkins, and beneath them lay a few nuts from the previous autumn. The moss grew thick on her father's engraved name, etching it in green letters onto the gray stone: Joseph Marie Auger.

Fox had come here often as a child. She'd pluck the grass from the damp soil, place wildflowers on the stone, and search the abandoned house for signs of the life she and her mother might have had there. This was where she'd met the vixen for the first time, and it was in the woods bordering the crumbled wall that she had saved the wounded fox and her pups from Gustave's and René's clubs.

"I know, I haven't been back in a while," she said. "I asked Maman for the ring. I'm not sure she used your gift wisely. Sometimes I wish you'd let her die and kept the years you gave her for yourself. You can only say this to a grave, but it feels good to say it. Maybe you could have protected me. I've found someone who did that for these past years. There's nobody I love more. He's looked out for me so often, but now it's my turn to protect him."

Fox gathered the nuts from the grave and put them in her pocket. Then she swung herself onto her horse. The sun was already quite low, and Jacob didn't have time to wait for her.

28. THORNS AND TEETH

The wolf's breath stank of the rotting flesh that was lodged between its teeth. The eyes were nearly as golden as the Goyl's. Jacob had heard of the wolves in these parts. Supposedly, they took their victims even from their beds and parlors. Not important—Jacob knew this was going to be messy. Maybe drowning wouldn't have been such a bad death after all.

There were now five wolves circling him. He tried to free one hand to get to his knife, but the choke vine dug its thorns into his flesh so relentlessly that the pain drew out a suppressed cry.

Scream, Jacob. Why not? Maybe Fox will hear you. No. She was probably already in Gargantua, waiting. What would she do if he didn't turn up? Search for him, as the

Goyl had said? But surely not for the rest of her life. The vixen would find out quickly enough what had happened to him. The thought was consoling in a way.

One of the wolves dragged its tongue over Jacob's face, getting a taste. Jacob tried to free at least one leg so he could kick at it, but the thorns clawed even deeper into his flesh. *Damn, Jacob, think of something.*

They stopped.

The larger one licked its mouth.

The end of the prelude.

Jacob threw himself to one side. He heard teeth snap at empty air. The next one bit into the vines, but they weren't going to protect him for long. Jacob desperately tried to remember what he knew about choke vines. He'd used them himself to slow down pursuers, though never to capture them. One of the wolves bit into the vines around his chest; another was pulling at the ones around his legs.

Choke vines, Jacob. How could you forget! What do they like most?

He threw himself around again, no matter how much it hurt, and he rolled around on the forest floor. The wolves let go with angry barks while the thorns tore through his skin.

Blood—the taste choke vines relished above all else. Of course, it also made the wolves even more frenzied. The next bite was so determined that the teeth actually found his flesh. Jacob howled as the teeth dug into his side. But the vines had also tasted the blood, and they began to grow even faster.

Fresh vines shot out toward the wolves, hardening as they grew. They clawed at the animals' fur and enveloped Jacob in an ever-thicker cocoon. He found it hard to breathe, and his clothes were sticky with his own blood, but at least the wolves couldn't reach him anymore. They howled with rage and dug their teeth again and again into the thorny branches, even though the vines were now also growing around them. Jacob fought for air. His fingers found the hilt of his knife, but he couldn't move his hands enough to get hold of it.

The lead wolf paused. It panted with lust for the flesh that smelled so deliciously of blood and the cold sweat of fear.

Then it snapped at the vines that had grown around Jacob's throat. Jacob tried to turn away, but the vines that protected him also held him like fly in a spider's web. After one more bite, the wolf's breath brushed over naked skin. Jacob could already feel the teeth on his throat, and then...

Nothing.

No crunching cartilage. No choking on his own blood. Instead, a shrill whine. And the sharp voice of a man.

Through the vines, Jacob could see boots and the blade of a rapier. One wolf dropped with a slashed throat. Another freed itself from the vines and attacked, but the blade killed it in midair. The others drew back. Finally, one of them let out a disappointed bark and they all ran, their fur peppered with thorns.

His rescuer turned around. He was hardly older than

Jacob. His rapier cut through the vines like a letter opener through paper. There weren't many blades that could make such short work of choke vines. Jacob clambered out from the chopped-up vines while the stranger picked the thorns from his gloves. His clothes were as fine as his blade. The lapels of his jacket were lined with the fur of a black fox. In Lotharaine, only the highest nobility was allowed to hunt these animals.

The fairy-tale prince. And he even looked the part.

Great. Just be grateful he wasn't busy saving Snow-White. The last time Jacob had felt so stupid was in the schoolyard, when a teacher had to free him from the choke hold of a girl.

"Choke vines are quite rare in these parts." His savior helped him to his feet. "Did the wolves bite you?"

Thank him, Jacob. Go on.

"It's not that bad." He touched the wound in his side. "How did you drive them off so fast?" *Stop it. You sound as if it was he who set the wolves on you.* Pride was so tedious. But his rescuer just shrugged.

"My lands are near Champlitte. There we used to have trouble with beasts that were much bigger than these." He offered his hand to Jacob. "Guy de Troisclerq."

Jacob wiped the blood off his hands. "Jacob Reckless." *Treasure hunter and certifiable idiot.* He could barely stand upright.

Troisclerq pointed at Jacob's torn clothes. "You'll have

to bathe in bark suds, or else the wounds will get infected. Those thorns can be nasty."

"I know!" *Jacob!* He forced his mouth into a smile. "It appears you saved my life."

Troisclerq threw the chopped-up vines into the center of the clearing. "I was in the right place at the right time—that's all."

And noble as well. *Stop it, Jacob! How is it his fault you stumbled into the Goyl's trap like an amateur?*

The lighter that Troisclerq held to the vines was one of the first ones Jacob had seen behind the mirror. They cost a fortune. He plucked a tendril from his hair and threw it into the flames. He was alive, but the head was gone.

The bite wound in his side hurt so badly that he had to ask Troisclerq to catch his horse for him. The sight of his plundered backpack filled him with such helpless rage that he wanted to ride after the Bastard on the spot. But his noble savior was right—he needed to have that bite looked at and to disinfect his shredded skin, or it would soon get septic. And Fox was waiting for him in Gargantua.

At least he managed to get into his saddle without Troisclerq having to help him with that as well. His rescuer rode a white horse that made all the mounts Jacob had ever owned look like nags in comparison.

"Where were you headed?"

"Gargantua."

"Excellent. That's where I'm going as well. I'm catching the evening coach to Vena."

Oh, perfect. Exactly what he'd planned to do as well. He hoped his savior would not tell their fellow travelers how they had met. *The heart in the east.* He had to find it before the Bastard did, or he might as well have let the wolves have their feast.

Jacob cast a final look at the clearing where the Goyl had caught him like a rabbit. It was a long journey to Austry, and Troisclerq's face would be there all the way, reminding him of his stupidity.

"Reckless?" Troisclerq drove his horse to Jacob's side. "Are you that treasure hunter who used to work for the Austrian Empress?"

Jacob closed his tattered fingers around the reins. "The very one."

And the idiot who let himself be robbed like a dilettante.

29. A NEW FACE

The inn where Fox was supposed to meet Jacob was one where they'd already stayed before. Back then, they'd come to Gargantua to search for a jacket made of donkey skin that hid its wearer from his enemies. Le Chat Botté was situated right next to the library, and it also stood in the shade of the monument erected by the town to commemorate the Giant for whom it was named. His effigy was as tall as a church tower, and it attracted travelers from far away, but Fox had no eyes for his silver hair, nor for the eyes made of blue glass, which supposedly moved at night. She longed for Jacob's face. Her excursion into the past had only made it clear to her once more that he was the only home she had.

The barroom of Le Chat Botté was much more elegant

than Chanute's Ogre. Tablecloths, candles, mirrors on the walls, and waitresses with lace aprons. The landlord boasted to have personally known the legendary Puss. A pair of well-worn boots hung by the door as evidence. Those boots, however, would have barely fit a child's feet, and every treasure hunter knew that Puss in Boots had been as tall as a grown man.

The landlord gave Fox and her men's clothes a disapproving look before he started searching the guest register for Jacob's name.

"Mademoiselle?" The man rising from one of the tables was so beautiful that more than one of the women present followed him with their eyes. Fox, however, only saw the black fur on his collar.

He stopped in front of her and touched it with his fingers. "A gift from my grandfather," he said. "Personally, I find no pleasure in that kind of hunt. I'm always on the side of the fox."

His hair was as black as the shadows in a forest, but his eyes were light blue, like a summer sky. Day and night.

"Jacob asked me to keep an eye out for you. He's at the doctor's—he's fine," he added when Fox gave him a worried look. "He stumbled into some choke vines, and some wolves. Luckily, we were on the same road." He bowed and kissed her hand. "Guy de Troisclerq. Jacob described you very well."

The doctor's practice wasn't far. Troisclerq explained the way to Fox. Wolves and choke vines... Jacob generally knew how to keep wolves away, and choke vines were supposed to have been eradicated from Lotharaine; after Crookback's niece was killed by choke vines, they'd been ordered to be burnt. Jacob met Fox halfway, his hands bandaged and his shirt splattered with blood. She'd rarely seen him as angry.

"The Bastard has the head." He flinched in pain as she embraced him, and she had a hard time coaxing out of him exactly what had happened. At least for now his injured pride had pushed away all thoughts of death, but Fox couldn't think of anything else. The haste, the dangers, the time it had taken them to find the head—for nothing! They were again empty-handed. Fox was sick with fear, and her hand clamped around the box in her pocket.

"And he's got the hand as well!" Jacob looked up at the monument. Flocks of birds were nesting in the Giant's ears. Fox knew that Jacob wasn't seeing the chiseled stone but the onyx-black face of the Bastard.

"Bastard!" he panted. "I will find the heart before him, and then I'll get the head and the hand. We're riding to Vena today."

"You can't possibly ride that far. Troisclerq says one of the wolves bit you in the side." Even a good horse would take ten days to reach Vena.

"Really? And what else did he tell you?"

"He didn't tell me anything else!" Oh, his pride. He'd probably rather have been eaten by wolves than have beeen saved by a stranger. "Why do we have to go to Vena? Did you hear from Chanute or Dunbar?"

"Yes, but what they know, I already knew myself. Guismond's daughter is buried in Vena, in the crypt of the imperial family. That's the only lead I have."

That wasn't much. And Jacob knew it.

"There's a coach tonight."

"That'll take us at least two weeks! You know those coachmen stop at every tavern. And the Goyl must be on his way already."

They both knew he was right. Even if they bribed the coachman, it would still take them more than ten days. The Bastard was going to be in Vena before them. All they could hope was that he didn't find the heart, though he'd already been quite fast with the hand.

Jacob held his wounded side. For a moment, Fox saw something on his face she'd never seen there before. He was giving up. It was one fleeting moment, but that moment scared her more than anything.

"You rest," she said, stroking his scratched face. "I'll get us tickets for the coach."

Jacob nodded. "How's your mother?" he asked as she turned.

"Fine," Fox answered, fingering the box in her pocket. She was so worried about him.

30. NOTHING GOES

Eight people in one badly sprung coach that smelled of sweat and eau de cologne: a lawyer from St. Omar with his daughter; two governesses from Arlas, who knitted through the entire journey even though their fingers got pricked on every bump in the road; and a priest who tried to convince them that the Goyl were direct descendants of the Devil. Jacob wished himself in the black forest, or back at the Blood Wedding, or even on board the sinking *Titania*... and they'd only been traveling for three days.

The coins his handkerchief produced were becoming ever more pathetic, but the coachman had accepted his with wide eyes. Compared to the copper coins he usually received, gold was still worth a fortune, even if it was paper-thin. The coin had spurred him so much that the other travelers soon began to complain about the lack of rest stops. Five days in, one of the wheels broke in a mountain gorge. It took them hours to unharness the horses and lead them along the icy road toward the next coach station. Jacob couldn't decide which was worse, his throbbing side or the voice in his head: *You should have taken a horse. The Bastard must be in Vena already. You're dead, Jacob....*

The stationmaster refused to send his men into the night to repair the wheel. He told them about wood sprites and kobolds that supposedly roamed the gorge. He charged them a fortune for his cold rooms, and he only sent his cook back into the kitchen after Troisclerq dropped a pouch full of silver on his polished counter. Troisclerq paid for them all. He arranged for the fire in the dining room to be stoked, and he put his coat around Fox's shoulders when he saw her shivering as she brushed the snow from her hair. Jacob did not miss the grateful look she gave him in return. She was wearing a dress she'd bought in Gargantua while they'd waited for the coach, and Jacob caught himself wondering whether she'd put it on especially for his rescuer.

Not that Troisclerq wasn't also taking care of Jacob. As soon as he noticed Jacob holding his hand to the bite in his side, he offered him two black pastilles. Witch-caramel. Not something people generally carried on them. It was made by the child-eaters, and one had better not ask about the ingredients. How did someone with such fine clothes and manners get hold of Witch-caramel? *Maybe the same way he learned how to drive off a pack of wolves, Jacob.* And anyway, Lotharaine was swarming with Dark Witches ever since Crookback had granted them asylum in return for straightening his spine.

The pastilles were even better than moor-root, and Witch-caramel had no side effects. Jacob had to admit he was beginning to like his rescuer. Troisclerq hadn't said a word about saving Jacob in the woods, not to Fox or to the other travelers. He might have given Fox a few too many looks, but even that Jacob could forgive. After all, he couldn't ask the man to pretend to be blind.

It was best not to drink wine with Witch-caramel, but not even the child-eater pastilles could soothe his injured pride, and Jacob could still see the Goyl sneering down at him. Fox shot him a worried look as he ordered his second carafe. He answered her with a smile that he hoped didn't give away too much of the humiliating self-pity he was wallowing in. Self-pity, injured pride, and fear of death. A nasty mix, and they still had several days of traveling in that stuffy coach ahead of them. He filled his glass to the rim.

The pain shot into his chest so suddenly that he thought he could feel his heart explode behind his ribs. Nothing would have soothed that pain. Jacob clawed at the table around which they were all sitting, and he suppressed the groan that so badly wanted to escape from his lips.

Fox looked at him. She pushed back her chair.

The pain blurred her face as much as the others', and he could feel his whole body begin to shake.

"Jacob!" Fox took his hand. She talked at him, but he couldn't hear her. There was only the pain as it seared another letter of the Fairy's name from his memory. Jacob felt Troisclerq's arms reaching under his, then Troisclerq and the coachman carrying him up the stairs, where they put him on a bed and examined the wound the wolf had torn into his side. He wanted to tell them they were wasting their time, but the moth was still feeding, and then he was gone.

❧

When he came to, the pain was gone, but his body still remembered. The room was dark. Only a gas lamp burning on the table. Fox was standing next to it; she was looking at something in her hand. The lamp's light made her skin as white as milk.

She spun around as he sat up, and hid her hand behind her back.

"What do you have there?"

She didn't answer. "The moth on your chest has three spots," she said. "When was the other time?"

"In Saint-Riquet." Jacob had never seen her face look so pale. He sat up. "What is that in your hand?"

She flinched.

"What's that in your hand, Fox?" His knees were still weak from the pain, but Jacob grabbed her arm and pulled the hand out from behind her back.

She opened her fingers.

A glass ring.

Jacob had seen a similar one in the Empress's Chambers of Miracles.

"You didn't put that on my finger, did you? Fox!" He grabbed her shoulders. "Tell me the truth. This ring was not on my finger. Please!"

Tears ran down her face. But then she shook her head. Jacob took the ring before she could close her hand. She reached for it, but Jacob put it in his pocket. Then he pulled her close. She sobbed like a child, and he held her as firmly as he could.

"Promise me!" he whispered. "Promise me you'll never try something like that again. Promise!"

"No!" she replied.

"What? Do you think I want you dead instead of me?"

"I just wanted to give you time."

"These rings are dangerous. Every second you put it on my finger will lose you a year. And sometimes they can't be pulled off before they have taken your entire life."

She struggled free and wiped the tears off her face.

"I want you to live." She whispered the words, as though she feared death might hear them and take them as a challenge.

"Good. Then let's find the heart before the Goyl does. I'm sure I can ride. Who knows when they'll get that coach repaired."

"There are no horses." Fox went to the window. "The

landlord sold his only riding horses the day before yesterday, to four men. He boasted to Troisclerq that one of them was Louis of Lotharaine. He had a Goyl with him, with a green-speckled skin. They only stopped briefly and rode on that same afternoon."

The day before yesterday. *It's even more hopeless than you thought.*

Fox pushed open the window, as if letting out the fear. The air that came rushing in was as cold and damp as snow. There was laughter from downstairs, and Jacob recognized the loud voice of the lawyer who'd sat next to him in the coach.

Louis of Lotharaine. The Bastard was hunting the crossbow for Crookback.

Fox turned around. "Troisclerq heard me ask about horses because we had to push on urgently. He bribed the landlord to send his workmen to the coach. I told him we'll pay him back, but he won't hear of it."

They would pay him back. Jacob pulled the handkerchief from his pocket. He was already too deep in Troisclerq's debt.

"I tried that," said Fox.

She was right. No matter how hard Jacob rubbed the fabric, the only thing the tattered handkerchief produced was the card on which were still the same words. FORGET THE HAND, JACOB. It had been good advice.

"We could ask Chanute to send some money," Fox suggested. “You still have some in the bank in Schwanstein, right?”

Yes, he did. But it wasn’t much. Jacob took her hand.

“You’ll get the ring back once all this is over,” he said. “But you have to promise me you’ll never use it.”

31. TOO MANY COOKS

The best! No, Nerron couldn't remember ever having felt that good. He'd taken Jacob Reckless's loot and had humiliated him like a rookie.

Not even the princeling could spoil his mood, even though Louis told everyone Nerron had let an Albian spy get away, and that after he, Louis, had brought him an impeccable virgin. A whole day long the prince refused to set off to Vena, and even now he kept sneaking off with every girl that let herself be dazzled by his diamond buttons. The Waterman spent his nights searching the barns and farmhouses for him. Eaumbre had begun to eye his royal charge with such distaste, Nerron wouldn't have been surprised if he'd found Louis drowned in a trough one morning. Of course, none of that was mentioned in the journal in which Lelou kept scribbling tirelessly.

Instead, it noted every castle they passed, every icy road, and every mountain gnome that threw a stone at them. Nerron checked the tutor's writings every night (luckily, the Bug wrote very legibly) and regularly fell asleep over them.

Yes, it was all going splendidly. Despite Louis. Despite Lelou. Despite Eaumbre's fish stench. They'd soon be in Vena; he'd find the heart, take the hand off Louis, and then toast to the memory of Jacob Reckless.

They were spending the night in a roadside inn in Bavaria—Vena was just a day's travel away—when it dawned on Nerron that the final leg of his hunt was probably not going to be quite as smooth.

He woke up to the feeling of cold steel on his neck. Louis was standing over him, an elven-dusted look in his eyes, holding his saber to the Goyl's throat.

"You lied to me, Goyl," he growled. He was holding a swindlesack, which Nerron, even though he'd drunk a lot of that spiced hot wine they served in Bavarian inns, immediately recognized as the one he'd taken off Reckless. Nerron needed just one glimpse of Lelou's bug face peering out from behind Louis's elbow to understand who'd put the princeling on the trail of the sack.

"It's the head!" Lelou observed accusingly. "It gave me a jolt. And it screams."

"It probably put a curse on you," Nerron said, pushing Louis's saber away.

Lelou grew a little pale around his pointy nose, but

Louis leaned even lower over Nerron's bed. "You tried to trick me, Goyl. How long have you had the head?"

"He wanted to show it to you." The Waterman was a dark outline in the open door. "The Goyl asked me where he might find you, but you weren't in your bed."

That was probably the worst lie Nerron had ever heard, but the Waterman's whisper made it sound like a weighty truth.

"I work for your father," Nerron said, pulling the sack from Louis's fingers. "Or have you forgotten that? I am just following his instructions. The head stays with me, unless you let me teach you how to shield yourself from its curses."

Lelou was still hiding behind Louis's back.

Just you wait, Bug Man. From now on, I'll be sending every mountain gnome we meet your way.

Louis stroked the blade of his saber, probably picturing how it might cut through Goyl skin. "Fine. You keep the head. For now."

Eaumbre was still standing in the door.

Lelou might have suspected that Nerron was lying. But the Waterman knew it.

Nerron went to Eaumbre's room as soon as he heard the Bug's cricketlike snores from his room, and a girl's giggles from behind Louis's door.

Eaumbre was lying on his bed, pouring a bowl of water on his scaly chest.

"What's your price?" Nerron asked.

"We'll see," the Waterman whispered.

32. THE HEART IN THE EAST

It took them fifteen days, despite Troisclerq's silver, and every one of those days only convinced Jacob more that the Bastard had already found the heart.

After his collapse, the other travelers had been reluctant to get into the coach with Jacob. (The pox was going around in Bavaria and Austry.) But Troisclerq made a point of sitting next to him. Yes, Jacob was beginning to like him. Troisclerq knew as much about horses as about the newest Goyl weaponry, and he didn't mind discussing for hours whether Albian or Catalunian blades were better. They shared a passion for fencing, though Troisclerq preferred the rapier over Jacob's saber. The other passengers probably cursed them for their endless discussions, their hour-long arguments over whether the dirtiest feint was the *in quarto* or the *sparita di vita*.

Outside, dark valleys drifted past, lakes reflecting castles on the snowy peaks above. In one of those castles, Jacob had found the glass slipper that had earned him a medal from the Empress. At some point they caught a glimpse of the forest where he'd stolen a pair of seven-league boots from a gang of highwaymen for one of the Wolf Lords in the east. This couldn't all be over, not yet. However, thanks to him, the Empress was now spending her days in an underground fortress, and that forest had shrunk to half its original size since its timber had begun to be used to smelt steel in the valley beyond. And the Goyl ruled in Vena. Nothing lasted forever, even behind the mirror.

The two governesses were blushing over one of Troisclerq's jokes. Jacob looked out the window to distract himself from the fact that Fox had also begun to regard his savior with increasing affection. To their left, the Duna was flowing languidly through flooded meadows, and the towers of Vena appeared on the horizon.

"Jacob?" Troisclerq put a hand on his knee. "Celeste asked me where Louis of Lotharaine usually stays when he comes to Vena."

Celeste. It was odd to hear her real name from the mouth of a stranger. Jacob had only learned it himself a few months earlier.

"I imagine Louis will be staying with his cousin,"

Troisclerq continued. "I know him quite well. If you like, I could arrange for him to receive you."

"Sure. Thanks."

Celeste...

The coachman reined in the horses. The road was flooded. The snowmelt in the mountains had caused the rivers to swell over their banks. In the Mirrorworld, rivers still picked their own beds, and every year entire villages disappeared into the floods. Yet Jacob loved the reed-lined riverbanks and the wooded islands mirrored in slow-flowing water. The rivers here were not only home to naiads and mud-gnomes; they also contained treasure and had turned more than one poor fisher into a wealthy man.

Celeste...

The coachman crossed the river over the same bridge the Goyl had used to leave the city after the Blood Wedding. Vena had subsequently surrendered to them without a fight, after the Empress's daughter had announced that her mother had been responsible for the bloodbath in the church. The Goyl were no crueler than other occupying forces, yet as the coach passed gray uniforms and houses with bricked-up windows, Jacob had an eerie feeling, wondering whether this ever would have happened without him.

The coaches still stopped behind the train station, though the noise of the arriving trains made the horses shy. Maybe the coach operators didn't want to cede the future to the iron carriages without a fight, but they had already lost. Next to the train station, the Goyl had opened an access to the catacombs, which they now used as living quarters. As the other passengers stared at the soldiers who guarded that entrance, they could barely conceal the disgust the stonefaces still elicited in most humans. Kami'en's marriage had done nothing to temper that.

The station walls were papered with dozens of wanted posters. There were anarchist groups in Vena who had called for resistance to the new Empress, for attacks on her ministers, on military and police barracks, or on the living quarters of the Goyl. Fox anxiously scanned the placards, but Jacob saw neither his nor Will's face on any of them. Whatever it was the Dark Fairy had told her lover, Kami'en was not searching for the Jade Goyl. *And once you're dead, Jacob, nobody will ever know where he disappeared to.* Maybe that was exactly the ending the Dark Fairy was hoping for.

A few cabs waited beneath the trees on the other side of the station concourse.

"You go look for the heart!" Fox whispered as Jacob flagged one of them. "I'll get Troisclerq to show me where Louis's cousin lives, and I'll find out whether the Bastard's there."

He didn't like that plan at all. The Goyl was dangerous, but Fox put her finger on Jacob's mouth as he tried to protest. "Let's not lose any more time," she whispered. "Please. I'll make sure he doesn't see me."

Behind them Troisclerq was bidding farewell to the other passengers. Fox looked at him. Jacob tried to ignore the sting that look gave him.

"Good. You take the cab. I'll walk." Fifteen days on a coach bench was more than enough. "We meet at the hotel."

It had sounded colder than he wanted. *Jacob, what are you doing?* Fox's eyes were asking the same question.

Troisclerq bought a bunch of daffodils from one of the flower girls in front of the station. He plucked one of the flowers and pinned it to Fox's dress.

"Are you all right?" He put his arm around Jacob's shoulder. "I know a good doctor here in Vena. Maybe you should have yourself looked at."

"No. I'm fine." Jacob waved the cab closer.

"You will find the heart!" Fox whispered to him. "I know it."

Troisclerq opened the cab door.

Fox gathered up her dress and looked at Jacob. "Will you telegraph Chanute about the money?"

"Sure."

She gave him a smile and climbed into the cab.

Troisclerq was looking at two passing women. They returned his glance. One of them blushed.

"There are so many beautiful women," Troisclerq murmured to Jacob, "but some are more than that. So much more." He went to the cab and threw his bag toward the driver. "I have to journey on today," he said to Jacob, "but I'm sure we'll meet again."

He joined Fox in the cab.

Celeste . . . Jacob liked calling her Fox.

He watched the cab until it disappeared behind a tram. *You will find the heart.* He looked around. *Where to first, Jacob?* To the state archives, where all of Austry's treasures were cataloged? To the mausoleum where Guismond's daughter rested among her imperial descendants? He tried to summon the rage he'd felt in the forest, the urge to get even with the Bastard . . . but he felt nothing. As though the moth were actually eating his heart.

33. DIFFERENT METHODS

Strange, how humans liked to do their forbidden deeds in cellars. As though crawling underground was enough to remain undetected. A Goyl always would have chosen the light of day.

The man, whose name Nerron had been given by an undertaker, plied his illegal business beneath a well-established butcher shop. The smells wafting through the door above were the perfect disguise for the kinds of goods he traded beneath.

The basement stairs that led down to his place of business were unlit. They ended in front of a door with an enameled sign: BY APPOINTMENT ONLY. The man who opened to Nerron's knock was the same undertaker who'd given him the address. He was as bald as an Amber-Gnome, and he was hiding a knife under his black frock coat. He waved Nerron into a room that was so dark that only a Goyl could immediately see what was sold there. Jars with eyes, teeth, claws of any kind; cabinets filled with hands, paws, hooves, ears, noses, and skulls of any shape and size. Potent ingredients for giving your neighbor a headache, or your philandering husband a pair of goat-hooves. Harm-spells. That's what this forbidden craft was called. The Witches dismissed it as human superstition, but even the Empress's daughter liked to have eyes or teeth placed under her enemies' beds to harm their health. Nerron, of course, noticed that this particular pharmacy also offered a considerable range of Goyl limbs, which when ground into a powder were supposed to cause paralysis.

The man who traded in all this looked as though he himself had become a victim of his craft. The yellow skin was stretched over his bones as if it had been worn by someone else before. He was wearing a white coat, like all the apothecaries who'd switched from the healing to the hurting kind of medicine because of its larger profits and because the clients could hardly come and complain if the sinister remedies failed to work.

"The undertaker told you what I'm looking for?"

"He did indeed." The surprisingly full mouth stretched into an obliging smile. "It's about a heart. A very special heart. Very expensive merchandise."

Nerron emptied a purse of red moonstone onto the spotless white counter. The smile grew even wider.

"That might be enough. It was quite a challenge to find the merchandise. But I have my sources."

The apothecary turned around and opened one of the enameled drawers behind him. It contained hearts of every size and shape; some were as small as hazelnuts, and the biggest one looked like the well-preserved heart of a Giant.

"You won't find a finer collection in all of Vena." Another smile, proud, like that of a florist praising his roses. "The spell that keeps my merchandise fresh is quite complicated and not without hazards, but that's, of course, not necessary for this heart. This, after all, is the heart of a Warlock. And I probably don't have to explain what that means."

He reached for a silver case next to the Giant heart. The heart the case contained was no bigger than a fig and had the consistency of black opal. Guismond's heraldic animal was etched into the smooth surface: the crowned wolf.

"As you can see, it's in pristine condition. It was, after all, in the possession of the imperial family these past centuries."

The undertaker first, Nerron.

Nerron spun around and smashed the man's head into the wall before the dolt even realized what was happening.

"How stupid does one have to be to try to sell a fake stone to a Goyl?" he hissed at the apothecary. "Do you think we're as ignorant as you people and can't tell an opal from a petrified heart? One stone's like any other, right? What do you think my skin's made of? Jasper?"

He swiped the case off the counter. Disappointing. Very disappointing. *Your own fault, Nerron. You're trying to find the heart of a King, and here you are, searching in the gutters.* Reckless never would've been so stupid.

He pointed his pistol at the trembling apothecary and nodded toward the glass jar by the register. Floating among the human and Dwarf eyes were also two Goyl eyeballs.

"Try the golden ones," Nerron said as he poured the moonstone back into the purse. "I'm sure they taste better. And who knows, maybe you'll end up seeing my kind with fresh eyes." The idea came to him as the apothecary was forcing down the first eye. It was a dirty idea, but he'd been looking for the heart for more than a week now, and patience had never been his strong suit. Nerron grabbed the pale, shaking hand before it went into the eye jar again. "You can skip the second one. Do you have a Witch tongue? But no fake this time!"

The apothecary hastily pulled open another drawer. He used a pair of pliers to pick out a tongue that differed from a human tongue only by a small slit at the tip. Nerron poured the fake heart out of the case and put the tongue inside.

He was already at the door when the undertaker began to stir.

But he never came after Nerron.

34. A GAME

It was less than a half hour's walk from the train station to the state archives, but all the big avenues leading to the palace were cut off by police blocks. The crowds on the sidewalks were nearly as thick as on the day of the Blood Wedding, and Jacob felt himself being washed along by the throng, like a piece of driftwood. Kami'en was in Vena. There was going to be a parade to celebrate the pregnancy of his human wife. The new Empress's guards were decorating the streetlights and facades with garlands. The guards were, without exception, Goyl. Amalie left her protection to her husband's soldiers. It was said she preferred to pick ones that had Kami'en's carnelian skin. The garlands were strung with moonstone flowers, and the barricades along the streets were decorated with silver branches.

Yet all Jacob saw was Troisclerq as he pinned a flower to Fox's dress. What was going on with him? *You're jealous, Jacob. Don't have enough problems already?*

He turned into the next alley—and ended up in front of another roadblock. *Damn.* Who was he fooling? The Bastard had long found the heart. *Stop it, Jacob!* But he couldn't remember ever having felt so tired. Not even the fear of death penetrated the fog in his head.

He pulled out the city guide he'd bought at the station. It was an unwieldy, chatty thing, as thick as a novel and filled with tiny print. But the Goyl had changed Vena so much that he hardly knew the place anymore. The archive was on a street that was also on the parade route. Maybe he should try the mausoleum first. He leafed through the densely printed pages—holding Earlking's card in one hand.

You're wasting your time, Jacob.
Museum of Austrian History.
Hall 33.
The man who was Guismond's eyes also knew his heart.

Jacob looked down the street. The pain in his chest was now constant, like a wound that wouldn't heal. *The price should be payable.* He flagged down a cab and gave the driver the address of the museum.

Columns shaped like the bodies of tethered Giants. The entrance a frieze of vanquished Dragons. Dwarfs and Heinzel as chiseled ornaments beneath the windows. The building that housed the Museum of Austrian History had originally been a palace. One of the Empress's ancestors had designed every detail himself. In his day he was called the alchemist prince, but it wasn't his statue in front of the museum; it was that of his great-grandson, flanked by the equestrian statues of two victorious generals. Jacob pushed through the stream of uniformed schoolchildren flooding down the steps. He put the entrance fee in front of the ticket lady. Luckily, a goldsmith had agreed to change a few of the pathetic coins Jacob's handkerchief still produced for brand-new guilders. The currency now bore Kami'en's profile instead of the Empress's.

Unlike the imperial Chambers of Miracles, the museum held no magical objects, but in its halls Jacob had learned more about the Mirrorworld than many who were born there ever did. Weapons and armor of Austrian knights, long spears for fighting Giants, Ogre claws, gilded Dragon saddles, a copy of the original Emperor's throne, and the head of the horse that had warned the Empress's mother of a poisoned apple. Thousands of objects brought the history of Austry to life. Jacob remembered his first visit very well. Chanute had taken him to find information on a castle that had sunk into a lake more than a century before. Jacob had stopped in front of every display until Chanute grabbed him by the neck and shoved him along. But Jacob had snuck back every time they stopped in Vena, usually while Chanute was sleeping off his cheap wine. Jacob could find his way through the halls blind, but the Goyl hadn't just changed the map of Vena. They'd done the same to Austry's history.

The room where Jacob stopped had, until a few months earlier, housed the robes of state of the deposed Empress. Now the room was dominated by her daughter's bloody wedding gown. The wax doll wearing it looked eerily like Amalie. The wax rendering of Kami'en's stone skin was not half as convincing. Jacob approached the wax figure next to the King. The Jade Goyl stared at him through golden glass eyes. It looked so much like Will that Jacob could hardly bear to look at it. There was, of course, also a wax effigy of the Dark Fairy. She was standing a little aside. Wax corpses covered with black moths were strewn around her feet.

It's in the past, Jacob. Like everything else here. Yet for a few breaths, he was transported back to the cathedral. Clara was again lying among the dead, Will was wearing the gray uniform soaked in Goyl blood, and his own tongue was forming the name that had planted death in his chest.

His brother's glassy glance followed Jacob from room to room. He nearly walked past the one with the number 33.

The red walls were covered with portraits of Austry's imperial family. They hung all the way up to the ceiling, frame on frame, countless faces with the brown patina of many centuries. The deposed Empress's great-grandparents, her grandmother's infamous brothers, the Emperor whom everybody called the Changeling (he'd probably been one). And of course there was also a portrait of Guismond. He wasn't wearing the cat-fur coat from the tomb's door, but was clad in the armor of a knight, though his helmet was shaped like the head of the crowned wolf on his crest. Next to his was a portrait of his wife with their three children. In the painting the children were still very young and stood very close to their mother. The pupils of Guismond's wife were not those of a Witch, but that didn't mean much. Every Witch could make herself look like a human woman. There were also portraits of Feirefis and Gahrumet as Kings, but Jacob just gave them a quick glance. He also passed Orgeluse's portrait, which showed her with her husband. The picture he did stop at was the one painting in room 33 that didn't depict a member of the imperial dynasty. Jacob had noticed it years earlier, because the man looking out from the heavy golden frame bore a slight resemblance to his grandfather. Hendrick Goltzius Memling had been the Witch Slayer's court painter, but it was not his art that had made him famous. He was also rumored to have carried on a passionate affair with Guismond's daughter. His was a self-portrait. Memling had painted it three years after Guismond's death, and he'd dated it himself. Hanging from his neck was a gold-set stone. Memling was touching it with the fingers of his right hand, which was crippled but had reportedly enabled him to handle the tools of an engraver better than anybody else. The stone was as black as coal.

The golden hearts and the black hearts. Chanute's voice had sounded almost devout when he told Jacob about them. "The golden ones are those of alchemists. At some point they got the silly idea to turn their hearts into gold to make themselves immortal. Many had theirs cut out of their living bodies." "And the black ones?" Jacob had asked. What did a thirteen-year-old boy care about immortality? "The black ones are the hearts of Warlocks," Chanute had replied. "They look just like black jewels. Whoever carries one around his neck supposedly gets anything he desires. But if you wear it too close to your heart, it will rob you not only of all joy but also of your conscience."

Jacob stepped closer to the painting.

Memling was looking down at him through cold eyes. There were stories that he had poisoned not only his wife but also Orgeluse out of jealousy. It might have been Orgeluse's downfall that she had given the man she loved her father's heart.

35. THE RIGHT KING

The Dragon's lair lay beneath the backyard of a brewery. Nobody in Vena had known of its existence until a Goyl patrol had noticed the unmistakable smell of sulfur and lizard fire.

Kami'en's bodyguards were hiding in the shadows of the brewery's gate. They were probably counting on their alabaster skin being mistaken for a shimmer of moonlight. They'd gotten too used to how easily human eyes were deceived. Sneaking past them was fun, and after the debacle with the apothecary, Nerron really could do with some cheering up.

Two more guards were posted where the Dragon's breathing tunnels opened behind the brewery drays. Nerron was past the guards before they could turn their heads, and he quickly melted into the darkness of the tunnel. The Dragon had been dead for centuries, but its smell enveloped Nerron as though it were still lurking in its lair below.

Quiet, Bastard. Like a snake.

At its end, the tunnel opened into a cave that was black from Dragon fire. Only in some places a little gold gleamed through the soot. The treasure cave. Better preserved than most Nerron had seen. He pressed himself against the cool rock.

And there he was, his skin like petrified fire—even in the darkness. The King of the Goyl.

Kami'en had his back to the tunnel. Just one well-aimed bullet. Or a poisoned arrow between his shoulder blades. How many assassins had the onyx hired in vain to stand right where he was standing? And it had been so easy. *Yes, you're the best, Nerron. Never mind that you haven't found the damn heart yet.*

"How long will it take?" Kami'en's voice sounded calm, as usual. As though he had nothing to fear in this world.

"The architect tells me two months, but I can make sure work is completed earlier." Of course. Hentzau was standing next to the King. Only a few years earlier, he would have caught Nerron's scent, but the years spent aboveground had made Kami'en's loyal dog half-blind and had dulled his sense of smell until it was barely better than that of a human.

"Hire some Dwarfs. They work fast." Nerron stepped out of the tunnel.

Hentzau spun around and positioned himself protectively in front of Kami'en.

Good dog.

"What is this?" he barked at Nerron. "You want me to put a bullet into your speckled skin?" His jasper face had turned even more craggy since the Blood Wedding. Compared to Hentzau, even Nerron could pass as attractive. Nerron bowed his head with a smile and pressed his fist over his heart, a gesture of obedience he usually had problems with, but not in front of this King.

"Be grateful, Hentzau. He's just demonstrating my need for better bodyguards." Kami'en turned around as leisurely as only one could who owned half the world. He was wearing the same uniform in which he'd survived his wedding. Moonstones for the human bloodstains, rubies for the Goyl blood. The Dark Fairy knew how to turn horror into beauty.

"He's right. Hire Dwarfs," Kami'en said to Hentzau. "I want work to begin immediately. I'm tired of that human palace. This will be my study. The guards in the sleeping cave. One tunnel to the palace, one to the train station, and a third one connecting to the road beneath the river." He shot a cool glance at Nerron. "You still haven't found the heart?"

"No. But I have the hand and the head."

"Good." Kami'en rubbed the sooty wall until the gold appeared beneath. "The Witch Slayer's crossbow. Maybe I should send my airplanes to the Dwarf mines. Teach them not to keep secrets from me."

"There are many places we should send them to," Hentzau growled. "Even in the east, the Doughskins are now joining forces against us. Ask him who's getting them all to sit around the same table. Without the onyx, they'd still be killing each other." He stared at Nerron. Like all soldiers, Hentzau never trusted anyone not in uniform, and especially not an onyx bastard who had the trust of the King's enemies. Maybe he sensed that Nerron, despite all his admiration for the King, served nobody but himself. Yet they owed him for the names of many spies, and his information had helped thwart two attempts on Kami'en's life. Even Hentzau realized they needed the Bastard, though he didn't trust Nerron as far as he could spit.

"Hentzau's spies tell me you have some serious competition for the crossbow." Kami'en's face was as impassive as the likeness they minted on his coins. Only once had Nerron seen the King less composed, and that was when he'd first heard from him how far-reaching the onyx conspiracy against him was.

"It seems you don't just need better bodyguards but also better spies." Nerron brushed Hentzau with a taunting glance. "That competition is no more."

"Indeed?" Hentzau's thin mouth moved. It nearly smiled. "My useless spies are reporting that your competitor is in Vena and very much alive. Jacob Reckless has a penchant for rising from the dead."

Nerron caught his heart doing a few extra beats.

Surprise. On the other hand . . . how disappointing would it have been if Jacob Reckless had let himself be devoured by wolves just like that?

The best…

"Reckless paid a visit to the history museum." Hentzau's left eye had that milky sheen that came from too much daylight. "I assume you know why?"

Nerron hadn't the faintest idea, but he hoped his face didn't give him away.

"I put an old friend on his trail. He'll take care of Reckless." Kami'en leaned down and inspected the gouges left by the Dragon's claws. "What a waste to exterminate them," he said, running his fingers through the crevices. "They were such great weapons. Though never very obedient. Machines are easier to control." Kami'en stood straight again. The gold in his eyes was brighter than that of the onyx. "Hentzau would like to kill Reckless, but since the wedding I've developed a weakness for him. Who is he hunting the crossbow for?"

Nerron shrugged. "It doesn't matter. Because it'll be me who finds it."

"Together with Crookback's son?" Hentzau's voice sounded harsh, as when he spoke to his soldiers.

Watch yourself, old man.

"We have to get back." Kami'en turned around. "Hentzau's right. From now on you search alone."

Hentzau threw a purse of silver toward him. Expenses. The King of the Goyl was a less generous employer than the onyx, but Nerron would have worked for him for free. Not everything was for sale. He listened until their steps had faded into the Dragon's breathing tunnel.

The parade would begin soon for the grumbling people of Vena. The Goyl showing off his pregnant human wife. Her subjects had already come up with many names for the child. "The monster," "the skinless prince"... everybody seemed to assume the child was going to be a boy. Human-Goyl mongrels didn't live long. You could sometimes see them in freak shows at country fairs. Some were so stony they could hardly move; others had a skin through which one could see the bones and organs, as through glass; some had no skin at all. But Kami'en was determined to keep this child alive. There were rumors he'd even asked the Dark Fairy for help.

What did Reckless want in the museum?

Nerron leaned against the claw-gouged stone. The darkness around him reeked of the Dragon's odor. He opened the medallion, and the spider crawled sleepily on his hand. Why hadn't he asked her earlier whether Reckless really was dead? Because he hadn't wanted to know the answer? Interesting...

He had to feed an extra helping of lapis lazuli to the spider before she began her dance.

No carriages... damn... roadblocks... flowers everywhere...

Nerron felt a smile sneak onto his face. Yes, Reckless really was alive. The spider kept dancing. *Cabby! What? No. To the spiny gate...*

He'd be damned. Maybe the Witch's tongue wasn't going to be needed after all.

36. DISAPPEARED

The gate to the jewelers' quarter only truly earned its name by night. Jacob's flesh had already felt the spikes the gate grew in the dark, but now it was midday and so the iron wings stood wide open.

The jewelers' quarter was one of the oldest parts of Vena. Its alleys were too narrow even for the lightest cabs, and its backyards still contained clusters of tiny houses from the days when jewelers used to employ Elves and when Heinzel were regarded as good-luck charms.

Hippolyte Ramée had driven his Heinzel away years ago after he'd caught them stealing. But he still worked with Elves. He hid them in his back room so he wouldn't be thought of as old-fashioned, yet the silvery dust they spread when they flew immediately settled on Jacob's coat as he opened the door.

The jewelry Ramée crafted was famous beyond Vena. The jeweler originally came from Lotharaine, where he'd trained under the infamous goldsmith of Pont-de-Pile. There were many stories, each more gruesome than the next, about how Hippolyte had lost both his feet in the goldsmith's service. Ramée maintained his silence about it. Jacob had actually seen the golden feet Ramée had wrought to escape his master. On this morning, however, they were tucked inside buttoned boots.

For the past thirty years, Hippolyte Ramée had been the official goldsmith to the imperial family of Austry, and as far as Jacob was aware, the Goyl had not changed that. The many years of setting tiny stones in gold and silver had not been kind to Ramée's eyes. The lenses on his spectacles were so thick, they made his rheumy eyes look as big as a child's.

"Do you have an appointment? If not, you may leave immediately." Ramée's temper was as famous as his jewelry. He was known to have thrown even emissaries from the Empress out of his shop. Yet the beauty of the pieces that were on display in glass cabinets all around the shop made most aristocratic treasure chambers look shabby in comparison. Necklaces, bracelets, tiaras, and brooches; rubies, emeralds, topaz, and amber, wrought so delicately into gold and silver that it looked as though they had simply grown from the fingertips of the old man behind the simple wooden table.

"It's me, Hippolyte."

Ramée lifted his head and put down the palm-sized magnifying glass through which he'd been inspecting a diamond the size of a pea. The suspicion on his face disappeared only after Jacob went to stand right in front of him.

"Jacob, of course," he observed. His mottled hand closed around the diamond. Ramée always expected to be robbed. The Empress was the only person he'd ever exempted from his suspicion. "Are you in need of another brooch to impress some imperial maid?"

"No." Jacob glanced at a tiara that looked like a web of silver woven around blossoms of carnelian. Ramée had adapted his craft to the new masters of Vena. "I presume you're still in charge of maintaining the imperial jewels?"

Ramée adjusted his glasses. "Of course. Say what you will about the Goyl, but they do recognize a man who knows his stones."

Jacob suppressed a smile. Hippolyte was a vain old man.

"A shame they don't like gold," Ramée added. "It means I have to work more with silver, but their King only recently ordered a few very tasteful pieces. The bracelet, he..."

"Hippolyte!" Ramée could ramble on for hours about the cut of a stone or the value of flawless elven glass, but Jacob was done wasting time he didn't have. Yet the old man carried on, in the heavy Lotharainian accent he'd never lost through all the decades of exile. He was obviously not only half-blind but also quite deaf by now.

"Hippolyte! Could you listen to me for a moment?"

Ramée abruptly fell silent, as though he'd swallowed one of his diamonds. "What?" he barked at Jacob. "I'm three times as old as you. What's the rush?"

"We never know when death might claim us, right?" Jacob flicked a spider off his sleeve. Her body was blue, like the amethyst rings Ramée was so famous for.

The old man swatted at the spider as she dropped between his fingers.

"Spiders, mice, cockroaches!" he muttered, wiping the spider off the table. "The cats can't keep up with them! I might have to get some of those thieving Heinzel back after all."

Another favorite subject. Heinzel.

"Hippolyte, can you tell me something about a piece of jewelry? I saw it in a portrait at the history museum. The stone is black, slightly larger than a grape, set in a mesh of golden tendrils."

Ramée stared at him, aghast. Then he dropped his head, and his shaky hands began to sort the tools on the table in front of him. When he lifted his head again, the eyes behind the thick glasses were swimming with tears.

"Why are you doing this?" he panted at Jacob. "Is that some kind of cruel joke? I confessed everything to the Empress back then."

He stood up so abruptly that the diamond he'd been working on was knocked off the table. "Did Amalie send you? Sure! What can you expect from a princess who gets herself knocked up by a Goyl!"

Ramée pressed his hand over his mouth as though he could stuff the words back inside. He shot a quick glance at the window, but the only one outside was a Dwarf standing in front of the shop window opposite.

What was the old man talking about? Jacob picked up the diamond and put it back on the table. It glistened like a frozen tear.

"Nobody sent me," he said. "I'm looking for this piece myself. I just wanted to ask you whether you could get me a look at it."

Ramée took off his glasses and agitatedly wiped the lenses with his sleeve. "Forget it!" The words burst out of him. "The stone is lost. Just like Marie."

Jacob took the glasses from his hands. He polished the lenses and handed them back to the old man. "Marie?"

Ramée's hands were trembling as he took the glasses. He pointed at a photograph on the wall next to the door. A black ribbon was tied to the frame. The picture showed a young girl, maybe eighteen years old. Jacob went to the picture. Past reality, frozen by light, acid, and silver. Behind the mirror you were still reminded what a miracle a photograph really was. The girl Jacob was looking at had hair so dark that it nearly melted into the sepia brown background. She looked a little stiff—after all, one had to sit still for a long time for a portrait like that—but her eyes were saying, "Look at me. Am I not beautiful?"

"It was her first ball." Ramée stood by Jacob's side. Only the heaviness of his steps hinted at the golden feet.

"I'd just received the necklace, together with a few other pieces from the palace. I still don't know what kind of stone it was. It had a strange consistency. But it looked so beautiful on Marie's white skin. 'Like a piece of night caught in gold, Grandpapa' is what she said. Who can refuse his own granddaughter? And it was only for the ball. She never returned. Gone. Just gone. As if she never existed. Her mother grieves so much, she now barely leaves the house. She tells herself Marie ran off with one of the officers who like to hang around those balls. She probably knows that the truth is far more unbearable."

Ramée pulled back his sleeve. He was wearing a golden bracelet. The fine links looked tarnished, black. "You've heard about bracelets like this?"

Jacob nodded. Not many goldsmiths knew how to make them. You added a drop of blood to the gold. If the one whose blood it was, was well, the metal stayed bright; if it turned red, the person was in grave danger. And black could mean only one thing.

"Dead." Ramée stared at the photo. "These photographs are a disconcerting invention, are they not? One always looks like a ghost in them. But at least I have her picture." He pulled his sleeve back over the black bracelet. "On that last day, when Marie came here, she had a flower pinned to her dress, and she was gushing over some stranger who was as beautiful as a prince. And of course he was clean-shaved. I don't have to tell you why she never came back."

No, he didn't.

A flower on her dress. Jacob felt his heartbeat quicken. *Have you gone blind, Jacob?*

"Bluebeards." Ramée rubbed his rheumy eyes. "You think they only exist in fairy tales, until one of them gets your granddaughter. Should you ever find the necklace you're looking for, shoot the one who has it, and then go and see whether there's a dead girl in his red chamber, with a ruby brooch. I made it for Marie's sixteenth birthday."

His red chamber. Jacob had seen such a chamber once. A memory he'd rather have forgotten.

How long since Fox had left with him? Three hours?

Ramée shouted something after him, but all Jacob heard was the blood rushing in his ears. Troisclerq had pinned the flower on her right in front of his eyes! They soaked them in forgetyourself oil.

He stumbled out into the alley. *Damned fool.* Had he forgotten everything Chanute had taught him?

Move, Jacob.

But he didn't get far. An arm came around his neck from behind, and someone dragged him through the next alleyway into one of the dark backyards that dotted the jewelers' quarter.

"And? Are you enjoying Vena under your new friends?" Donnersmarck was no longer wearing imperial white but the gray uniform of the Goyl. The last time Jacob had seen him, he'd been a prisoner. Now his old friend was the personal aide to the new Empress. She obviously didn't hold his service to her mother against him.

Donnersmarck had been drinking. Not a lot, but enough to lose control. He hit Jacob in the face so hard that he tasted blood on his tongue. Jacob responded by ramming his knee into Donnersmarck's stomach. Jacob struggled free, but again he didn't get far. Blocking the alleyway was Auberon, the former Empress's favorite Dwarf. He aimed a pistol at Jacob's head. Auberon loved to show off his marksmanship by shooting people through the forehead. The Empress's Dwarfs were all excellent shots, but Amalie preferred to be guarded by her husband's men, and so her mother's former bodyguards now protected jewelers, bankers, and rich manufacturers.

Jacob raised his hands.

"Let me go, Leo!" He was going to be too late.

Donnersmarck pushed him against the nearest wall. "You're not going anywhere. I made a promise to the Empress, in that filthy hole the Goyl have locked her in: I will find Jacob Reckless, and he will pay for what happened in the cathedral."

"Why don't we shoot him right here?" Jacob remembered Auberon's swollen face as he'd stumbled out of the cathedral. Yes, the Dwarf would probably love to pull the trigger, but Donnersmarck ignored him.

"For months I've had the train station and the coach stations watched for you."

"Really? Yes, I can see you're still a powerful man. Congratulations on the Goyl uniform. It suits you!"

Jacob knew Donnersmarck would hit him for that

remark, and that he was drunk enough to lose his footing. Before Donnersmarck could regain his balance, Jacob already had his pistol to the man's head. Auberon proved once more that nobody was as inventive at swearing as the Dwarfs. He tried to get a clean shot, but Donnersmarck was very tall and provided excellent cover.

"It was about my brother!" Jacob hissed into his ear. "What would you've done? You put on their uniform so you wouldn't have to end up in a dungeon like your former Empress. So drop the self-righteousness and tell me what you know about a Bluebeard who's been hunting in these parts."

He could feel Donnersmarck take a deep breath.

Bluebeard. They'd hunted one together. Years before.

"Tell me. You're Amalie's watchdog. You know the answer."

"That's a filthy trick!" Donnersmarck's voice had turned hoarse, roughened by ghosts only he and Jacob had seen.

"Spit it out!" Jacob let go of Donnersmarck so his old friend saw the fear in his face. "Is there a Bluebeard in Vena?" Donnersmarck stared at him. *Show him your fear, Jacob, even though you're usually better at hiding it.*

"Yes." Donnersmarck spoke haltingly. "He took the first girl ten years ago. There have been four so far. He's supposedly from Lotharaine, but he prefers hunting here. You know what they're like—never in their own backyard. Why are you looking for him?"

"He's got Fox." Jacob pushed past him. Always the

same image: Troisclerq's hand pinning the flower on her dress. Why did he do it in Jacob's presence? So he'd be haunted by it every night? He had fallen for Troisclerq's charms, just like the women he killed. *But Fox only went with him because of you, Jacob. You handed her to him like a gift.*

"Where in Lotharaine?"

"It's all just rumors."

"For example?"

"That he lives somewhere near Champlitte."

Champlitte. Troisclerq hadn't even tried to lie. *What if I take what's dear to your heart, Jacob? Will you come to get it back?*

He shoved the Dwarf out of the way and stepped into the alley. Donnersmarck quickly caught up with him, despite the limp he had from fighting his Empress's wars.

"Where did you see her last?"

"At the train station."

He had to find the cabdriver. . . .

None of the moth's bites had made his heart beat as fast. Reason drowned in fear. He'd never known he could be that scared.

You will find her. And she'll be alive.

If only he could believe himself. He just knew one thing: He was going to kill Troisclerq.

He'd kill him.

37. FLOWERS

Wilted flowers, in a cab and on a station platform. No. Troisclerq wasn't even trying to cover his tracks. Donnersmarck was by Jacob's side as he picked up the flowers from the platform. Bluebeard. The one word had turned Donnersmarck's hostility into the unquestioning support Jacob had always been able to count on until the Blood Wedding.

It was three years since the Empress had asked Jacob to find a Bluebeard who'd taken one of her maids. Donnersmarck had requested to be his military aide. The maid was his sister. They'd found her in an abandoned castle, together with seven other girls, all dead. The killer had already left. They had searched for him for months, but then he'd lured them into a trap from which they'd barely managed to escape alive. After that his trail had gone cold, and he died, years later, peacefully in his bed—having killed six more girls.

Bluebeards always went on the hunt clean-shaved so the blue facial hair they were named after wouldn't give them away. Supposedly, there had never been fewer than a dozen of them, but Chanute had always maintained there were hundreds. It was said they all shared one common ancestor, a man with black blood and a blue beard who'd found a way to live forever by feeding off the fear of others. Bluebeards only killed their victims after they had milked all their fear. That was Jacob's hope: Fox wouldn't easily give Troisclerq what he craved.

One of the station supervisors remembered a young red-haired woman who'd been so tired that her husband had to support her as they boarded the train. The effects of the flower...

That train stopped in Champlitte. The next one wouldn't leave before the following morning, but Jacob couldn't wait. When he asked the cabdriver to take them to the outskirts, where the air was thick with soot and destitution, Donnersmarck did not have to ask why. They needed fast horses, even faster than the ones in the Empress's stable, and Donnersmarck knew as well as Jacob that such horses could only be found in the darkest corners of Vena. The farmers called them devil-horses because they ate raw meat and their breath was hot enough to scald you. They were caught in swamps and moors—pale white nags, their manes hanging like a tangle of roots around their necks.

They were twice as fast as normal horses, but they also ate unwary owners in their sleep.

Jacob purchased two that even their Giantling handler could barely control. Donnersmarck hadn't said much since their brawl, but they both knew the house of a Bluebeard should not be entered alone. Darkness was falling as they turned their backs on Vena and rode westward together.

38. AIR

Air. They had disappeared into thin air. Both Reckless and the man Kami'en had put on him. Not even Hentzau knew where they were. And the spider had pulled her legs under her blue belly and refused to dance.

And, Nerron, still glad the wolves didn't get him?

He returned to the palace of Louis's cousin, his mood as dark as his skin. The building looked like one of the overwrought cakes sold in Vena's bakeries. It had more rooms than Lelou had hairs on his head. But Louis was always easy enough to find. You just had to follow the giggles of his current favorite.

There. The linen room. Louis left no room untouched. Nerron pressed his ear against the door.

Time to move beyond civilized methods. He needed the hand. He needed the heart before Reckless could find it. And he needed to get rid of his companions. There was only one way to accomplish all of that. Three birds with one stone.

"What are you doing?" Eaumbre's whispers sounded even more damp than usual. Nerron turned around.

The Waterman's wet hair stuck to his angular head, as though he'd just climbed out of a pond. And he probably had. Nerron thought he could detect a slight scent of goldfish. Watermen dried out if they didn't take a dip in a pond every now and then, the muddier the better. They also dried out if they were fed firemoths. Probably an interesting sight. *Stop it, Nerron. Stay on good terms with him. He's much more useful that way.*

Nerron pointed at the door to the linen room. "Your royal master is getting impatient. Crookback wants the crossbow, but how can I concentrate on the search while his son does nothing but try to seduce every girl in Vena?"

Eaumbre's face stayed as inscrutable as ever. Only his eyes hinted at what he felt on the inside: six eyes, filled to the rim with boredom and injured pride. Louis had let everybody in Vena know that his Waterman was nothing but an annoying babysitter his father had forced on him. There could be no doubt that Eaumbre despised his princely charge, but that didn't mean he liked anyone else. And he was strong. Very strong. He could easily break every bone, even in a Goyl body, with one hand. Probably not a pleasant experience.

"And? What should we do, in your opinion?" The whispers filled Nerron's ears like pond muck.

Through the door came a sigh that made even the portraits on the walls blush.

"Bring Louis to the library in one hour. I'll talk to him." *Hopefully, that sounded harmless enough.* "And tell him to bring the hand."

"Why?"

Careful, Nerron.

"I want to see whether it can point us to the heart."

Six eyes. They were saying, *You're lying, Goyl. And I know it.*

"The library," the Waterman repeated. "In one hour."

The Snow-White method had severe side effects—so severe that in Albion you got hanged for using it. Crookback probably had an even more painful method of execution in store, should he ever learn that it had been used on his son. But Nerron counted on the fact that its effects were easily confused with those of an overdose of elven dust.

One of the kitchen hands boiled the Witch tongue for him in the palace kitchen. The fool thought it was a calf's tongue. Nerron prepared the apple himself. The fruit was the reason the formula was named after Snow-White, even though her apple had been prepared with a different kind of potion. Nerron cut out the stalk and the core and poured the tongue-broth into it. Black magic was a rather unappetizing craft. He sealed the opening with dark chocolate to sweeten the deal. Louis could never resist chocolate.

The shelves were lined with rows of books as neat as those found only in libraries that were never used. Louis's cousin loved to give himself the appearance of an educated man.

One hour. The Waterman delivered on time. The crown prince of Lotharaine did, of course, not knock.

"The Waterman says we have something to discuss?" As usual, he reeked of elven dust and the disgusting eau de toilette he applied as liberally as water. "Stay outside!" he ordered Eaumbre as the Waterman tried to follow him. "You stink of fish again. Go and find my cousin. I want to go out."

Eaumbre's eyes brushed Nerron with a bland glance before he closed the door. Lelou obviously hadn't taught Louis anything about the pride of Watermen. Quite a dangerous knowledge gap.

"Did you bring the hand?"

Louis held up the sack.

"I hope you keep it well away from yourself?"

"Why?" Louis frowned. The elven dust made thinking even more difficult than it usually was for him.

"What is Lelou teaching you? Black magic is not particularly healthy. And it'll be me who'll have to answer to your father for any side effects!" Nerron offered him the apple. "Here. The antidote tastes disgusting, but I asked the cook to make it a little more palatable."

"An apple?" Louis flinched. "I never touch apples. Two of my aunts were poisoned that way."

"As you wish." Nerron put the apple on a lectern, next to a book on the family history of Louis's Austrian relatives, which was gathering dust. "Go see a doctor if you don't believe me. And keep an eye on your fingernails. Once they turn black, it may be too late already."

Louis stared at his fingers.

"I'm sick of treasure hunting!" he burst out. "All that magical nonsense. I'm so over it."

He took the apple and eyed it so warily that Nerron nearly gave up hope. "Is that chocolate?"

One bite and he slumped over. Nerron caught him before he hit the marble floor. Not so easy, considering Louis's weight.

He leaned over him and blew into his sleeping face. "Where is the heart of Guismond the Witch Slayer?"

"What?" Louis mumbled.

Nerron cursed so loud he had to press his hand over his own mouth. Compared to the princeling, the vagrant on whom he'd tried the formula six years earlier had turned into a veritable font of wisdom.

"Guis-mond the Witch Slay-er," Nerron whispered into the royal ear.

Louis wanted to roll on his side, but Nerron held him;

he had to apply quite a lot of force against the princely weight.

"Lotharaine," Louis mumbled.

"Where in Lotharaine?"

Louis shuddered. "Champlitte," he whispered. "White as milk. Black as a sliver of night. Set in gold."

Then he began to snore.

He'd be doing little else for the next ten years. Clairvoyance had its price.

Nerron got up. Champlitte. White as milk. Black as a sliver of night. Set in gold. What the devil? He sprinkled Louis's clothes and hands with elven dust and tucked a few more sachets into his pockets. Then he dropped the apple into the swindlesack with the hand, and stuffed that into the saddlebag that already held the sack with the head. He opened the door—and found himself staring at the Waterman's uniformed chest.

Eaumbre looked over Nerron's shoulder.

"What did you do to him?" His voice grated on Nerron's skin like a wet rasp.

"He overdid the elven dust." Nerron surreptitiously put his hand on his pistol.

"I wouldn't do that," the Waterman whispered. "Where are you going? You think Crookback will get any joy from his crossbow if he gets his son back as Snow-White?" The scaly face stretched into a grim smile. "But Crookback was never supposed to get the crossbow, was he? You want to sell it to the highest bidder."

Well, at least he hadn't guessed the whole truth.

"And what if?" Nerron's fingers closed around the grip of his pistol.

"I want a share. I'm tired of the bodyguarding business. Treasure hunting is so much more profitable."

And Watermen came with plenty of experience, in their very own way. The girls they dragged to their ponds could vouch for that. The scale-faces showered them with gold and silver to make their slimy kisses more bearable.

Three birds.... *Seems like you're going to be holding on to one, Nerron.* The fattest and scaliest of the three.

A quiet cough.

Bug-quiet.

"Can any one of those present tell me where I might find the crown prince?" Lelou was standing at the end of the corridor, his notebook under his arm. What would he be writing at the end of that day? *And the prince slept for ten years, his snores echoing through his father's palace....*

Nerron pointed at the library door. "Eaumbre just found him. I think you should take a look at him. We were already wondering what he's doing in the library without a girl."

They were out on the street before Lelou's cries alerted the guard by the entrance.

Crookback would find a particularly gruesome way to dispatch the Bug. But Nerron wasn't going to miss Arsene Lelou.

39. FRIEND AND FOE

The devil-horses lived up to their name. On the second night, one of them snuck up to Jacob with bared teeth; and Donnersmarck scalded his hands as he tried to feed the horses rabbit meat. But they were fast.

Border posts, icy passes. Lakes, forests, villages, towns. Jacob felt his fear for Fox eating through his body like a poison. The thought of finding her dead was unbearable, and so he tried to lock it away, just as he'd done with his longing for his father when he was a child. But he failed. With every day that passed, every mile they traveled, the images became more gruesome, and his dreams became so vivid that he'd wake up and search his hands for her blood.

To distract himself, he asked Donnersmarck about the Empress and her daughter, about the child who should not be, and about the Dark Fairy. . . . But Donnersmarck's voice kept turning into Fox's: *You will find the heart. I know it.*

All he wanted to find now was Fox.

When finally they crossed the border into Lotharaine, more than six days had passed since he'd watched Troisclerq help her into that cab. They crossed rivers, passed white castles, rode through villages with unpaved roads, and heard flowers sing in the dark like nightingales. . . . The heart of Lotharaine still beat to the old rhythm while the engineers in Albion were already building the new, mechanical one.

Then Donnersmarck reined in his horse. A meadow. White flowers dotted the short grass. Forgetyourself. The livestock avoided the flowers, which gave off the narcotic oil Bluebeards put on the flowers they pinned to their victims' clothes or hair. They also rubbed it into their clean-shaved cheeks.

A little later they came to a signpost. Three miles to Champlitte. They looked at each other, the same images in their heads. But in Jacob's memory, even Donnersmarck's dead sister now had Fox's face.

40. THE GOLDEN TRAP

Wake up, Fox! She thought she could feel the vixen's pointy snout prodding her forehead. *Fox! Wake up!* But when she opened her eyes, she found herself alone in her human body.

Above her she saw a canopy, blue like the evening sky, and the dress she was wearing was as strange to her as the bed she was lying on. Her head ached and her limbs were heavy, as though she'd slept too long. Images flooded her head. A cab. A train. A carriage with golden cushions. A servant at a gate with iron flowers and—

Troisclerq.

She felt dizzy as she sat up. High walls covered with golden silk. Hanging from a wreath of white stucco flowers on the ceiling was a red crystal chandelier. As a child she'd fantasized about rooms like this. But the windows were barred. She pushed her hand beneath her pearl-embroidered décolletage. She wasn't wearing her fur dress anymore.

Calm, Fox.

But her heart wouldn't listen.

Try to remember, Fox. A labyrinth. Troisclerq had led her through it. To a house with ivy-covered walls of gray stone. No matter how hard she tried, she couldn't remember any more than that.

Had he put something in the water he'd offered her in the cab? Elven dust? A Witch's love potion? But she felt no love. Just anger at herself.

Where had he taken her? And where was her fur dress?

Jacob...

What would he think? That she'd abandoned him for a flower on her dress and a smile from Troisclerq?

She gathered up the far-too-wide skirt. The dress was sumptuous enough to be worn to a royal ball. *Who put it on you, Fox?* She shuddered. She'd also never before seen the shoes she was wearing. She pulled them off and walked barefoot across the wooden flower patterns in the waxed parquet floor.

The door was unlocked.

Outside it, a corridor with a dozen doors. Which direction had she come from? *Remember, Fox!*

No. First she had to find the fur dress.

She could still feel Troisclerq's hand on her arm. So gentle. So warm. What had he been thinking? That he could seduce her with a big house and a new dress? Had she returned his smile too readily, laughed at his jokes too often? Laughing had been so easy with him. His glance had let her know how beautiful she was. Did he try to kiss her? Yes. The images were coming back to her like the memories of a stranger. He had kissed her. On the train. In the carriage. *What have you done, Fox?*

So many doors.

She tried to open them, but they were all locked. The portraits hanging between the doors all showed women.

The corridor led to a staircase. Fox thought she could remember it. She was just about to go down, when a servant came up the white steps toward her. It was the same one who'd opened the iron gate. He was so tall that he kept his head bowed between his broad shoulders.

The room she'd woken up in...the dress...the portraits...the servant in his black velvet coat. It was as though she was lost in one of the games she'd played for hours as a child in the woods.

"Where is your master?"

The servant just silently took her arm. His hands were covered in dull brown fur. Lotharaine was full of stories of noblemen who kept enchanted animals as servants, for they were more loyal than any human.

The house was huge, but they met no one. The door at which the servant finally stopped was made from dark wood; the same wood lined the walls of the dining room the servant waved Fox into. Red lace curtains caught the evening light coming through the windows.

"Welcome to my home." Troisclerq was sitting at the end of a long table. It was the first time Fox saw him unshaved. The skin around his mouth and chin had a bluish hue.

Breathe, Fox. In and out. As the vixen does when death is staring at her.

Bluebeard.

There were ten plates on the table. They always laid their table for the number of their victims.

Troisclerq smiled at her. He was wearing an immaculate white shirt, as usual. Even during their endless coach journey, he'd always been dressed as though he traveled with a manservant.

"Do sit down." He waved at a chair to his left. "The dress looks nice on you."

The servant pulled out the chair for Fox. As she sat down in front of her empty plate, she thought she could sense the presence of all the dead girls who'd sat before her on these black velvet chairs. She tried to remember the faces that had looked at her from the portraits.

Breathe, Fox. In and out.

She had to find her fur dress. She couldn't leave without the dress. Troisclerq took her hand. He kissed her fingers gently, as though his lips had never touched anything more beautiful.

"I usually give my female guests the keys to all the doors in my house, and I ask them not to use one particular key. It's an old tradition in my clan. You may have heard about it?" He put the key ring on the table. All the keys were silver-plated except one. That one was somewhat smaller than the others, and its head was golden and shaped like a flower.

"Yes," said Fox. "Yes, I've heard about it."

"Good." Troisclerq pushed the bunch of keys next to her plate. "Not that you'd need the keys to find out what's behind each door. The vixen would smell it anyway."

Of course. He'd seen the fur dress. Fox tried not to wonder whether it was he who'd taken it off her. She closed her hand around the key ring as if that could prove she wasn't afraid. The servant poured her a glass of wine. The wine was so red, it looked as though he was filling her glass with blood.

"This time you caught the wrong girl."

She sensed the strange dress on her skin. *Done up for the portrait on his wall, Fox.*

"Really? And why is that?"

The servant filled her plate. Duck. Baked potatoes. She realized how hungry she was.

"I've never been afraid of death." Fox looked Troisclerq straight in the eyes so he could see she was telling the truth. Those eyes with the shadows that should have warned her. *But you liked how he looked at you, Fox. You liked how he kept reaching for your arm or touching your shoulder as if by accident.* All the things Jacob was avoiding more carefully these days. She carried her longing for him like a secret beneath her skin, but maybe Troisclerq had sensed it, as he'd sensed the dress beneath her clothes, like a trail of blood in the woods, though his hunger was of a different kind. So what? Whatever it was that had attracted him to her, she would know how to die. The vixen had taught her. She lived with death, both as the hunter and the hunted.

"The wrong girl? Oh no." Troisclerq was as soft as moss in the woods. "Don't fret. I always select my prey carefully. It's what has kept me alive for nearly three hundred years." He nodded at his servant. "You will give me what I want. Like all the others. And even more so."

The servant placed a pitcher on the table. The evening light glistened through the crystal like splinters of a dying day.

Troisclerq got up and stroked Fox's naked shoulder. "Fear has many colors, did you know that? White is the most nourishing kind, the fear of death. For most, it is their own death they fear more than anything. But I knew right away that you are different. And that made the hunt even more enticing." Troisclerq scattered a handful of withered flowers on the table. "I left a very clear trail. I'm sure he's already on his way. Wouldn't you think so?"

Jacob.

No. Fox would forget his name, so Troisclerq could never find it in her heart. She felt her fear choking her.

A few white drops materialized at the bottom of the pitcher.

Troisclerq gently stroked her cheek. "The labyrinth

that surrounds my house," he whispered, "will let only me pass. Everybody else gets hopelessly lost. They forget who they are, forget why they came, and they just wander aimlessly between the hedges until they starve to death. They end up eating poisonous leaves and licking dew off the gravel."

Fox splashed her wine into his face. She gripped the glass so tightly that it shattered in her hand. The wine turned Troisclerq's shirt red, as red as the blood that now trickled down Fox's fingers. Troisclerq offered her his napkin.

"He loves you, too, you know. Even though he tries hard not to notice it." No voice could have sounded more tender. He pushed back his chair. "From here you have a good view of the labyrinth. If a swarm of pigeons rises from it, that means he's caught in it. I'm not expecting any other guests apart from Jacob."

The floor of the carafe was now covered with a milky white puddle.

Troisclerq walked down the long table. Past the empty plates. Before he closed the door, he said to her, "It may be a consolation to you that the fear will kill you as well. Love is a deadly affair."

She wanted to bite his throat. Choke his velveteen voice with blood. But the vixen was as lost as Celeste.

41. THE HUNTER'S TERRITORY

As soon as they entered Champlitte, Jacob knew they'd found the right place. Many of the houses were freshly painted, and the evening streets were glowing under gaslights—a luxury usually found only in the largest cities behind the mirror. Bluebeards made good neighbors. They never hunted where they lived, and they gave money for roads, churches, and schools. The silence thus purchased was their best protection. Jacob was sure many eyes were following him and Donnersmarck from behind the curtains of Champlitte.

Most Bluebeards lived in remote country houses surrounded by sweeping landholdings. There was only one house nearby that fit that description. It lay to the south of the town. Jacob turned his horse northward, so none of the good citizens would deem it necessary to notify Troisclerq of their arrival.

They left their horses in a little wood. Even wolves would leave devil-horses alone, and Jacob had replaced their reins with chains to keep them from freeing themselves. His stallion had actually befriended him and snapped amicably at his hand as Jacob pulled the backpack from his saddle.

The evening smelled of blooming trees and freshly plowed fields. Everything around them seemed peaceful, a sleepy paradise. But they didn't have to walk long before they came upon a sycamore-lined avenue where a carriage had left deep tracks in the wet gravel. A little later, an iron gate appeared between the trees.

The deceptive peacefulness, the locked gate... even the avenue had looked similar when they'd been looking for Donnersmarck's sister. They'd come too late then. *Not this time, Jacob.*

He could have thrown up with fear. He'd lost count of how often during that endless ride he'd caught himself looking around for Fox. Or thinking he could hear her breathing next to him in his sleep.

"What's the greatest treasure you ever found?" Chanute had asked him not too long ago. Jacob had shrugged and named a few objects. "You're an even greater fool than I," Chanute had growled. "I just hope you won't have lost it by the time the answer dawns on you."

The gate was covered with iron flowers. Donnersmarck

silently pulled a key from his pocket. Jacob had once owned one just like it, but he'd lost it, together with too many other things, in the fortress of the Goyl. A key that opened any lock...Some worked only in the country where they were forged, but this one worked fine here. The gate swung open as soon as Donnersmarck pushed it into the lock.

A coach house, stables, a wide driveway between dripping-wet trees, and at its end the house they'd seen from a distance. It was surrounded by evergreen hedgerows.

The labyrinth of the other Bluebeard had been dead and wilted because he'd already escaped. Jacob and Donnersmarck had hacked their way through it with their sabers. This labyrinth, however, was still alive. *Good, Jacob. That means he's still here.* The hedgerows rustled as the pair approached, as though the evergreen branches wanted to warn the murderer they were shielding. Troisclerq. This time he had a name and a familiar face. All the evenings they spent together in coach stations, drunk together, exchanged stories about the jealousy of Fairies and merchants' daughters, about duels lost and won, good blacksmiths and bad tailors. *And he saved your life, Jacob.*

He wanted to kill Troisclerq. He'd never wanted anything as badly.

A flock of pigeons fluttered up from the hedgerows. Jacob looked after them with apprehension. What if Troisclerq killed Fox as soon as he noticed him and Donnersmarck? *Stop it, Jacob. She's still alive.*

He repeated it to himself over and over. *She's still alive.* He'd go crazy if he allowed himself to think anything else.

I'm sure we'll meet again.

He was going to kill Troisclerq.

42. WHITE

Pigeons. Their feathers as white as her fear. Their wings writing it across the evening sky.

Fox pressed her hands against the window. She whispered Jacob's name, as though her voice could guide him through the Bluebeard's labyrinth. He had freed her from a trap before, but back then she'd been the prey. Now she was the bait.

She was so happy that Jacob had come.

She wished so badly that he'd never found her.

Behind her, between the empty plates, the carafe was filling with her fear.

43. LOST

Jacob wished he had a ball of untearable yarn, or one that could find the way on its own if he placed it on the graveled path that disappeared into the hedgerows ahead. But Donnersmarck had searched the Chambers of Miracles in vain for such an item. The yarn Jacob was now tying to a bush at the entrance of the labyrinth came from a tailor's shop in Vena, and there was nothing magical about it except for the skill involved in spinning common sheep wool into a firm thread. This was going to be their thread of life, their only hope of not losing themselves between the shrubs.

Jacob carefully ran the thread through his fingers as he and Donnersmarck stepped into the twilight between the branches. The predator had cast his green web very wide. Just a few turns in, they stumbled over a rusty saber. They found bones that had been nibbled clean, rotten boots, an old-fashioned pistol. Soon enough they no longer knew which direction they'd come from, yet their greatest worry was the white flowers growing in the shade of the shrubs. Forgetyourself. No point in crushing them or pulling them out. Their effect just got stronger when the blossoms wilted. Jacob and Donnersmarck tied kerchiefs in front of their mouths and noses and walked on, repeating each other's names, or places and things they'd done together. But their memories faded with every step, and their only connection to the world they were fast forgetting was a thread of yarn.

Leaves. Branches. Paths ending in evergreen walls. Again and again.

Jacob had escaped from places where one lost oneself, but not even the Fairy island had turned his world into such a nothing. He touched the scar on his hand, which the vixen's teeth had once left there so he wouldn't lose himself in the arms of the Red Fairy.

Don't forget her, Jacob.

Forget yourself, but not her.

And again the path ended in the shrubs. Donnersmarck cursed, ramming his saber into the thicket. Left. Right. The very words seemed to have lost all meaning. Jacob rolled up the thread so it would lead them back to the last fork.

Don't forget her.

How many hours had they been wandering like this? Or was it days? Had there ever been anything but this labyrinth? Jacob spun around and reached for his pistol. A man was standing behind him with his saber drawn.

The stranger lowered his weapon. "Jacob! It's me!" Donnersmarck. *Repeat the name, Jacob.* No, there was only one name he couldn't forget. Fox. *She's still alive.* Again and again. *She's still alive.* He leaned against the evergreen leaves. The perfume of forgetyourself filled his head with sticky nothingness.

He stumbled on—and suddenly he clutched his chest.

The fourth bite.

No. Not now.

The yarn fell from his hand as the pain forced him to his knees. Donnersmarck stumbled after the ball of wool and just managed to catch it before it disappeared beneath the hedge.

The pain set Jacob's heart racing, yet all he could think was *Not now, not here!* He had to find her.

"What is it?" Donnersmarck leaned over him. *It'll pass, Jacob. It always passes.*

The pain was everywhere. It flooded his flesh.

Donnersmarck dropped to his knees beside Jacob. "We'll never find a way out of here."

Think, Jacob. But how, with the pain numbing his senses? He pushed a trembling hand into his pocket. Where was it? He found the card in the folds of his gold handkerchief. It didn't stay blank for long.

Do you need my help?

Jacob pressed his hand to his aching chest. The answer didn't come easily. A bargain that could only end badly.

"Yes."

"What are you doing?" Donnersmarck stared at the card.

It filled with new words.

Anytime. I hope this is the beginning of a fruitful collaboration.
Are you ready to pay my price?

"Whatever you want." It could hardly be higher than the Fairy's price. As long as he got out of this labyrinth.

I will take you at your word.

Green ink. Nearly as green as Earlking's eyes. Guismond had sold his soul to the Devil. Whom was he selling his to?

The pain eased, but Jacob was still nauseous from the smell of the forgetyourself, and he barely remembered his own name.

The card stayed blank.

Come on!

The letters appeared painfully slowly.

Twice left and then right.
Twice right and then left.
So goes the web the Bluebeard weaves.

On your feet, Jacob! It was a pattern. Nothing but a pattern.

Donnersmarck stumbled after him. Left and left again. Then right. Jacob let the thread run through his fingers. Right. And right again. And left.

Through the hedges came the light of a lantern. They rushed toward it, both certain it would disappear again. But the hedgerows opened up, and they were standing in the open.

The house in front of them was old. Nearly as old as its owner's ghastly clan. The crest above the door was weathered, but the centuries had not diminished the splendor of the gray walls and towers. Their dark outlines nearly melted into the night. There was one lantern shining next to the entrance, and there was light behind two windows on the first floor.

Behind one of them stood Fox.

44. BLUEBEARD

No. Troisclerq's labyrinth could not catch Jacob. Fox wished him far, far away; and she was so happy to see him. So happy.

Jacob was not alone. Fox recognized Donnersmarck only at second glance. She always thought his sister had been a fool for getting seduced by a Bluebeard.

Troisclerq's servant dragged her away from the window. She bit his furry hand, even though her human teeth were so much blunter than the vixen's, and tore herself free. The pitcher was already half-full. Fox pushed it over before the servant could stop her. He grabbed her hair and shook her so hard that she couldn't breathe. She didn't care. Her fear was trickling white across the table. Jacob was here, and they were both still alive.

"So it's just like everyone says. Not that I would have

doubted it." Troisclerq was standing in the doorway. He went to the table and caught the dripping liquid in his hollow hand.

He didn't seem alarmed that Jacob had escaped his labyrinth.

"You cannot kill him!" What was she thinking? That if she spoke the words loudly enough, they would become the truth? Fox felt her fear return.

Troisclerq touched the white liquid in his hand. "We shall see." He nodded at his servant. "Take her to the others."

Fox kept screaming Jacob's name while the servant dragged her down the corridor. What for? To warn him, to call him, to wrap herself in his name, the way she would wrap herself in the fur the Bluebeard had stolen from her. *Don't call him, Fox.*

The servant stopped.

Take her to the others.

The door was no different from the other doors, but Fox could smell the death behind it as clearly as if there was blood actually seeping through the dark wood.

"You forgot something." Troisclerq was standing behind her. He was holding the bunch of keys he'd put next to her plate. Maybe he wanted to see her hands tremble as she tried to put the golden key into the lock.

Jacob hadn't let her inside the house where the Bluebeard had killed Donnersmarck's sister. Fox had mocked him for it. The vixen had herself killed too often to be shocked by death, yet the sight awaiting her behind the door still filled her with dread.

This hunter never let go of his prey.

Nine women. They hung, held up by golden chains, like string puppets killed by their own fear. Their eyes were empty, but the terror was forever written on their pale faces. Their killer kept them in his red chamber like jewels in a casket. Frozen remnants of the pleasure they'd given him, of the life they'd fed him, of the love that had lured them to him.

The servant wrapped the golden chain around Fox's neck and wrists as though he wanted to adorn her one last time for Troisclerq. There wasn't much space left in his horrible dollhouse. Her elbow touched the arm of the dead girl next to her. So cold and still so beautiful.

"They won't let me go." Troisclerq put the empty pitcher on a table by one of the shrouded windows. "They become part of me. Maybe that's part of why I kill them—to free myself from them. But they remain, silent and still, and they remind me. Of their voices. Of the warmth their skin once had."

The gaslights that illuminated the chamber cast the shadows of the dead on the red wall. Fox could see her own among them. She was already one of them.

Troisclerq approached her. "You're still afraid more of his death than of your own?"

"No." Fox didn't care whether Troisclerq knew that was a lie. "He will kill you. For me. And for the others."

“Many have tried.” Troisclerq nodded at his servant. “Bring him to me,” he said. “But only him.”

Then he leaned against the silk-covered wall that gave the room the color of the insides of an animal. Troisclerq waited.

And Fox saw her fear trickling into the pitcher.

45. THE WRONG RESCUERS

In a well. They threw him into a damn well.

Why? All he did was repeat Louis's unintelligible mutterings in a few shops around the market square. White as milk. Black like a sliver of night. Set in gold.

And, Nerron? Shouldn't the way the fat butcher stared at you have been warning enough?

He clawed at the slippery wall. Eaumbre was drifting in the briny water deep below. The Waterman was staring up at him as though it was his fault they'd ended like that. Eaumbre could probably survive for years down there in his scaly skin.

The best? My foot! No more eternal glory as a treasure hunter. Into a well, Nerron, a well! The good people of Champlitte now clearly used it only to dispense of unwelcome visitors. Running water, gaslights... wherever all that wealth came from, they didn't like strangers, and definitely not ones with a stone skin.

Nerron put his forehead against the damp wall. *Do not look down.* Water. The Goyl's ultimate fear.

He'd tried to heave up the iron plate they'd placed over the well, but after that landed him next to the Waterman, he refrained from any further attempts. His clothes were still damp and as slimy as a snail's flesh.

His only consolation was that now Reckless wouldn't get the crossbow, either. Maybe someday one of those scholars who dug up old stones would fish his well-preserved remains from the well and would wonder why he'd been carrying a golden head and a severed hand.

Nerron groaned—by now his claws were aching as though they were being slowly pulled from his fingers—and he pressed himself against the cold wall as he heard voices above. Were the townspeople coming back because they'd decided to burn him alive instead, as they used to do with his kind in Austry?

The iron plate lifted. It had been afternoon when they were thrown into the well, but the piece of sky that now came into view was already darker than Nerron's skin. His golden eyes squinted as the light of a lantern beamed down the well shaft.

"What a picture!" A twangy voice echoed into the well. Arsene Lelou was staring down at him, thrilled, like a child staring at a captured insect. Nerron never thought the sight of the Bug would make him that happy.

His aching fingers barely managed to grab hold of the rope Lelou threw down the well. Someone yanked him so roughly over the well's wall that he grazed his stony skin. Nerron knew the oafish face from the household of Louis's cousin. One of the kitchen hands. Milkbeard. He even used that name himself. He threw Nerron on the ground as though he'd spent his whole miserable existence waiting to lay his lumpish hands on a Goyl.

"By all means, hurt him. But don't kill him!" Lelou stabbed the tip of his boot into Nerron's side. It smelled of wax. The Bug spent hours polishing his buttoned boots. "What did you expect?" he hissed. "That I'd return Crookback's son as a Snow-White and get myself executed in your stead? That wasn't the deal. Elven dust! You really have to try a bit harder if you want to fool Arsene Lelou."

The Bug loved speaking of himself in the third person.

"Take his backpack!" he ordered.

The kitchen boy pressed his boots so hard into Nerron's back that he thought he could hear his spine crack.

"I hope you still have the head and the hand," Lelou purred. "Otherwise I'll have to throw you right back into that well. We will find the crossbow together, and should you try to sneak off again, I'll immediately telegraph Crookback about what you did to his son."

Milkbeard dragged Nerron to his feet. They had an

audience. Despite the late hour, half of Champlitte had gathered around the well. The butcher wasn't the only one who looked disappointed that the stoneface was still alive. Nerron was probably the first Goyl they'd ever seen in the flesh. He wanted to scream at Kami'en: *Forget Albion! Start invading Lotharaine already.* Nerron wanted to see them dead, all the brave burghers of Champlitte who'd tried to drown him like a cat.

Lelou pressed his pistol into Nerron's side.

"Go on. Fish the Waterman out as well!" he barked at the boy. How, by the Devil and all his golden hairs, had he found them?

The answer was standing in front of the butcher's shop. The gold ornaments on Louis's cousin's carriage would have fed not only the butcher but the whole of Champlitte for a year. Sitting on the coachman's box was the dog man who trained the princely cousin's hounds. In Vena, he already used to stare at Nerron in a way like he'd love nothing more than to set his dogs on a Goyl for a change. And he'd brought two of them with him. Bloodhounds. They sat next to him on the coach box and bared their fangs as soon as they caught sight of Nerron. Damn. He hadn't even tried to cover his tracks. He'd clearly underestimated the Bug.

"Get in!" Lelou shoved him toward the carriage.

Louis was lying on one of the gold-upholstered benches with his mouth open, uttering grunting snores. Lelou shook him by the shoulder. "Wake up, my prince. We found them!"

Wake up? Hardly.

But Louis did indeed open his eyes. They were swollen and bloodshot, but the princeling was awake.

Lelou gave Nerron a triumphant look.

"Toad spawn!" His lips pouted into a self-satisfied smile. "Two treatises from the seventeenth century list it as an antidote to Snow-White apples."

Nerron had never heard about that, but the spawn seemed to work. Never mind that Louis looked even more moronic than before.

"How did the dogs find our trail so quickly?"

Lelou looked at him with compassionate disdain. *Your pathetic performance in the well has forever negated the effect of your Three Souvenirs, Nerron.* "We didn't need the hounds. Louis has been saying nothing but 'Champlitte' for days."

Yes, Snow-White apples did have that effect. Most victims, should they ever awaken, spoke nothing but the words they'd said as oracles.

Louis began to snore again.

Lelou frowned. "I think we may have to up the dose," he said to the dog man. "Fine. That obviously takes care of the question of whether we still need the Waterman. I'm sure he's very qualified to find us more toad spawn."

He looked at Eaumbre, who was just being hauled out

of the well by Milkbeard. The people of Champlitte shrank back as the dripping Waterman was shoved across the market square.

"Right then, Goyl." Lelou looked at Nerron. "Before I might wonder whether you're still any use to us. Where is the heart?"

"Show the hounds the sack with the head," Nerron said.

If they were lucky, it would still have enough of Reckless's scent.

46. BRING HIM TO ME

The window behind which Fox had stood was dark by the time they reached the house. Jacob forced himself not to think what that might mean. Donnersmarck leaped up the steps as though if he only hurried, he could have his sister back. The heavy door simply swung open as he pushed his shoulder against it. Donnersmarck did not need Jacob to explain that an unlocked door on a house like that was best treated with caution. Both drew their sabers. Pistols were as useless against a Bluebeard as they were against the Tailor in the black forest.

The entrance hall smelled of forgetyourself, even more so than the endless paths of the labyrinth. Jacob plucked the flowers from the vases by the door, and Donnersmarck pushed open the high windows to let in the night air.

Several corridors led away from the hall, and a broad

staircase swung up to the second floor. What now? Should they split up?

They didn't have to make that decision. A servant stepped from one of the corridors. Judging by his hairy hands, he hadn't always been human.

Jacob drew his pistol. It was useless against the master, but it might work on the servant.

"Where is she?"

No answer. The eyes staring at him were uniformly dark, like an animal's.

Donnersmarck grabbed the servant by his stiff collar and put the tip of a saber to his throat. "If she's dead, then so are you. Understood? Where is she?"

It happened too fast.

Antlers sprouted from the servant's head. They tore through Donnersmarck's body before he could parry them with the saber. Jacob shot, but the bullets had no effect, and the Man-Stag deflected Jacob's saber effortlessly, as though it were nothing but a stick wielded by a child. Jacob had read about them—stag calves that took the form of a man if human hair was mixed into their hay. It was said they were mindlessly loyal to their masters.

The Man-Stag wiped Donnersmarck's blood from his brow and made a summoning gesture toward the corridor he'd come from. Jacob ignored him. He reached into his belt pouch and knelt down next to Donnersmarck. Yes, he still carried the Witch's needle with him. Jacob pressed it into his friend's bloody hand. It wouldn't be able to heal a wound as terrible as this, but it could at least close it. The Man-Stag snorted impatiently. Only his head had changed. The blood was dripping from his antlers onto his black tailcoat.

"Go, Jacob!" Donnersmarck's voice was a croaky rattle. Maybe the needle would keep him alive long enough. *Long enough for what, Jacob?* He got up.

The servant pointed at the corridor again. Jacob thought he could hear Chanute berating him: *"Damn it, Jacob! What did I teach you about Bluebeards? You seriously believed you could just barge into his home and steal his quarry?"*

Doors. At each one, Jacob thought Fox might be lying behind it, dead. But every time he stopped, the Man-Stag just uttered a menacing grunt.

The door he led him to was open.

Jacob already saw the red walls from many steps away.

And the dead on golden chains.

And Fox among them.

47. LIFE AND DEATH

For an instant, Fox feared that the blood on Jacob's shirt was his own, but then she saw the servant's bloody antlers, and that they'd come without Donnersmarck.

Jacob just brushed her with a quick glance. He knew they were both lost if he let his concern for her distract him from the murderer who was waiting for him among the dead. Jacob was unarmed. His face was blurred by the tears in Fox's eyes. Tears for her own helplessness. Tears for her fear for him. As they ran down her face, she nearly expected them to be as white as the liquid that was filling Troisclerq's pitcher.

The Bluebeard pushed himself off the bloodred wall. Lost in his house of death. Guy. He briefly regained his name. He went to Fox and touched her cheek as though he wanted to feel her tears on his fingertips.

"You may go," he said to the servant, who was still standing in the door with his bloody antlers. The Man-Stag looked puzzled.

"I said, you may go!" Troisclerq's voice sounded composed, as though time was his. And it was his. The dead bodies around them had procured it for him.

The servant bowed his horned head. Then he hesitantly stepped back and disappeared into the dark corridor.

They were alone. With the dead and their murderer.

Fox recalled all the hours Jacob had sat next to Troisclerq in the coach, relaxed, as though they'd been friends for years. She could still see a trace of that friendship on Jacob's face. He liked Troisclerq, and he despised his heart for it.

"No one has made it through the labyrinth in more than eighty years. The last one was a police constable from Champlitte. I kept his weapon as a souvenir." Troisclerq pointed at a rapier hanging on the wall behind the dead girls. "Help yourself. I'm sure he wouldn't mind. I know you prefer a saber, but since this is my house, I hope you'll respect my choice of weapon."

Jacob went to the rapier. He still avoided looking at Fox. *Yes, forget me,* she wanted to whisper. *Forget me, Jacob, or he will kill you.* She saw her fear trickle into the pitcher.

Troisclerq saw it, too.

"Only nine?" Jacob looked at the dead. "I'm sure you killed many more than that. Am I right?"

He took the rapier from the wall.

"Yes. I only bring the prettiest ones here." Troisclerq brushed back his black hair. "I killed my first ones during the Giant Wars. A long time ago. A very long time."

"You forget their names, don't you?" Jacob pointed the unfamiliar blade at the dead girl with the red ruby brooch on her dress. "Her name is Marie Pasquet. She was the granddaughter of a famous goldsmith. I promised her grandfather I'd kill you when I found her."

"And I know you usually keep your promises." Troisclerq smiled. "I already knew we'd end up here when I cut you out of those vines. A downside of such a long life. After just a hundred years or so, everybody becomes so predictable, transparent, like glass. Every virtue, every sin, every weakness...nothing but endless repetition. Every ambition—seen it a thousand times. Illusions, lost a hundred times over, all hope childish, all innocence a joke..."

He lifted his rapier. "What remains is death. And the search for that perfect thrust. Death in its most...immaculate form."

He struck out so suddenly that Jacob, trying to dodge the thrust, stumbled into the hanging dead. Fear. How much could one have? The dead girls, watching the duelers through empty eyes, knew the answer. Fox died with every stumble, with every cut Troisclerq's blade left on Jacob's skin. He was toying with Jacob. And he let Fox see it. He left himself open so that Jacob would charge into his blade; he drew bloody lines on Jacob's skin, sketching his death before he'd fill it in with red. And the pitcher filled with white fear—more lifetime for the Bluebeard.

Fox had often watched Jacob fight, but never against such an adversary. It only dawned on her slowly that he was Troisclerq's equal—and he wanted to kill the Bluebeard. Never before had Fox seen that desire so clearly on Jacob's face.

The rapiers snagged on silky robes; they slashed through the golden chains and dead flesh. The two men were breathing heavily. Their wheezes and the silence of the dead... Fox knew both would stay with her until the end of her life. If she'd have a life. She tried to free herself so desperately, blood streaming down her arms, and she screamed when Troisclerq's blade nearly pierced Jacob's throat. So much fear. She closed her eyes, trying not to choke on it. But the next scream did not come from Jacob.

Troisclerq pressed his hand against his slashed knee. "That was dirty," Fox heard him gasp. "Where did you learn that?"

"In another world," Jacob replied.

Troisclerq stabbed at his chest, but Jacob slashed his blade through the other knee, and as Troisclerq collapsed, Jacob rammed his blade so deep between the Bluebeard's ribs that the thrust was only halted by the hilt of the sword. Troisclerq cowered on the floor, spitting his own blood on his chest. Jacob dropped to his knees and pulled the key from the Bluebeard's pocket.

It is over, Fox.

Troisclerq reached out with his bloody hand and grabbed Jacob's arm.

"I'll see you," he whispered.

His hand didn't let go, but his eyes went as blank as his victims'. Jacob pried the fingers from his arm. Then he staggered to his feet and dropped the rapier. The blood on the blade was black.

His hand trembled as he unlocked the chains around Fox's throat and arms with the Bluebeard's key. Then he held the pitcher to her lips.

"Drink!" he whispered. "Forget about him. Drink as much as you can. It will be all right."

48. TOO LATE

A Bluebeard's house. Of course. At least now some of Louis's ramblings had made sense. *White as milk.* Not clear enough? Nerron cursed his own thick-wittedness as he caught a glimpse of the withered hedgerows and the stag standing forlornly in front of the unlit house. He ran off before the bloodhounds could get him.

The Bluebeard was laid out in his red chamber, surrounded by nine women. They lay next to their murderer as though they were sleeping. Lelou threw up in the corridor. The Bug had a sensitive stomach when confronted with death. Even Eaumbre looked rather distraught at the row of beautiful corpses, but then he quickly went off in search of the Bluebeard's treasure chamber. Watermen at least kept their girls alive—though some would probably prefer death over a life in a pond.

Black like a piece of night set in gold. You're a fool, Nerron. Louis had told him everything he'd wanted to know. Wherever the heart had been hidden in this horrible place, Reckless had found it. Nerron would have bet the head and the heart on that. Just as he was certain the blood in the entrance hall was not that of his rival.

They found some thoroughly wiped tracks in the driveway, but making yourself invisible wasn't easy when you were transporting an injured man. And it slowed you down.

They'd catch up with them soon enough.

49. TWO CUPS

The house, which Fox had found in a dark pine forest barely two miles from Champlitte, smelled neither of cinnamon nor of molten sugar. There also were no gingerbreads on the walls—and you didn't need a fur dress to scent the dark magic wafting around the house like a bad smell. Jacob would have preferred a Witch like Alma, but Donnersmarck was as good as dead, and child-eaters could heal even the most terrible wounds. It was just best not to ask what went into their potions.

The woman who opened the door was very beautiful and very young. Most Dark Witches showed themselves in that form even if they were hundreds of years old. Jacob and Fox put Donnersmarck on her kitchen table so she could inspect his wounds. The nails on her fingers were so long and sharp, they made Jacob grateful his friend was already unconscious. Donnersmarck was paying a high price for helping him, and Jacob was not just worried about the wounds inflicted by the Man-Stag. The Witch confirmed his fears. When Jacob described to her who had attacked his friend, she shook her head with a vicious smile.

"I can save his life," she said. "But I can't do anything about him maybe wearing antlers one day. You can stay in my stable. This will take a few days, and you know the price. His life will cost you two cups of blood." The Witch cut off Fox before she could protest. "Careful now! Or I might also ask for the dress that's out there in that devil-horse's saddlebag. I'm sure it gives you a beautiful fur."

The Witch cut Jacob's arm expertly, and the two cups were quickly filled. Then she rushed them out of the house. Dark Witches never allowed anyone to witness their craft. The cups had taken a lot of blood. Fox and Jacob chained the devil-horses to some trees, and Fox took the saddlebags with her. Jacob had found the fur dress in the servant's room—and only then had the fear finally disappeared from Fox's face.

She caught a few will-o'-the-wisps before she bandaged his arm in the dark stable. It was barely more than a shack, and definitely not the kind of place he'd wanted to take her to after the Bluebeard's chamber. But the woods out there were no better. *This will take a few days.* Jacob had wanted to return to Vena as quickly as possible, to start searching for the Bastard. The moth on his chest was missing only two more spots, and the heart was no good to him as long as the Goyl had the head and the hand. But they could hardly repay Donnersmarck for all his help by leaving him alone with a child-eater. The Witch's needle had kept him from bleeding out, but there wasn't much life left in him. Jacob didn't tell Fox about the fourth bite in the Bluebeard's labyrinth. He was so relieved to have her by his side again, breathing and unhurt, that the moth seemed nothing but a nightmare, and death was something they'd both left in Troisclerq's red chamber.

Fox was so exhausted that she was asleep before Jacob could explain to her why he'd taken the necklace off one of the dead girls. She probably hadn't even noticed—all she'd been concerned about was whether Troisclerq had destroyed her fur dress.

Jacob lay down next to her on the filthy straw, but he couldn't sleep. He just listened to her breathing. At some point a crowned snake crawled into the stable, a kind found only in Lotharaine. The black lily on its head was worth a hundred gold talers, but Jacob didn't even lift his head. He didn't want to think about treasure, or about the crossbow, or about having to die soon. Fox was sleeping a deep sleep. Her face was peaceful, as though she'd left all her fear behind in the Bluebeard's house. She was back in the men's clothes she'd worn on their trip to Albion. She'd left the Bluebeard's dress next to her sisters-in-death. Jacob couldn't take his eyes off her sleeping face. It finally erased all the images that had been tormenting him since Vena. It felt like a miracle that she was still alive, a magic that would pass. No Fairy island, no Larks' Water, just a bed of filthy straw and her rhythmic breathing—yet nothing had ever felt better.

Jacob had spent years looking for one of the hourglasses that stopped time, for the Empress. He'd never understood why this was one of the most coveted treasures one could find behind the mirror. There had never been a moment he'd wanted to hold on to forever. The next one always had more promise, and even the most glorious day began to taste stale after a few hours. But now he was lying in the stable of a child-eater, his arm sliced open and death in his chest, wishing for an hourglass. He waved away a will-o'-the-wisp that had settled on Fox's brow—they often brought bad dreams—and brushed the hair from her sleeping face.

His touch woke her. She reached out and ran her finger over the cut Troisclerq's rapier had left on his left cheek.

"I am so sorry," she whispered.

As if it was her fault he'd been too blind to protect her from Troisclerq. Jacob put his finger on her lips and shook his head. He had no idea how to apologize for all the fear and terror she'd never be able to forget. There was no consolation in that they'd both been Troisclerq's prey, that they'd given Troisclerq a death he might have even been longing for after all the stolen lifetimes. Was it possible to escape death too long? Could there be too much life? It was hard to believe that on a night like this.

"You heard the Witch," he said quietly. "We'll be here a few days. So sleep! It's not the coziest of places, but much better than the one we came from, don't you think?"

Fox didn't answer. Her eyes wandered to his chest, to where the moth was hiding beneath his shirt. She hadn't forgotten about death. From his backpack, Jacob pulled the necklace he'd taken from Ramée's granddaughter. Her face incredulous, Fox touched the black heart.

"Two treasures in one go," Jacob whispered. "I'll tell you the whole story. But now you have to rest."

She was so pale. He felt as though he could see through her skin.

Outside, one of the devil-horses whinnied.

Fox sat up.

The horse was quiet again, but it wasn't a good silence.

She was quicker to the stable door than he. His eyes couldn't make out anything suspicious between the dark trees, but Fox reached for the saddlebag with her fur dress.

"Someone's there."

"Let me take a look."

She just shook her head. Jacob watched the trees while she put on the fur dress. The horses were still restless. Maybe they just smelled the Witch.

No, Jacob.

It was a moonless night, and he barely noticed the vixen dart off. There was still light behind the Witch's window. A dog was barking somewhere.

Why did you let her go, Jacob? She was too weak. He

could still see the pitcher, filled to the rim with her fear. Again, a dog barking. His hand reached for his pistol. He was just about to go after her when the fur of the vixen brushed against his leg.

"They are over there, to the left, between the trees. The Bastard and five others." Fox pulled Jacob away from the stable door. He thought he could still feel the fur on her hands. "You can smell the Waterman from miles off. And they have two bloodhounds."

Damn. How did the Goyl get there? Jacob seemed unable to shake him off, like a shadow. Jacob rubbed his bandaged arm. It was his left—the heart arm, as the Witches called it. Sadly, it was also his better shooting arm. Not to mention the blood he was missing, and he still had the fight with Troisclerq in his bones. The Bastard would take the heart, and it would be like taking it off a child.

"Maybe the Witch can help us," Fox whispered.

"Sure. But I can't afford to give another two cups of blood. And have you forgotten about the Waterman?" Witch magic was as powerless against Watermen as a lit fuse thrown into a pond.

"I can try to lure them away."

"No."

She knew him well enough to know that this "no" was final.

Jacob looked toward the devil-horses. Even if he and Fox managed to get away, what about Donnersmarck?

Damn. Too little time in the wrong place.

He took the black heart from his pocket. Fox flinched as he put the necklace around her neck. Jacob had wrapped the stone in a piece of cloth so it wouldn't touch her.

"Take it off before you go to sleep, and make sure the stone never sits on top of your heart!" he whispered. "The cloth will only protect your skin. I'll try to get you at least an hour's head start."

"No!" She wanted to take the necklace off, but Jacob grabbed her hands.

"Nothing will happen to me. I'll surrender myself before things get too hot."

"And then what? That Goyl already tried once before to kill you!"

"He won't, as long as I am his only chance of getting the heart! You just can't get caught. Meet up with Valiant. Let the Dwarf deal with the Bastard. There's an empty watchtower by the Dead City. I'll tell the Goyl that's where you'll be waiting for him."

She leaned her head against his shoulder.

"It'll be all right," he whispered.

"When?" she whispered back. "Let's try together. Please! We'll be on the horses before they can start shooting."

"And Donnersmarck?" Jacob brushed a will-o'-the-wisp from her hair. An hourglass. He'd find one. But the moment was now lost.

"Take the rear." He drew his pistol. "The wall's so rotten, I'm sure you'll find a crack over there."

Fox turned around, but Jacob pulled her back once more. He wrapped his arms around her and buried his face in her hair. Her heartbeat was like his own.

Something stirred outside between the trees.

"Run!" Jacob whispered.

Red fur where just a moment before was pale skin.

She was gone before he had turned around again.

50. A TRADE

Yes, the vixen had spotted them. However, the stable she'd disappeared into had only one door, and Louis would hit anything that came out of there. He yawned as often as he breathed, but his eyes were halfway clear again, and he was a decent shot.

"Shall I let them go?" The dog man could barely hold his panting charges.

"No. Not yet." The thought of them tearing the vixen to pieces made Nerron nauseous. It wouldn't take much and soon he'd be throwing up at every turn, like Lelou.

Speaking of the Devil...

"Are you sure he's in there?" The Bug stared at the stable as though he were trying to burn a hole into the brittle walls. He was very proud of the pistol he'd started to carry in his belt.

"Yes. He's standing right behind the door."

Reckless thought the darkness hid him, but he'd forgotten he was dealing with a Goyl.

"I best hit him straight in the head." Louis trained his rifle. "Or do we need him alive?" His clan's passion for the hunt. The excitement even made him forget to yawn. They still believed the story about the Albian spy.

"No. Just shoot him dead," Nerron replied. He didn't want Louis to think he was softer than him. And, anyway, Reckless wouldn't be so stupid as to run out in front of his rifle. Nerron was sure he had the heart. Once more, Reckless had been faster. *Two to one for him, Nerron.*

Lelou nervously licked his lips. The pistol on his belt had not made a warrior out of him. Eaumbre was with Milkbeard by the Witch's house. After what had happened in Vena, Louis had become even harsher toward the Waterman, but Eaumbre bore the insults with a stoic expression, and he kept acting as if he'd never given up the bodyguarding business.

At Nerron's sign, Eaumbre kicked in the Witch's door. Yes, he was useful, though one could never be too sure which side he was on. Probably his own. The child-eater fluttered past him and landed on her roof with a loud croak. The magpie was the Dark Witches' bird of choice; the White Witches preferred swallows. Reckless had probably been watching, but there was no movement behind the stable door.

“One thing’s for sure,” Louis muttered. “When we find that crossbow, I get the first shot.”

“Yes? And who would that be aimed at?”

Louis gave Nerron an icy look. “A Goyl, of course. And with the second shot, I’ll wipe out the Albian army.”

Eaumbre stood in front of Nerron. “Just one wounded man. He’s sleeping some kind of Witch sleep. Shall I bring him here to flush out the other one?”

“No. I’ll get him out anyway.” Nerron drew his revolver and checked the ammunition. Nothing wrong with having a bit of fun.

Eaumbre stood by his side. The well had obviously not dampened his lust for treasure hunting.

“I’m coming as well.” Louis suppressed a yawn.

To hell with Lelou and his toad spawn! Luckily, even the Bug understood that a dead prince meant a dead Arsene Lelou. “Best to let the Goyl handle this, my prince!” he purred. “Who’s going to shoot the spy if he gets away from Nerron and the Waterman?”

Louis yawned once more. “Fine.” He pointed his rifle at the stable door again. “What are you waiting for, Goyl?”

Nerron badly wanted to give him some of the lizard venom the onyx used to turn human skin into translucent slime. *The crossbow, Nerron. It’ll be worth it all!* He could already feel its wooden shaft in his hands. It would give all the treasure hunters sleepless nights. His ugly face would be on the front page of every newspaper, and princes and

Kings would beg him for his services. Only the onyx would wish him dead, once Kami'en put the crowns of Lotharaine and Albion on his head. They would curse the day they'd sent a five-year-old bastard home instead of to his death.

Nerron left the dog man and Milkbeard with Louis. They were both loud and stupid, not worthy of this enemy. But he did give Milkbeard orders to set the devil-horses free. It would be far too humiliating should Reckless manage to escape on them.

Nerron stayed under the trees until he could no longer be seen from the stable door. Reckless didn't have eyes that could see in the dark, and his skin wasn't as black as the night, but the vixen was with him, and her senses were as sharp as a Goyl's.

A few quick steps across the yard. The back against the stable wall. Reckless was no longer standing behind the door. Nerron could see that much.

Cat and mouse.

He squeezed through the door.

A cart. Bales of hay. Brushwood, the kind Witches used for their brooms. Especially the vixen could be hiding anywhere. Would Reckless shoot him without warning? Maybe. Though Reckless was more into rules than Nerron was. According to what people said about him, he had old-fashioned ideas about honor and decency, though he probably would've never admitted it.

Where were they?

Nerron briefly worried they might have escaped through some kind of spell—but here, in the Dark Witch's territory, no magic worked besides her own. Hopefully, Lelou made sure Louis didn't fall asleep.

The Waterman was still standing in the doorway. What? Was he suddenly afraid of the dark? *Go search, you idiot!*

Nerron rammed his saber into the brushwood.

"I see you're also quite good at playing hide-and-seek!" His voice sounded like ground-up granite. The damp well was still sitting in his bones. "I just want the heart. Then I'll let you and the vixen go." He might even keep that promise, but of course he couldn't speak for Louis.

A follet ran past him, and there were rats in the hay. A cozy place, but the vixen's company without a doubt even turned the filthy stable of a child-eater into a romantic venue.

There. He could hear someone breathe. *You have him now, Nerron.* All that hassle, just because he'd trusted the wolves.

A sound made him spin around, but it was only the Waterman who'd stepped into one of the Witch's rat traps. *Scaly fool.* He groaned and cursed as he freed his boot from the iron jaws. The noise distracted Nerron for a fraction of a second, but that was enough. Before he could turn again, he heard the click of a pistol's hammer.

Reckless was standing a step away, aiming at Nerron's heart. Where had he been? Between the hay bales? Eaumbre took a hobbling step toward him.

"I really wouldn't." Reckless's left hand was wet. His whole sleeve was dripping with blood.

"Was that the payment for your wounded friend? How noble." Nerron waved the Waterman back. "Yes, child-eaters cut deep."

Reckless shrugged. "Don't worry. I can still pull a trigger."

"Yes, but how often? You'll be dead before you get out that door." Nerron cast a quick glance behind Reckless, but the vixen was nowhere to be seen. "Come on now. Where is the heart?"

Reckless smiled.

Oh, Nerron, you are a fool.

51. RUN

Fear. And more fear. Too short had been the peace in between.

She was so tired that even the fur gave her no comfort. Fox had drunk her own fear, but she could still feel it. Like a tremor deep inside her.

Places, clinging to her heart like mold . . . the shabby house that smelled like the sea. The red chamber. They couldn't just be left behind. No matter how fast the vixen ran. Jacob was the only one who protected her from them.

Fox wanted to sleep by his side. Just be with him and feel his warmth wash away the memory of the red chamber. And the house that smelled of salt.

But she had to run.

She was carrying his life around her neck.

Nothing had ever weighed more.

52. CUNNING AND FOLLY

"You should have let the dogs loose! My father puts vixens in their cages when they are puppies, so they learn to like the taste. You should see what they do with them!"

The same angry rant, every time they stopped for a break. The Snow-White apple had made Louis even more unpredictable—or was it the toad spawn? If it hadn't been for Lelou, the princeling would have killed Reckless as soon as Nerron led him out of the stable. The future King of Lotharaine really was as stupid as he looked. *No, Nerron, much stupider.*

"Foxes are smarter than dogs." The Waterman was sitting in the grass, examining his injured foot. He had smeared on it some ointment that he'd found in the

Witch's house, and now the scaly skin around the wound had turned as white as a mushroom.

"You're treating that filthy swine like a raw egg!" Louis rammed his sword so hard into the flame that the sparks singed Nerron's skin. "He's been giving us the runaround for weeks. Have you already forgotten everything you learned as my father's bodyguard?" he barked at Eaumbre. "He has you treat prisoners who think they're smarter than he very differently."

Eaumbre pulled the boot over his injured foot.

"Fetch him!" Louis ordered.

The Waterman got up quietly, but Nerron stood in his way.

"He's my prisoner."

"Really? Since when?" Louis got up. He was swaying a little, but the arrogance on his face was truly regal. Every evening, Eaumbre tied Reckless to one of the carriage wheels. Nerron liked to picture swapping him for Louis and letting the horses have the whip.

The Waterman pushed past him and hobbled to the carriage.

Reckless was still pale from the Witch's bloodletting, and the Bluebeard had cut a few bloody patterns into his soft skin, but his face still had the same infuriatingly fearless expression it had worn when he faced the wolves.

He even offered his tied hands to Nerron. "The Waterman ties the ropes so tight that my fingers are dying off. How about you take these off me? I'm not planning on running."

"And why not?" Louis wiped some grease from his mouth with his velvet sleeve. The dog man had shot two rabbits, and Louis had eaten them both himself. "You know what my father does to spies from Albion?"

Reckless shot an amused glance at Nerron. His eyes were asking, *Really? A spy? You owe me, Goyl.*

"Oh that...that's just a sideline," he said out loud. "I'm actually a treasure hunter, like the Goyl. And I'm afraid we'll have to join forces for this hunt. You have the head and the hand. I have the heart. And if that's not enough, then ask the Dwarfs whether they know where Guismond's body is."

Oh, the cunning dog.

It took Louis a few seconds to comprehend what Reckless was saying. He was now swaying so much that he nearly fell into the fire as he staggered toward him. Lelou fed him toad spawn thrice daily (the Waterman was often gone hours to find it), but the effect always wore off toward the evening. And the princely breath again smelled of elven dust as well.

"You obviously forget whom you're talking to!" Louis tried very hard to sound menacing.

Reckless gave the hint of a bow. "Louis of Lotharaine. I worked for your father, but you probably don't remember. He needed an antidote to a love potion. Your cousin was the perpetrator, and you were the victim. Didn't she turn you into a frog?"

"That story was spread by my father's enemies." Louis

nearly swallowed his tongue with rage. "I was against leaving your friend with the Witch. You would have called the vixen back if the Waterman had cut off his fingers one by one."

"My prince!" Nerron wasn't sure whether Lelou's voice sounded indignant or impressed.

Louis paid no attention to him. "Call her back," he panted. "Now! Or I'll order the Waterman to cut off your fingers. My father usually has them start with the thumbs."

He nodded at the Waterman. Eaumbre's scaly face didn't show what he thought of the order, but he did draw his knife.

"Call her back? How am I supposed to do that?" Reckless asked. "Fox is probably miles ahead of us. Her paws are faster than your golden carriage. She'll be waiting for me by the Dead City. Ask the Goyl. I'm certain the crossbow is there. And I bet you the heart that without me and the Goyl, you won't survive more than three steps in those ruins."

Louis's face turned as white as curdled milk.

"Forget his fingers," he barked at the Waterman. "Cut his throat!"

Eaumbre hesitated. But then he put his knife to Reckless's throat.

Enough. Nerron grabbed Louis and pulled him away.

"Aren't you listening?" he hissed. "He doesn't just have the heart! He also has Guismond's body. What good do you think the hand and the head are without it? Kill him, fine, but then you explain to your father why we couldn't find the crossbow."

Louis stared at him as though he was going to cut off Nerron's fingers next. *Not so easy with a Goyl, princeling.* "He insulted me. I want to see him dead. Now!"

The Waterman was looking at them, his knife still on Reckless's throat. In times of emergency, Nerron's mother used to pray to some mysterious Queen who lived in a copper mountain and wore a dress of malachite. Nerron would have loved to ask her to put just a grain of reason into the crown prince's head, but salvation already came scurrying to Louis's side in the shape of Lelou.

"My prince!" he whispered with an appeasing smile. "I'm afraid the Goyl is right. From time to time, even your father has to collaborate with his enemies. You can still kill Reckless later."

Louis frowned (touching, how humans' skin creased up when they tried to think) and gave their prisoner a menacing look.

"Fine. Keep him alive for now!" he ordered the Waterman. "But tighten those ropes."

53. SOMEHOW

The vixen didn't count the days it took her to reach the mountains where the Dead City lay. But there were too many.

Fox only shed the fur to sneak some restless hours of sleep. With her human body came the memories, but she also caught herself missing the feeling of the wind on her bare skin. She even missed her vulnerable heart. Animal, human, vixen, woman. She was no longer sure what she was more. Or what she wanted to be more.

She had telegraphed Valiant from a train station. The aging telegraph operator had eyed her as though he could see the fur dress beneath her stolen clothes.

The Dwarf had suggested they meet in a mountain village not far from the Dead City. One could see the ruins from the market square: collapsed towers and domes, pale walls, laid out along the slopes of a mountain like bleached bones. Dark clouds hung over the dead streets. They had drifted in over the entire valley, and Fox felt their cold shadow as she stopped in front of the tavern where she was supposed to meet Valiant.

The goat horns above the door were meant to ward off the kinds of ghosts that were particularly feared in this area: tegglis, wax-ghosts, mountain Witches... they were blamed for every dead goat and sick child, even though most of them weren't half as vicious as their reputation. Fear flourished like weeds in these mountains.

Fox stepped into the dark taproom. The look she got from the landlord was as filthy as his apron, and she was glad Valiant didn't keep her waiting too long.

"You look like death!" he observed as he pulled up one of the chairs the landlord kept ready for his Dwarf customers. "I hope Jacob's looking even worse. Shall I show you the telegrams that lying dog has sent me? 'No trace yet... will keep you posted... this hunt may take years...' You know what? As far as I'm concerned, that Goyl can drag him here by a rope."

Tired. She was so tired.

The landlord served the tea she'd ordered, and he took a glass of milk to the child at the next table. Fox felt her hand begin to tremble at the sight of the white liquid.

"What the devil..."

Valiant grabbed her arm and looked in shock at the

grazed wrists. She'd be carrying the scars from Troisclerq's chains for the rest of her life. Tears welled up inside her, but the vixen wiped them away. They were as useless as her fear for Jacob. *You will save him. Somehow.* How?

Valiant handed her a handkerchief embroidered with his initials.

"Don't tell me you're worried about Jacob!" The Dwarf shook his head and sneered. "That Goyl's not going to hurt a hair on his head. Jacob is unkillable. I know what I'm talking about. I dug his grave once."

That memory didn't really make things better. Jacob had dodged death so many times. *But not this time*, she heard a whisper inside her.

Be quiet.

The child at the next table was drinking her milk. Fox wanted to look away, but she forced herself to watch. Or did she now want to start running from moths and flowers as well?

The wind pushed open one of the windows, blowing hailstones across the wooden tables. The landlord quickly closed it with a worried look on his face. He'd been talking with a farmer who'd told him stories of landslides and drowned sheep—and that one of the crazies who lived in the Dead City had been to his farm, announcing the end of the world. They were called Preachers, men and women who'd lost their minds in the ruins and who believed that the abandoned city housed the gateway to heaven. Fox had met one of them at the edge of the village. They adorned their clothes with tin and glass, turning them into a kind of bizarre armor.

The farmer gave Valiant a dark look.

"You see that?" the Dwarf whispered, returning the look with a gold-toothed smile. "They blame the mines for the bad weather. If those goat-herding imbeciles had any idea how close they are to the truth. Since we found that tomb, it's not only the weather that's gone crazy. We're having more accidents in the mines. Those Preachers are popping up everywhere, prattling about the end of the world, and the farmers keep their livestock locked in the stables, claiming the Dead City's come alive."

Fox rubbed her scuffed wrists. "Where did you take the body?"

Valiant held up his hands. As small as children's hands, and strong enough to bend metal. "Not so fast. Jacob is like a brother to me, but we need to renegotiate. There'll be additional costs now that the fool has let himself get captured."

Fox hissed across the table, "Like a brother? You'd probably sell Jacob for the silver fingernails of a Thumbling! I wouldn't be surprised if you joined forces with the Goyl if he offered you a bigger share."

That thought brought a flattered smile to the Dwarf's face. He took any reference to his cunning as a compliment.

"We should discuss all this in a less public place," he purred. "My chauffeur is waiting outside. Chauffeur..."

He gave Fox a meaningful wink. "A wonderful word, isn't it? Sounds so much more modern than 'coachman.' "

As they stepped into the street, the wind nearly blew the ridiculously high hat off the Dwarf's head. The houses were cowering in the shadow of the mountain, their walls dark with rain. The chauffeur was anxiously wiping the water off the dark green paint of his enormous automobile. He was, of course, human. The horseless vehicle looked even more alien on a village road than the ones Fox had seen in Vena.

"Impressive, isn't it?" Valiant said while the chauffeur rushed toward them with an umbrella. "I am a man of the future. The speed's still a little disappointing, but the looks I get more than make up for that."

The chauffeur held the umbrella over Fox's head, though the wind nearly tore it out of his hand. He helped the Dwarf onto the much-too-high footboard.

"Whatever the reason for this weather," Valiant whispered as the shivering Fox sat down next to him on the brown leather, "this cold does make keeping a headless King fresh much easier."

54. THE SAME TRADE

The Bastard came every night—whenever he had the watch and the others had fallen asleep. He gave Jacob food and sometimes even some of the wine the prince had left over.

Tell me. How did you get through the labyrinth? How did Chanute survive the Troll caves? And to make yourself invisible... which method do you use? Did you ever find one of the candles that call the Iron Man with their flame?

During the first night, Jacob answered him with silence or some lie. But by the second night that became boring, so he followed every answer with a counterquestion: How did you find the hand? How did you figure out where to catch me with the head? Where do you catch the lizards whose skins you use for your bulletproof vests?

The same trade.

Of course, the Bastard searched his pockets, and when the Goyl rubbed the gold handkerchief between his fingers Jacob was glad for once that it had stopped working properly. Nerron. Just one name, like all Goyl. His meant "black" in their language. Who'd given him that name? His mother, to deny the malachite in his skin? Or was it the onyx, who usually drowned their bastards? Nerron even checked Earlking's card, but in the Goyl's fingers, it just showed the printed name.

Nerron held up the ballpoint pen Jacob always carried because it was so much easier to write with than the quills or the old-fashioned fountain pens used behind the mirror.

"What do you do with this?"

"Wishing ink." The Goyl had brought meat, and Jacob put some of it in his mouth. The Waterman had, despite Louis's orders, loosened his ropes. The Bug Man seemed to be the only one who was unquestioningly loyal to the prince. But it was probably still best not to underestimate Louis. He had the same cunning face as his father, though he was probably only half as smart.

"Wishing ink?" The Bastard put the pen in his pocket. "Never heard of it."

"Whatever you write with it will come true someday." Not a bad lie. Somewhere in the east was a goose feather that supposedly did just that.

"Someday?"

Jacob shrugged. He wiped the grease off his tied hands. "Depends on the wish. One, two weeks..."

Hopefully, their paths would have parted by then. They'd been traveling for four days. The Witch must have finished with Donnersmarck by now, unless she'd killed him or turned him into some insect. But taking him before she finished her magic would have meant certain death.

They rested in caves at night. The Goyl always found one, and Jacob was glad for it. The nights were still so cold that he froze, despite the blanket the Bastard had brought him. His arm hurt from the Witch's knife, and the cuts from Troisclerq's rapier burnt his skin. But what really robbed him of his sleep was the uncertainty of whether Fox had made it to safety. He kept seeing her weary face. *You're asking too much of her, Jacob.* Too often had his only gift to her been fear—experienced together and conquered together, but fear still. Yet in the child-eater's stable, all of that had been forgotten. Then he'd just wanted to protect her. But in the end, and like so many times before, it was she who had to help him.

"Don't you wish it was just the two of us?" The Goyl had lowered his voice, though the other three seemed to be fast asleep. "No prince, no Bug, no Waterman, not even the vixen. Just you and me, against each other."

"The prince could be useful."

"What for?"

"He's related to Guismond. What if you need to have the blood of the Witch Slayer to get into the palace? It is, after all, awaiting his children."

"Yes. I thought of that as well." The Bastard looked up

at the bats stirring under the cave ceiling. "But I hate the idea of having to drag that blue-blooded airhead with me until the end. No. There's always another way."

Jacob closed his eyes. He was tired of how the Goyl's face reminded him of his brother's jade skin. Even the cave looked like the cave where he and Will had argued.

The pain was stirring again in his chest, so suddenly that he could barely suppress the scream that wanted to explode from his lips.

Damn.

He clutched his bound hands to his chest. *It will pass. It will pass.* How many times now? *Try to remember, Jacob!* Five. This was the fifth. One more bite. There couldn't be much left of his heart.

"What is this?" The Bastard looked anxiously at Jacob's pain-stricken face. "Did Louis give you anything to drink?"

Jacob could have laughed, if he'd had any breath left. Not a baseless suspicion. The royal house of Lotharaine had a long tradition of poisoning its enemies.

The Bastard pulled Jacob's hands from his chest and tore his shirt open. The moth was now as black as the onyx in Nerron's skin, and the red outline of its skull-spotted wings looked like fresh blood.

Nerron recoiled as though he was afraid to contaminate himself.

Jacob leaned against the cave wall. The pain was subsiding, but he probably made quite a pitiable sight. Was this what the Red Fairy had in mind when she'd whispered her sister's name in his ear? Had she pictured this while she kissed him? That he'd be writhing like a wounded animal, paying with his agony for her pain? Only that she wasn't going to die of her broken heart.

She has no heart, Jacob.

Nerron poured out the wine he'd brought, and filled the beaker with a brown liquid. "Drink slowly," he instructed Jacob before putting the beaker in his bound hands. "I'm not sure your stomach can take Goyl spirits."

It tasted like sugared lava.

The Bastard pushed the cork back into the bottle. "I have to be careful Louis doesn't find this. He'd kill himself with it, and his father would execute me. This was the Dark One, I assume? I always wondered how you managed to steal your brother from under her nose." He put the bottle back in his sack. "The third bolt...you want the crossbow for yourself! What if that story is just a myth?"

"I tried everything else." Jacob forced down another gulp of Goyl liquor. It warmed better than any blanket.

"The apple? The well?"

"Yes."

"What about Djinn blood? The ones from the north. Quite dangerous, but..."

"Didn't work."

The Bastard shook his head. "Don't your mothers tell you to stay away from the Fairies?"

"My mother knew nothing of Fairies." Jacob ignored the curiosity in the golden eyes. What was the matter with him? Was he now going to tell his life story to the Goyl? Just one more bite. Maybe he'd die before he saw Fox again. He'd always assumed she'd be with him when he died. Not Will. Not the Fairy. Always the vixen.

Nerron got up. "I hope you're not so stupid to think I'd let you have the crossbow as some kind of noble gesture."

Jacob pulled his shirt over the moth. "You haven't found it yet."

The Goyl smiled.

His eyes said, *I shall find it. Before you. And you will die.*

"What would you be searching for? If you weren't busy trying to outrun death?"

Yes, what, Jacob? He was surprised by his own answer. "An hourglass."

The Bastard rubbed his cracked skin. "I wouldn't be racing you for that one. Which moment could be worth holding on to forever?" He touched the rock as though searching his memory for one that might have been worth it.

"What would you like to find most?" Jacob's chest was still numb with pain.

The Goyl looked at him. "A door," he said finally. "To another world."

Jacob suppressed a smile. "Really? What's so bad about this one? And why should another be any better?"

The Bastard shrugged and looked at his speckled hand. "It's my mother's fault. She told me too many stories. The worlds in them were all better."

Behind them, Louis was beginning to snore. He was turning more moody and irascible with every day. A side effect of toad spawn, as Jacob had learned from Alma. Paranoia was another. Both not uncommon character traits in a King's son.

"I don't ask much!" Nerron said. "Having no princes would already make it a better world. And no onyx lords. I could also do without Thumblings...and it should have deep, uninhabited caves."

He turned away. "We all have our dreams, right?"

55. NOT THE PLAN

"And where in this mess is the palace supposed to appear?" Louis pulled the spyglass from Nerron's hand and pointed it at the ruins of the Dead City, which were barely visible beneath the dense clouds that had settled between the mountains.

"The palace stood above the city." Lelou brushed some hailstones from his thin hair. "At the end of that road with the Dragon kennels." Of course. The Bug could probably draw an exact map of the Dead City.

The dog man brought Reckless. He had tied Jacob's hands behind his back and had, on Louis's orders, also tied a noose around his neck. Louis still resented their prisoner for having questioned his treasure-hunting abilities.

"Lock him in the carriage!" he ordered, rubbing his red eyes.

The dog man obeyed his orders more readily than Eaumbre did. He used every opportunity to treat the prisoner worse than his dogs. A casual kick here, an elbow to the ribs there, or a shove with the butt of his rifle. Even now he pushed Reckless so hard that he smashed his face bloody on the side of the carriage. It was obvious that Louis was enjoying the show.

"What is this?" Nerron hissed at him. "He's only useful to us alive. Do I really have to keep explaining this?"

The toad spawn had turned the princely smile green.

"You don't have to explain anything to me, Goyl," he hissed back. "I've had enough of your explanations for a while now."

Nerron felt the muzzle of a pistol in his back. Judging from the height, it was Lelou who was pressing it into his spine.

"I told my father a hundred times! The Goyl should all be roasted until their stone skins crack. Sadly, the old man is afraid of your lot!" Louis sneered. "Lelou tells me you've been sitting with Reckless every night. You're suspiciously friendly to him, but you can't fool me. What's the plan? Even splits when you both sell the crossbow to Albion?"

The dog man yanked Nerron's arms back, and Milkbeard trained his gun at Eaumbre. He was as dumb as he was strong, but he was a surprisingly good shot.

Louis gave Nerron a look that contained all the arrogance of his ancestry, and also the recalcitrance of a seventeen-year-old who still felt immortal. A dangerous mix.

"I will find that crossbow for my father," he announced while the dog man tied up Nerron so tight, it felt as though he was trying to cut his stone skin with the rope, "and Albion will finally stop acting like they own the world. But first we deal with the Goyl."

Oh, it would have all been so easy had he just killed Louis and Lelou in Vena. *Your aversion to killing is becoming a hindrance, Nerron.*

"Who plotted this?" He tasted his own rage like blood on his tongue. "Lelou?"

The Bug blushed, flattered. "Oh no. This is entirely the plan of His Highness." He shot Louis a nervous smile. "He's not very experienced in treasure hunting, but he was right to point out that we are searching for the crossbow of his ancestor. I merely suggested we don't kill you and Reckless quite yet. After all..."

"...we still have to squeeze you for everything you know." The dog man exposed his teeth, which were as yellow as those of his charges. "About the hidden palace...about the crossbow. And all that...The prince thinks I should be in charge of that." He gave Louis a devoted smile and managed a plump curtsy. "The Waterman is the expert," he added, "but the prince is convinced, and rightly so, that you can't trust the scale-faces any more than the stone-skins."

"Yes, yes, that's fine. Why are you telling him all that?"

Louis dabbed a pinch of elven dust into his nose. The stash in his saddlebag seemed inexhaustible. "First we take the heart off the vixen. Lock the Goyl in the carriage with Reckless."

It took all three of them to tie up the Waterman. They tied him to one of the wheels, just as they used to do with Reckless. The dog man dragged Nerron to the carriage.

"The prince is right, Goyl!" he whispered before slamming the door shut. "You should all be roasted. Those will be good times, when he is King."

"Get the horses!" Nerron heard Louis say with a heavy tongue.

Reckless was lying on one of the benches, his face swollen from its encounter with the carriage.

"That wasn't quite the plan, was it?" he asked.

56. GIANTLING RAGE

There they came. Fox stepped back from the fence, which the farmers had erected to keep their livestock away from the cursed ruins. The wind blew from the direction of the dead streets, and it drove ice and hail into her face. Everything around her was spelling one word into the night: calamity.

The men riding toward the watchtower were the same ones Fox had seen behind the Witch's stable, but as they rode closer, she noticed that the Goyl wasn't among them. Nor was Jacob.

"Calm!" Valiant whispered to her. "It means nothing. Absolutely nothing."

Yet Fox felt as though someone were forging iron rings around her heart.

He wasn't with them.

They had killed him.

No, Fox!

They were four. All well armed. The Waterman was also missing, but they had brought the bloodhounds, and Fox was glad she wasn't wearing fur. One of the men was very young, and another one was barely taller than Valiant. Fox recognized Louis of Lotharaine from the pictures of him standing by his father's side. In the pictures he'd looked much taller. Fox could smell elven dust and toad spawn as he reined his horse just a few steps away from her.

"You're the vixen."

It was half question, half stated fact. Louis's voice was as unpleasant as his face. "A Dwarf? Is that all the reinforcements you could muster?"

The man with the dogs uttered a barking laugh.

Valiant gave Louis an indulgent smile. It was every Dwarf's curse and blessing to be underestimated for his size. "Evenaugh Valiant. And with whom do I have the pleasure?"

Louis swayed in his saddle as he pushed back his jacket to reveal the gem-encrusted hilt of his saber.

"Louis Philippe Charles Roland, crown prince of Lotharaine."

"Impressive!" Valiant replied. "But we Dwarfs, we're all republicans. I hope you don't take it personally. Anyway"—he looked searchingly past the prince—"we had actually arranged to meet a Goyl."

The bloodhounds were watching Fox. They were not as easily deceived by her body as humans were.

"Where is Jacob?" She'd promised the Dwarf to leave the talking to him, but she was done waiting.

The prince stared at her with that mixture of disgust and desire every shape-shifter was all too familiar with.

"Where do you have the heart?" he barked at her. "I bet you have it hidden under your clothes, like your fur."

The hounds bared their fangs, and Louis gave the dog man a nod.

Valiant turned to the watchtower and gave a shrill whistle.

Two lumbering figures stepped out of the shadows behind the tower. The Giantlings had ice all over their clothes, and they stared rather unkindly at Louis. Nowhere had Giants once lived in as large numbers as in Lotharaine, and nowhere had they been hunted with as much abandon. Crookback had a collection of Giants' heads, which he still liked to show off during state events.

"Yes, I was forewarned," Valiant said while Louis tried to calm his shying horse. "I've had the dubious pleasure of doing business with your father. Why should I trust his son any more?"

The taller of the Giantlings gave a disapproving grunt, and one of the horses reared up.

It was the dog man who fired the shot. Maybe he was afraid for his bloodhounds, who were barking so furiously at the Giantling that he took a lumbering step toward them. The bullet hit him in the center of his broad brow. His collapsing hulk buried the shooter as well as his dogs.

The other Giantling howled out with rage.

He yanked the prince from his saddle and shook him like a rag doll, his other fist blindly flailing about. He killed the baby face with one swipe; Fox could hear his neck snap. Valiant only just managed to jump to safety, and she retreated between the shying horses to find some shelter from the raging Giantling. In his fury, he trampled the rifle that had killed his companion, until its metal stuck to his soles like wilted leaves. Then he threw himself to his knees next to the lifeless body and wiped the blood from the shot-up forehead.

"Like a Giantling's vengeance," the saying went—for good reason.

Louis was spread-eagled on the trampled earth, and like the servant with the baby face, he was not moving. But the Bug Man was crawling on all fours to his master, staring in distress at the waxen face. Behind him, Valiant was groaning as he struggled to his feet, cursing all Giantlings.

The prince had two swindlesacks on his belt. Fox took them before the Dwarf got hold of them. She put her pistol to the Bug's head.

"Where is your prisoner?"

Louis stirred. The Bug Man sighed with relief and ran his spidery fingers over his master's face. "The carriage," he stammered. His eyes were full of tears. Fox couldn't tell whether they were tears of rage or of fear.

She caught one of the horses, ignoring Valiant's calls.

The trail was easy to follow. A herd of cows wouldn't have left clearer tracks, but the dark clouds over the mountains made it hard even for her to spot the carriage beneath the pines. The Waterman was tied to one of the wheels. Good. The scent of his scaly skin reminded Fox of the many damp caves she and Jacob had searched for abducted girls. When the Waterman spotted her, he started yanking angrily at his fetters, but Fox just walked past him.

Her hands trembled as she tore open the carriage door. The Bastard was all but invisible; only his eyes glinted through the dark like coins. Jacob's face was streaked with blood, but he seemed unhurt otherwise. Fox cut his ropes. He stumbled as he climbed out of the carriage. Fox had seen this kind of exhaustion before.

"How often?"

He rubbed his battered face and attempted a smile. "I really am glad to see you. Where is Valiant?"

"How often, Jacob? Answer me!"

He took her hands. His fingers were cold. *It's a cold night, Fox. It means nothing.* But she could see death all over his face.

"One bite to go."

Just one.

Breathe, Fox.

She pulled out the two swindlesacks she'd taken off Louis. She also gave Jacob the leather pouch where she kept the heart. This time his smile wasn't quite as weary.

"You also look exhausted." Jacob stroked her face. "Just as well this will all be over soon, one way or another. Right?"

He tucked the sacks into his coat pocket and leaned into the carriage.

"Keep searching," Fox heard him say. "There is a door. No onyx on the other side, no Thumblings, but there are some princes. Only few of them wear crowns, though."

"Cut me loose!" the Goyl replied with a hoarse voice. "Let's find out once and for all which of us is the best."

Jacob stepped back.

"Another time," he said. "This one I can't afford to lose."

"You would have lost a long time ago if the vixen didn't keep saving your skin!" The Goyl sounded like he was choking on his rage.

"That's correct," Jacob replied. "But it's also nothing new."

Then he slammed the carriage door shut.

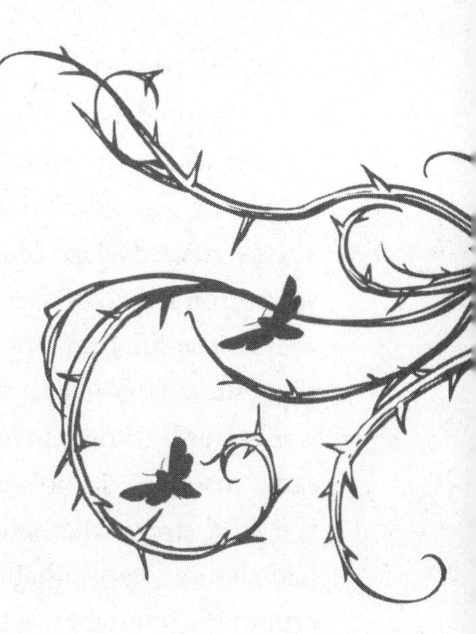

57. HEAD. HAND. HEART

The Giantling had already covered the body of his companion with stones. He'd also arranged the bodies of the other dead at his feet like offerings: the kitchen hand, the dog man, and his two bloodhounds. The two who'd survived his rage lay bound and gagged by the wall of the watchtower: Louis and the Bug. Valiant was pacing up and down in front of them. He didn't look happy at all.

"Look at that!" he yelled at Jacob. "What've you gotten me into this time? The Lotharainian crown prince! Luckily, he's still alive, but that probably rules out Crookback as a buyer. Wasn't it enough to make the Empress your enemy?"

Jacob felt Fox's arms around him before she slipped off the horse. Her warmth lingered like a promise as he swung himself from the saddle.

All will be well.

He ignored Valiant's muttering and went to the fence behind which the ruins lay. The Dead City. Not a place he'd ever wanted to see this close. Even Chanute had always steered clear of it. Jacob thought he could hear voices, some kind of chanting, interrupted by hoarse howls. Maybe the lunatics who lived among those ruins sensed that this was going to be a special night. Supposedly, it was enough to merely touch the walls to succumb to the same madness. Jacob's eyes searched for a path through the dead streets that led up the mountain. The city once had thousands of inhabitants. He saw stairs and bridges, crumbling churches. He saw towers and houses, their empty windows outlined by will-o'-the-wisps, and palaces with walls pocked with the nests of plague-finches—the only kind of bird that thrived in places like this. If the palace really appeared, it was going to be a long way to reach it. And Jacob could feel his life slipping away with every breath.

"I hear the Goyl's still alive?" Valiant appeared by his side. "Why didn't you shoot him? Competition's good for business?"

"I'm not quite as quick with the shooting as you, remember?" Jacob looked at the watchtower.

Fox was waiting by the door.

"Did you have the body brought here?"

"Indeed." Valiant let out a pitiful sigh. "I hope you have at least some idea of how difficult that was! I had to bribe the Giantling guard by the tomb with a year's supply of elven dust, and then I had to hire the other two to bring the coffin here. I had to give a master performance in front of the Dwarf council to convince them that I was as disgusted as they were by the sudden disappearance of the body. I neglected my other business interests to come here. I want that crossbow. And I want to make a fortune off it! I'm planning on traveling to Albion myself, as soon as you have it. Wilfred the Walrus seems to be our most likely buyer, don't you agree?"

"Sure," Jacob answered.

He was just glad that Valiant didn't know about his promise to Robert Dunbar. If that crossbow really did save his life, then he'd have to be careful the Dwarf didn't shoot him.

The inside of the watchtower was empty, except for a few rusty lances and the remnants of a goat that had perished in its walls. The Witch Slayer's body lay in one of the simple wood coffins in which the Dwarfs buried their dead mine workers.

Fox helped Jacob open the lid.

The simple coffin made the gown on the headless corpse look even more sumptuous.

Fox looked at him.

It had been a long hunt. But they'd made it this far, together. Just as they had promised each other in Valiant's castle. Just the way their fellowship had shaped not only his but also her life for more than six years. There was hardly a memory from those years that was not shared by both of them. His second shadow. By now she was so much more than that. Nothing had ever made that clearer than these past months. She was a part of him, inseparably connected. Head, hand, and heart.

"What are you waiting for?" His impatience was making Valiant stand on tiptoes in his bespoke boots. They had not only high heels but also soles that made him taller. Dwarf cobblers were very skilled at giving their customers a few extra inches.

Jacob first pulled the sack with the hand from his bag. As with the head, he barely felt anything when he touched the dead skin. He felt a brief twinge of worry that Guismond's magic might have lost its potency after so many centuries. *You'll know soon enough, Jacob.* The fingernails still had remnants of gold on them, but they were not moldy, as one usually saw on the hand of a Warlock. Maybe Guismond had found a way to protect himself from that effect. The regular intake of Witch blood had terrible consequences. It attacked the brain and caused strong hallucinations. All Warlocks went mad at some point. If the archives in Vena were to be believed, already years before his death Guismond had began to distrust even his most loyal knights, and he had friends and enemies executed indiscriminately, usually by starving them to death in golden cages he'd hung from the walls of his palace.

The hand in the south.

Jacob leaned over the body. The hand was stiff and cold, but it fit perfectly onto the stump of the arm, as though he were assembling a sinister doll.

The wind that came rushing through the tower's windows was cold and damp like snow, and it made the lantern Fox was holding over the casket flicker.

Jacob opened the leather pouch that contained the necklace with the heart. He tucked back the burial gown until it revealed the gold-lined hole in the chest. The black heart Ramée's granddaughter had worn around her white neck. Jacob felt nothing but a faint warmth as he took the jewel off the chain. It almost seemed to welcome his touch.

The heart in the east.

It fit into the gold-lined hole as though Guismond had a stone heart beating in his chest even when he was alive. And he may well have had.

The Goyl had kept the head in the same swindlesack Jacob had carried it in.

The head in the west.

Like the hand, the face was stiff and lifeless as Jacob pulled it out of the sack, but as soon as he put it on the stump of the neck, the golden lips parted.

The gurgle that emanated from the open mouth sounded like the last sigh of a dying man. The corpse's pink skin turned gray, and the face began to crumble as though someone had shaped it from golden sand. The neck, the hands, the entire corpse crumbled into itself. Even the gown rotted in front of their eyes, until the casket was filled with nothing but gray dust mixed with a few specks of gold.

"What the devil?"

Valiant stared down at it, aghast, but Jacob breathed a sigh of relief. The Witch Slayer's magic was still working. And he had found himself a new abode, like a bird that's been let out of its cage.

Fox was already by one of the windows, looking at the ruins.

A shadow, manifested from the darkness of the night. It took shape very slowly, for what was molding itself there was huge. Towers, battlements, walls. At first they were transparent, like smudged glass, but then they became stone, as sallow as the dust in the coffin.

The palace, which kept growing into the night like a stone thistle, had not been built to impress through its beauty. It was meant to do only one thing: inspire awe. Even from a distance, one could see the cages on the crenellated walls where Guismond had let his friends and foes starve to death. Beneath them Jacob could make out the Iron Gate. If the stories passed down from the times of the Witch Slayer were true, then the gate came to life with lethal force whenever an enemy demanded entry. A treasure hunter trying to steal Guismond's crossbow was unlikely to be considered a friend.

Well, first you have to get to that gate, Jacob.

❦

Outside, the Giantling was still piling rocks on his companion's body. The higher he piled them, the more importance he accorded to his dead comrade. Every friend and relative who visited the grave of a Giantling added a stone, so that the graves often grew to the size of a small hill.

The prince was still unconscious. The Giantling had given him quite a thrashing, but he'd survive. Jacob wasn't sure whether that was good news or bad. Imagining Louis on the throne wasn't necessarily a comforting thought.

"His father will feed you to his dogs!" Lelou was screeching with a shrill voice. "He'll have your hearts served for breakfast...."

"...and roll cigarettes from our skins. I know." Jacob pulled out his knife and leaned over Louis.

Lelou watched him in speechless horror, as though he'd suddenly swallowed his tongue.

"Yes, it's a pity he can't come with us," Jacob said, cutting a few strands of Louis's pale blond hair. "I'm sure the Iron Gate would welcome him more warmly than me."

"What's that supposed to be for?" Valiant asked. "Are you going to sell a strand to every girl you find pining at the prince's portrait, dreaming of becoming Queen of Lotharaine?"

Jacob left that question unanswered. Never had he felt

more grateful for the things Alma had taught him—things that Witches usually never divulged to a human. She had once pulled out one of his hairs and wrapped it around her bony finger. "This here tells me more about you than your blood," she told him. "Every single hair reveals who you are and where you come from. Yet you humans leave it in combs and brushes without realizing that even a few strands of it give any stranger the chance to put a very powerful part of you in his pocket. For a Witch, the hair you leave on a hairdresser's floor is enough to create a doppelgänger in just a few hours."

He didn't have enough for that. But maybe it would make Guismond's gate accept him as a distant descendant. It was worth a try.

"You have no right!" Lelou's voice trembled with rage. "Treasure hunter? You're all filthy thieves. The crossbow belongs to Guismond's heirs."

Jacob got up.

"Yes, but why did his children never come to claim it? What do you think, Lelou?" He put Louis's hair in one of the empty swindlesacks. "Maybe they never even came to his tomb. How do you explain that? Just with the fact that the Witch Slayer was a terrible father and quite mad toward the end? Did he, as some say, have their mother killed, and was that why they rejected him? Or were they simply too busy waging war against one another?"

Arsene Lelou pressed his colorless lips together. Still, as

expected, he couldn't resist the chance to show off his knowledge.

"They thought their father wanted to kill them all!" he twanged. "That's why they never came to the tomb. That's why they never searched for the crossbow. They were convinced Guismond would find a way to kill them."

Valiant uttered a skeptical grunt. "Why should he? He needed an heir."

Lelou rolled his eyes. "The Witch Slayer was crazy. He didn't want anybody on his throne, not even one of his children. He wanted the world to stand still after his death. It was supposed to begin and end with him."

Fox went to Jacob's side.

"We should get going," she said quietly.

Yes, but Jacob was still thinking about what Lelou had said. Maybe taking Louis's hair wasn't such a good idea?

He pulled Fox away.

Behind them, Lelou was reciting every horror story ever written about the Dead City. Jacob knew them all.

From his pocket he took the chain Ramée's granddaughter had worn—and possibly Guismond's daughter before her.

"I will get you a pendant for it," he said as he put it around Fox's neck. "The most beautiful one I can find in Guismond's palace. But let me go alone. Please! It's too dangerous. I'll come back with the crossbow. I promise."

Fox replied by placing her hand over where the Fairy's

moth covered his heart. “What could be worse than the Bluebeard’s house?” she asked. “Or worse than having to wait here for you?”

At a signal from Valiant, the Giantling kicked an opening in the fence.

The Dwarf handed Jacob two candles.

“They weren’t easy to find,” he said. “Your debts are growing and growing. I will wait here for you. The tomb was enough for me, but don’t get any ideas. I’ll find you, whatever you may try to cheat me out of my share. Believe me, I can be much more unpleasant than Crookback.”

“I remember,” said Jacob. He followed Fox across the trampled fence.

58. HEAD START

Pale blood was dripping from the Waterman's fingers as he cut Nerron's ties. He'd scraped the scales off his arms to free himself. Some of his olive-green flesh was probably still stuck to the carriage wheel, yet he never even flinched.

They had, of course, taken all their weapons.

Tricked by a prince dumber than any horse you've ever ridden, Nerron.

They saw the palace already from afar. So the Dwarf had brought Guismond's body with him. Nerron was sick with rage as he pointed his spyglass at the watchtower where the exchange was supposed to have taken place. A pile of stones that looked suspiciously like the grave of a Giantling, and a few dead bodies in front of it. He couldn't make out who they were, but the Giantling crouching over them was hard to miss. He was quite a hefty specimen. What, by Crookback's hangman, had happened there?

"Can you see Louis?" Nerron was glad the hatred in the Waterman's voice was not aimed at him.

He shook his head.

"I want to hear his princely neck snap," Eaumbre whispered. "Or crush his throat until his stupid face turns as blue as the sky."

Some Watermen spent years hunting down a man who'd insulted or cheated them. Eaumbre had been very patient with Louis. But Nerron didn't care whether the prince was still alive. All he cared about was whether Reckless was among the dead. But not even that information was worth tussling with a Giantling for.

He pushed the spyglass back into his belt.

Eaumbre eyed the ruins and the palace that was built around the mountain like a crown. "The Witch Slayer had more treasure than just the crossbow, right?"

"Probably."

Eaumbre rubbed his raw arms. "If Louis is there, he's mine," he whispered.

"And if not?"

The Waterman bared his teeth. "Then hopefully I'll find enough gold to compensate me."

59. THE DEAD CITY

Weathered facades. Cracked pillars. Arched doorways. Stairs leading nowhere. Even the skeleton of the Dead City still showed how opulent it had once been. The street they were following wound steeply past crumbled houses. The silence was as black as the moonless night. Jacob thought the first face he saw was an embellishment, the legacy of a talented mason. But they were everywhere, staring out of the gray walls like fossils. Women, men, children.

The stories were true. Guismond had taken the whole city with him to his death. *"He wanted the world to stand still after his death."* It was supposed to begin and end with him. Smart Bug!

The Witch Slayer had locked them into the stones of their houses. What had killed them? His final breath? Had he died with a curse on his lips? Jacob thought he could hear their voices as the wind brushed through the empty streets. It groaned and sighed, driving dead leaves in front of it, loosening weathered stones from walls that had been bleached like bones by the passing centuries. Swarms of will-o'-the-wisps dotted them with light, and a few plague-finches were frantically hopping around on the cracked paving stones. Apart from that, the deserted streets with their hemline of dead faces were still.

They were picking a path through the debris of a collapsed tower when a man jumped out from behind the remnants of a statue. Jacob hacked off his arm before he could ram his rusty scythe into Fox's back. His clothes were covered with pieces of glass and metal. A Preacher. His eyes were as empty as those of the dead in the walls. Six more were waiting beneath a triumphal arch, its weathered marble celebrating Guismond's victories over Albion and Lotharaine. They fought as stubbornly as if they were defending a living city, but luckily their weapons were old, and the men weren't very well fed. Jacob killed three and Fox shot another before he could push Jacob against the hexed walls. The others fled, though one of them stopped after a few steps to scream curses in the local dialect of the surrounding mountains. He didn't stop screaming until Fox put a warning shot in front of his feet. The curse was superstition, born of the helpless fear of real magic, but the screams attracted more of the ragged figures. They appeared everywhere between the ruins. Some just stood there, staring or throwing stones at them. Others stumbled into their path with rusty pitchforks and shovels they must have stolen from some farmer nearby.

Jacob and Fox had to kill four more before the others left them in peace, and Jacob was sure there'd be more of them waiting at the palace. Guismond's modern knights. Jacob wondered whether it was the magic that pervaded this ruined city that told them to guard it, or whether it was the fear of their own mortality that had brought them to this place of death—the hope that these ruins might harbor the secret of how to escape the ultimate end.

Not much different from the hope that brought you here, Jacob.

They only made slow progress toward the palace. Their path was often blocked by debris, collapsed bridges, crumbled stairs—Jacob felt as though he was again trapped in a labyrinth. This time, however, Fox was with him, and even the fear of his own death was nothing compared to the fear he'd felt for her in the labyrinth of the Bluebeard.

The ruins grew ever higher into the night sky. Some had walls that were constructed like stone grids. Dragon kennels. They were located right beneath the palace. The street climbed ever steeper up the slope. Jacob felt how much even the short fights with the Preachers had exhausted him. *You're dying, Jacob.* But the words no longer had any meaning, as if he'd thought them too often.

Another Dragon kennel. Instead of faces, these walls showed huge muzzles, spiny necks, wings, and barbed tails. Guismond was said to have captured hundreds of

Dragons to use in his wars. Instead of the stone they usually ate, Guismond had fed them peasants and enemy soldiers, Witches, Trolls, Dwarfs. It had driven them insane, like cows fed on meat.

One last kennel. The street in front of it was gouged by giant talons. The stairs at its end were even wider than those that had led them down to Guismond's tomb. These went up, and they were so long that a whole army could have deployed on the steps. *A hundred steps to the Iron Gate, and beyond a hundred ways to die.* Jacob couldn't remember where he'd read those words. He was so exhausted that he barely remembered how he'd gotten here. His chest ached with every step, but Fox stayed close by his side.

The stairs led to a snow-covered plaza. The clouds hung so low that the palace's towers were hidden in their haze. Suspended from the gray walls were the golden cages, and through the bars they could still see the remains of Guismond's prisoners. The whole palace looked as if it had been cursed just the day before, not centuries earlier.

The Iron Gate stood out from the walls like a seal. The iron shimmered like the breastplate of a King. Jacob could see neither a lock nor a latch, just a garland of skulls and the crest they'd also seen on Guismond's tomb.

The ragged corpses in front of the gate were more recent than the sad remains in the cages. Some had charred hands, or whole arms burnt to their elbows. Others had terrible bite marks. The Preachers must have thought the entrance to heaven had finally revealed itself; instead, they had knocked on the gate of a Warlock.

Jacob felt the same darkness he'd encountered in the tomb, like a clenched fist behind the gate. And all he had was a handful of princely hair and whatever he'd managed to learn about this world in his twelve years of treasure hunting. Fox dragged one of the corpses out of the way. *And you have her, Jacob.*

As soon as Fox approached the gate, it began to glow like the metal in a smithy's forge.

Jacob took the sack with Louis's hair from his pocket. His only hope of getting the gate to let them pass as friends. *And a faint hope it is, Jacob.* Clinging to the pouch was Earlking's card:

You don't need the prince's hair.

Fox looked over Jacob's shoulder. The green ink kept writing.

Hurry, my friend.
You should have shot that Goyl.
The crossbow is so close.

Friend—the word never seemed more fake. Jacob looked up at the Iron Gate. The Red Fairy was also once that helpful. He threw away the card and took the prince's hair from the pouch.

Another Preacher appeared on the steps. Fox aimed her

pistol at him, but he kept walking until he saw the bodies. His grimy coat was covered in thick layers of metal and glass—it really did look like armor. The gate to heaven. Fox struck him down as he stood and stared at the dead. Jacob and Fox had been there too long already. A few more hours and they'd start pinning glass and tin to their own clothes.

Jacob took a step toward the gate. It was so high that a Giantling could have carried him through on his shoulders. Most of the gates from Guismond's era had been built to accommodate Giants. Guismond had some in his service. Their graves were in the mountains, not far from the Dead City.

Jacob put his hand into the pouch. His fingers were going to smell of Louis's cologne. Not a pleasant thought. He closed his fist around the ash-blond strands. Louis was only very distantly related to Guismond, so his hair would work like a quietly whispered password. But this was their only hope of not being treated like intruders.

Jacob wouldn't have been surprised if the gate had melted the skin off his fingers. There were legends of monsters that came forth from its iron. The bodies around them did look like they'd encountered just that. Yet as soon as he reached out his hand, the metal burst open like the skin of an overripe fruit. It split into two wings, and each wing sprouted a handle, like an iron bud. They were shaped like wolves' heads, and even as their teeth were still growing from their pointy snouts, Jacob could feel the wind brushing across the glowing metal until the entire gate was again back to its cool, shimmering gray.

You don't need the prince's hair.

What had Earlking meant by that? A lie, to see Jacob killed like the ragged men around them? Whatever...

Fox and Jacob exchanged a glance.

The passion for the hunt. Was that what bound them, more than anything else?

She smiled at him. Fearless. Yet Jacob could still recall the white fear he'd made her drink in the Bluebeard's chamber. Over the past months, they had both learned the limits of their fearlessness.

He closed both hands around the wolves' heads. He thought he'd need all his remaining strength to open the heavy iron gates, but they opened without resistance, with a sigh that sounded like the death rattle from the gilded lips of Guismond's head.

The air rushing toward them was icy, and the darkness that awaited them behind the gate was so complete that Jacob was blind for a few steps. Fox took his arm until his eyes had adjusted to the darkness. The hall they had entered was empty, except for the pillars that supported a ceiling somewhere in the darkness above. The echo of their steps bounced between the high walls like the flapping of stray birds.

Fox looked around as the cries of a child came through

the silence. The screams of a woman soon joined them. Then the voices of quarreling men.

"Stop!" Jacob whispered to Fox.

The voices faded, as though they were moving away, but they would be audible for hours before they died away completely. The Steps of the Dead. A Dark Witch spell. Every step they took stirred the past: words spoken, screamed, or whispered in the palace. And not just words. Pain. Anger. Despair. Madness. Every emotion would become manifest. The darkness surrounding them was woven from sinister threads. They were going to have to be very quiet, lest they get choked by them.

Jacob could make out three corridors in the dark. As far as he could see, they were in no way different from one another. He pulled from his pocket the pale yellow candles Valiant had given him. He and Fox had used candles like these before in places where they'd had to split up. If one of them was snuffed out, so was the other. Fox got out some matches. Then she silently took the burning candle from Jacob's hand. The voices again grew louder as their steps rang out on the tiles. Guismond had killed most of the Witches, whose blood and magic he'd stolen, in the dungeons of this palace. The screams were becoming so loud that Fox clearly had trouble walking on. She looked around at Jacob one last time, and then the light of her candle disappeared into one of the corridors. She had chosen the middle one.

Left or right, Jacob? He turned left.

60. THE RIGHT SKIN

One of the Preachers had a fresh sword wound. Nerron shot him dead before his filthy fingers could write his madness onto the Goyl's skin. The Waterman had already been touched by one, but that didn't seem to worry him. Maybe he felt immune to human madness. Eaumbre had soon realized that the tracks they were following were not Louis's, but he didn't turn around. The palace that had risen above the ruins was too tempting.

It reminded Nerron of the fortresses a clan of moonstone Goyl had built a long time earlier against the onyx. Kami'en now used the strongholds as prisons, for they were particularly deep underground.

The ragged lunatics were the only danger they faced in the empty streets, and most of them just let themselves get shot by the Waterman like clay pigeons. It seemed the centuries had weathered the Witch Slayer's magic, like the city he'd once ruled. Eaumbre was disconcerted by the stone faces staring at them from the walls, but Nerron was not affected. They just proved how much the Doughskins were like his own kind.

When they reached the stairs that led up to the palace, they found Reckless's and the vixen's prints like scorch marks on the snowy steps. The snow was now falling ever thicker, tiny icy flakes that felt like stings on Nerron's stone skin. He hated the cold, and he felt such a sudden longing for the warm womb of the earth that it made him sick. The Waterman, however, just mutely rubbed some snow into his dry skin before he started the ascent.

The scene that awaited them at the top of the stairs proved that the stories about the Lost Palace and its Iron Gate were not just the fruit of some poet's lively imagination. The charred and ravaged corpses were real, but Nerron could see neither Reckless nor the vixen among the dead.

Where were they? The tracks on the snowy plaza allowed only one conclusion: His rival was already inside the palace.

Damn. How?

Nerron approached the gate, and the iron began to glow immediately. Eaumbre pulled him back as the metal warped to form a mouth. Mouths, claws. The whole gate was coming alive. Spiny necks arching, scaly paws sprouting lava-red claws of iron.

The Waterman stumbled backward over the bodies.

But Guismond had not expected a treasure hunter with a stone skin. In his time, the Goyl had been nothing more than a dark fairy tale.

To protect him from the claws, Nerron wore the kind of lizard shirt that had already saved Hentzau's and Kami'en's lives at the Blood Wedding. And the jade machete that he'd had made especially for the Iron Gate by a Goyl smithy sliced through the necks and paws as though Guismond's gate produced only monsters of wax. Nerron hacked and pierced until his clothes were stiff with cooling metal. Reckless was not among the dead, so there had to be a way in. Nerron split a head before its muzzle could swallow his head; he cut off paws barbed with dozens of needle-sharp talons. Reckless was not among the dead. There had to be a way!

His arms were already growing heavy when the Waterman finally came to his aid. The heat of the iron scalded his skin, but he fought valiantly. Soon they were both standing to their knees in shattered metal. Their own panting rang in their ears. *Reckless is not among the dead, Nerron. Damn it, there has to be a way!* And indeed, suddenly the iron was just iron again, and the gate formed a frieze of skulls. Guismond's crest appeared on the glowing surface, and a barely visible crack appeared.

Touching the hot iron was painful, despite his stone skin. It hurt so much that Nerron felt as though his bones were melting. But pain was something the Goyl cared much less about than humans did, and finally Nerron managed to force his finger through the crack. The opening he wrestled from the iron was barely big enough to squeeze himself through. The Waterman smelled of burnt fish by the time he joined Nerron on the other side. Behind them, the gate closed itself with a sound like the dull gong of a bell.

The cold that greeted them brought a relieved sigh from the Waterman, and even Nerron was grateful for the respite it gave to his scorched skin. Through the darkness that surrounded them like the fur of a black cat, Nerron caught the scent of Witch magic. Eaumbre gave him a startled look when he heard the voices, but Nerron smiled. A Step-Spell. He once knew a treasure hunter who was driven to madness by it, but nothing left a clearer trail. Once the voices were aroused, they could be heard for hours. You simply had to follow them.

"You stay here and watch the gate!" he said to the Waterman. Maybe Reckless was already on his way back with the crossbow.

But Eaumbre shook his head. "No, thank you!" he whispered. "I've been the doorman for far too long. Anything I find is mine, right?"

"As long as it isn't the crossbow."

The scaly face stretched into a scornful grin.

"Right. I'd forgotten. A crossbow is not what you're after," Nerron muttered. "But I'm sure you can find treasure you can lay at some girl's feet. There should be enough for a dozen."

The look from Eaumbre's six eyes grew icy. "We only ever love one, for a whole life."

"Sure. Just that they don't tend to live very long under your care." Nerron went to the first corridor and listened. Nothing. But the voices of the dead echoed out of the other two. Reckless and the vixen had obviously split up. Couldn't afford to waste any time when you had death lurking in your chest.

The Waterman disappeared without a word into the first corridor. Nerron decided on the one to the left.

61. AT THE GOAL

Jacob had been in many enchanted palaces. Every door could mean danger, and every corridor could end in a trap. Stairs disappeared. Walls opened up. But not here. Open doors, halls, courtyards. Guismond's palace breathed him in like an animal whose stone innards were fermenting the past like an indigestible poison.

Horses scraping in empty stables. Weapons clanging on empty courtyards, the stars above still hidden behind dark clouds. Children's voices from deserted nurseries. Invisible dogs growling. And all the time screams, echoing through the dark halls and corridors. Screams of fear. Screams of pain...Jacob felt Guismond's madness like grime on his skin.

He found rooms filled to the ceiling with treasure, armories with such precious swords that every one of them would have fetched enough to renovate Valiant's castle. But Jacob barely looked at them. Where was the crossbow?

He wondered whether he should have taken one of the other corridors. He kept glancing at the candle in his hand, but its flame kept burning steadily. Fox was having no more luck than he.

Hurry, my friend.
You should have shot that Goyl.
The crossbow is so close.

He spun around a dozen times, thinking he'd heard steps, but all that followed him were the ghosts he'd aroused. Maybe that was Guismond's magic: to make them roam his palace until they lost themselves in his past, becoming one of the ghosts whose voices were haunting them.

Another door.

Open, like the others.

The hall behind it seemed to have been an audience chamber once. The tiles on the floor were worn from countless boots, and the weathered stucco was streaked with the soot of long-snuffed torches. Jacob could feel anger, like acrid smoke, despair, hatred. The voices were whispering, dampened by fear.

Carry on, Jacob.

The door at the end of the hall bore Guismond's crest.

He stepped through it—and took a deep breath.

He'd reached his goal.

Guismond's throne chamber also brought the past to life, but not through voices. Jacob heard only his own steps echo through the silence. Here, just as in the tomb, Guismond's lost world was evoked in paintings on the walls and ceiling. Their color was hauled out of the darkness by swarms of will-o'-the-wisps. Battlefields, castles, Giants, Dragons, an army of Dwarfs, a sinking fleet, the city that was now crumbling outside, filled with people. The frescoes were painted so masterfully that Jacob forgot for a few breaths what he'd come here for. On the wall to his left was one particular picture that made him pause. A band of knights was galloping, swords drawn, through a silver archway. Their livery was white, like that of Guismond's knights, and it was emblazoned with a red sword, but also with a red cross above the sword. Where had he seen this before? *The Livonian Brothers of the Sword, Jacob.* A knights' order from his world, disbanded more than eight hundred years earlier, after they had usurped large parts of northern Europe. Jacob looked at the archway. It was covered with silver flowers.

Jacob had always wondered whether there was only the one mirror.

The answer was obviously no.

He looked around. The throne stood in the center of the room. Narrow steps led up to the stone chair. The armrests and the back were upholstered in gold. An effigy of Guismond was staring at Jacob from empty eyes. But Jacob was looking for a mirror. And there it was, at the rear end of the room. It was huge, nearly double the size of the one in his father's room. The glass was just as dark, but the flowers on the frame were not roses; they were lilies, just like on the archway in the picture. A skeleton stood next to the mirror, holding a golden clock in its bony hands. No clocks had existed in this world in Guismond's time. But they had on the other side.

Jacob! Only the pain in his chest finally reminded him why he'd come here. He turned his back to the mirror and went to the throne.

The statue sitting on the throne wore the Warlock's catfur coat, but it also showed Guismond as a warrior King. The helmet, which encircled his face, was shaped like the mouth of a wolf. Beneath the coat Jacob saw knee-length chain mail, as well as the white tunic with the red sword. Jacob had so often looked at the silver ringlet that surrounded the sword and never thought anything of it. Guismond sat with his legs apart, like a man who'd conquered a world. After he'd arrived here from another.

At the bottom of the steps stood a stool, and on it, on a golden cushion, lay a crossbow.

Jacob blew out the candle.

The tiles beneath his feet formed a round mosaic with Guismond's crest. The stool with the crossbow stood right on top of the crowned wolf's head.

Jacob was just a few steps from the stool when the moth took its final bite.

He dropped to his knees. He saw, heard, felt nothing, only pain. It seared the final letter from his memory like acid. The Dark Fairy had her name back. Then the moth rose from his skin. It peeled its furry body from his flesh as from a bloody cocoon and began to flap its wings. Jacob heard his scream echo through the throne room, and he flailed in agony on Guismond's crest as the moth fluttered off, back to its mistress, taking her name—and his life—with it. All she left behind was the imprint on his raw flesh, and Jacob lay there and waited for his heart to stop. It stumbled and raced, clinging to the last bit of life left in his body.

Get up, Jacob! But he didn't know how. He just wanted the pain to end, this hunt to be over, and Fox to be with him.

Get up, Jacob. For her.

He felt the cold of the tiles through his clothes and on his pain-numbed skin.

Get up.

62. EXTINGUISHED

The voices were terrible. They quarreled. Screamed. Cried. They were waiting behind every door, and as Fox drifted from room to room, from hall to hall, she found gold and silver, haphazardly piled loot from plundered cities, chests filled with precious clothes, golden plates on empty tables (which briefly brought back the memories of the Bluebeard's dining room), beds under bloodred canopies, jewel-encrusted furniture. The light of her candle peeled them out of the darkness like unreal images—and the opulence just whispered of Guismond's madness. The entire palace was a ghost. All the voices, the sinister hunger permeating it…the dead life that didn't want to die.

The trembling flame lit a writing room. Books. Maps. A globe. The hide of a black lion spread out on the floor.

The patterns on the carpet that hung on the wall announced that it could fly.

The candle died.

Fox felt her heart beat faster.

He'd found it.

Jacob had found the crossbow.

She shifted shape. The vixen would get to him much faster.

Jacob would live.

All was well.

63. THE TRAP

On your feet, Jacob. The pain began to subside, but his heart was sputtering as though every beat could be the last.

Never mind, Jacob. Just a few steps.

Take the crossbow. Fox will be here soon.

He actually managed to get up.

What if she didn't find him in time? *Do you want to shoot that bolt into your own chest, Jacob?* The thought was almost funny.

From this close, the figure on the throne looked so life-like, as though Guismond had created it from flesh and blood. The dead eyes stared right through Jacob as he stepped toward the stool. *Heavens.* His feet were stumbling as badly as his heart.

"You're really not making death easy on yourself." The

Bastard stepped out of the shadows, as quietly as he had in the tomb.

Where did you have your ears, Jacob? The oldest mistake in the world: to forget all caution once the treasure is within reach. He was going to die like an amateur.

The Bastard looked at the pictures on the walls as he walked toward his rival. Jacob reached for his gun, but death was slowing him down, and the Goyl had a pistol trained on him before Jacob could pull his own from his belt.

"Don't force me to further shorten these final minutes of your life," Nerron said, aiming at Jacob's head. "Who knows? Maybe you even have an hour. How did you open the gate? That damn iron even burnt my hands."

"I don't have the faintest idea." The crossbow was so close, all he'd have to do was reach out, but Jacob could see that the Goyl would shoot. He'd learned to read the speckled face. It reminded him, even now, of his brother's. "Who freed you?"

"The Waterman. I had a feeling it would prove useful to keep him alive. Though there were a dozen times in the past weeks when I'd have loved to wring his scaly neck." Nerron looked around. "Where is the vixen?"

Draw your gun, Jacob. At least try. What have you got to lose?

But maybe there just wasn't enough life left in him.

Nerron stopped in front of him.

"She is very beautiful, and I don't usually say that about

human women. You think she'll allow me to comfort her? After all, she also went with the Bluebeard."

Yes, Jacob would have loved to shoot him.

"I'm sure the obituary for the great Jacob Reckless will be in all the newspapers." Nerron stepped closer to the crossbow. His pistol was still aimed at Jacob's head. "Maybe they'll come to me, to hear how you breathed your last. I promise, I'll describe it most touchingly."

Jacob touched the bloody imprint on his shirt. So close. His hand trembled. "Whom will you sell it to?"

"I'm sure you'd be surprised." Nerron reached for the crossbow.

Snap.

The ticking began as soon as the Goyl had lifted the weapon off the stool. But he paid no attention to it. He still didn't realize, even as he walked toward the edge of the circle and ran into the invisible wall. The curse he uttered would have made a Dwarf blush. He tried to step out of the mosaic in another place, but of course the stones wouldn't let him go.

Jacob derived little comfort from the fact that the Goyl had been just as blind. At least he had the excuse that impending death didn't make you smarter.

It was a trap. From the beginning. They'd been caught in it from the moment they read the words in the tomb, and whosever body they'd found there, it was not the Witch Slayer's. *The fingernails should have made you suspicious, Jacob! No sign of decay? Where did you have your senses?*

He looked at the figure on the throne. The Witch Slayer was sitting in front of them, and the trap he'd set more than eight hundred years ago had finally snapped shut.

The Bastard threw the stool against the invisible wall so hard that it broke.

"Damn! What gave us away?"

Jacob dropped to his knees. "Nothing," he said. "He thinks we're his children. That's the problem."

He pulled out the pouch with Louis's hair and threw it far from him, even though it was already too late. "The trap was meant for them, but they were smarter than us. It's a time spell."

The Witches used hourglasses, but Guismond had used the clock he'd brought from the other world. *You saw it, Jacob! Where was your head?* A magic circle and a clock. That's all it took.

"Time spell?" The Goyl struck out at the invisible wall. It sounded as though his claws were hitting against glass. "Never heard of it. How does it work?"

"Every minute will cost us a year." He was going to be an old man after all.

The Witches used the spells to dispatch of particularly despised enemies, but the Witch Slayer wasn't out for revenge. *You should have already seen this in the tomb, Jacob!*

"If you catch your own children in the circle"—his voice was already sounding hoarse—"then you can use the years you take from them for yourself. You're just taking back the life you gave them in the first place. The more of it, the better. After all, Guismond didn't want to be reborn as an old man. So he tried to lure all three of them here."

"Reborn?" The Bastard stared at Guismond's effigy.

"Yes. That's not a statue. It's his body. The Witch Slayer wanted to return from death, even if that meant killing his children." Tick-tock. The clock's whirr sliced through the silence and Jacob felt his flesh wither. "It might have worked with Louis," he said, "but we won't do him any good. It'll still kill us, though."

And Fox couldn't do anything to free them. Only Guismond could break the circle. Jacob wasn't sure what he wished for more: that she found them while he still lived or when it was all over.

"Did you hear, Witch Slayer?" Nerron screamed at the corpse on the throne. "You caught the wrong prey. Let us go! Your children weren't as stupid as we are, and they are now as dead as you."

Every minute a year.

The Bastard sank to his knees. His breathing grew as labored as Jacob's, but the spell wouldn't show as clearly on him. Goyl skin barely aged.

"Admit it!" he panted. "Admit it. I won!"

Jacob closed his eyes. No, he didn't want Fox to find him like this. He wished she'd never find him and that none of this had ever happened. But how had it all begun? With him going through the mirror. And had he never done that, he'd have never met her, and the vixen would have perished in the trap.

He lifted his hand. It looked like that of an old man.

He didn't want her to find him like this.

64. LIFE AND DEATH

Fox didn't comprehend. What she saw was too terrible. Jacob on the floor, the Goyl next to him. She shifted as she ran toward them. Only as she got closer did she see the crossbow lying between them.

Jacob.

She tried to reach him—and was stopped by an invisible force. The air around him was made of glass, and Fox saw the mosaic that had caught him and the Goyl in its circle. A magic circle, but what was it doing to them? The Bastard seemed unchanged, though his breathing was shallow, like a dying man's. Jacob's face was so haggard that Fox barely recognized it. His skin was like parchment, and his hair as white as snow. He stirred as she called his name, but his cadaverous body shuddered as a clock's tick cut through the silence.

The spell that stole years, made people wither like leaves.

Fox looked around desperately.

The ticking came from the back of the room.

The hourglasses of the Witches stole their victims' time silently, but it befitted the cruelty of the Witch Slayer that he was taking Jacob's lifetime with a snarling clockwork. Fox heard the hands move forward as she ran toward the clock.

A golden dial, held by bony fingers. Fox tried to push the hands backward, but they wouldn't budge. She gave up, fearing Jacob would never get his years back if she broke the clock. She implored the vixen and everything that had ever given her strength, but the hands kept moving.

Please!

Fox lifted the housing from the bony hands, but not even her knife could crack it. The mirror that hung next to the clock showed her the despair on her own face. It was so large that its glass reflected the entire room.

At first Fox didn't quite realize what she was seeing in the mirror.

The figure on the throne was moving.

The gloved hands closed around the armrests, and the mouth gasped raspingly for air. Guismond turned his head. Fox hid behind a column before his eyes could find her. The face was barely visible beneath the helmet, but she remembered the gilded image staring from the door to the tomb. Whose had been the body in the sarcophagus? A double Guismond had created through witchcraft? A soulless hull that had taken his place in the coffin, soaked with enough black magic to make everybody think the corpse was his?

The Witch Slayer staggered to his feet, but the clock in Fox's hands was still ticking. *Good, Fox. That means it is still finding life to steal.*

Guismond looked around. He steadied himself on his throne and felt for the sword that leaned against it. His hands were shaking. Of course. The life he was stealing came from a dying man.

Fox pulled out her knife, wishing she had Jacob's saber. A knife against a long sword. No. She tucked it back into her belt and pulled out the pistol. The Witch Slayer was not a Bluebeard, nor was he the Tailor from the Hungry Forest. He was human.

He moved unsteadily as he climbed down the steps from his throne. With Jacob's breath, his heartbeat. The cats' hides dragged behind him, and he held his sword in his hand.

Only he can break the circle, Fox. And then she would have to kill him. And hope that Jacob got back the life the Witch Slayer had stolen from him. She ducked behind another pillar as Guismond looked around once more. She longed for her fur. *Not yet.* The vixen wouldn't be able to kill Guismond.

His steps were unsteady, like those of a sleepwalker. He stopped on the last step and stared down at the men caught in his magic circle. Only two men. Strangers. Fox thought she could smell his disappointment. His body yearned for more life.

He looked around.

No. They are not here.

What was he feeling? Did his madness leave room for the desire to see his children, even though he'd wanted to kill them? Was that the other reason he'd built the trap, to force them to his side, even if they came only to seek power, not love? A motivation he probably understood better, anyway.

The Witch Slayer took off his helmet. He still moved painfully slowly, as though his dead body didn't want to wake up. The hair revealed beneath his helmet was gray, the face wrinkled and pale. Guismond. Guismonde...his name was pronounced differently in Lotharaine. But his bynames were the same everywhere: the Cruel, the Greedy. And, of course, they'd also called him the Great.

He'd forgotten about the circle. He stumbled against it, felt the invisible wall with his wrinkled hands...and he remembered.

Go on! Your victims are already too weak to escape, and you must want your crossbow back.

The words came across his lips almost silently. Witch words.

The magic circle broke with the sound of shattering glass. Guismond kept the sword in his hand as he approached Jacob and the Goyl. The tinkling of his chain mail was the only sound Fox could hear. Guismond's rasping breath. And the ticking of the clock. But Jacob wasn't moving. He was so still. What if he was dead already?

No, Fox. The clock's still ticking.

She laid it on the floor behind the pillar before she stepped out from its cover. Guismond was just reaching for his crossbow.

Fox shot the arm holding the sword. Yes, he still was just a human being. The scream from his sallow lips sounded like the screams that echoed through the corridors of the palace. Not alive, not dead. A man who'd wanted to kill his children so as not to get lost in his own darkness. The Witch Slayer turned to face her and to stare at the weapon that had injured him.

The next bullet got stuck in his chain mail.

You have to aim better, Fox!

His lips moved while he picked up his sword with his uninjured arm. She shifted shape before his curse could find her. It merely brushed through the vixen's fur like frost. She ran toward him. *Quick, Fox.* Too quick for his body, which still belonged to death more than to life. Guismond struck out at her with his sword, but he had no strength, and Fox thanked the Fairy for the death she had planted in Jacob's chest. The vixen dug her teeth into the flesh. It reeked of putrefaction. She jumped back while Guismond dropped to his knees, and she shifted shape once more. Vixen and woman, forever one. One was nothing without the other.

The Witch Slayer rubbed his hand over his face. His skin began to wilt. He thrust his sword at her, but his attack was so feeble, she could have parried it with the knife. And before he could utter his next curse, Fox rammed her blade into his unprotected throat. The blood gushing out of the wound turned to dust even as it dripped onto the white tunic, and the hands clawing at her coat withered before the fingers could close.

Fox stepped back from the body. The face was stiff, as if carved from wood, and the eyes were as empty as glass. An old man, nothing more. But she could sense him in the walls surrounding her, and in the darkness filling the room. She wanted to be far away.

She lowered her knife and listened.

The clock was silent. And Jacob stirred. His hair was dark again, and his face was the face she loved, but the Bastard stood next to him, and he was holding the crossbow.

No.

Fox drew her pistol, but she'd used all her bullets on the Witch Slayer.

The Bastard smiled. "Never trust a vixen. How often I heard my mother say that! They are cunning, and like you, Nerron, they are not afraid underground. What would she have said about a vixen saving my stone skin?"

"Give me the crossbow." Fox drew her knife. Guismond's dusty blood was on the blade. "You'd be dead without me."

"And?"

A scaly arm came around her neck.

"They say shape-shifters can do magic," the Waterman whispered. "Prove it, vixen."

He was wearing a dozen necklaces, a coat of Unicorn skin, and rings on all his fishy fingers. Fox struggled to free herself, but Watermen were strong.

Jacob tried to get up. His blood was painting the outline of a moth onto his shirt.

The last bite.

Too late, Fox. Where have you been?

65. THE THIRD SHOT

Fox... Jacob heard her voice and felt her hands. But death was battling life in his body, and death was stronger. It was spreading through him, even though his skin was no longer that of an old man. The Fairy's price had not been paid yet.

Let go. It's over.

"No!" Fox grabbed him by the shoulders. "Jacob!"

He opened his eyes.

The Bastard was standing just a few steps away. "The Witch Slayer as a loving father..." He stroked the crossbow's gold-plated shaft. "Nonsense. I never believed that story about the third shot."

The bolt in the crossbow was as black as his skin. He nodded at the Waterman. "Get her out of the way."

Fox tried to pull her knife, but the Waterman struck it

from her hands. Jacob was too weak to even lift his arm to shield her. He felt his life dissipating with every breath. What would become of Fox? It was all he could think of as the Bastard's face blurred in front of his eyes. What would they do to her? Was the Waterman going to drag her into some pond, or would the Goyl shoot her? No, she'd escape. Somehow...

"Look at the shaft. Just as I thought. It's made of alder wood. Do you know what that means?" Jacob heard the Bastard's voice as though from a great distance. "No. You forgot all about them. But the Goyl remember. They lived even deeper under the earth than us, in their silver castles. Alderelves. Immortal. Devious. And masters at making magical weapons. The Fairies destroyed most of them, but there's supposed to be a sword, somewhere in Catalunia, that was made by them.

"The magic is always the same: The weapon brings death to its bearer's enemies and life to his family. I always suspected that the crossbow is an Alderelf weapon, ever since the first time I heard the story about the third shot." The Goyl ran his finger over the reddish wood. "Who knows, maybe Guismond actually wanted to kill his son. He was probably already mad back then. After all, he'd been drinking Witch blood for years. But the crossbow wouldn't allow it."

He went to Jacob's side.

"How did he open the gate?" he asked Fox. "It was easy, wasn't it? It simply let him in."

Fox didn't answer him.

The Bastard drew the bow.

"He himself explained it to me. The time spell only gives back life if it captures a relative. I most definitely don't qualify, but Guismond was quite alive. Which means . . . ?"

Jacob could barely hear what the Goyl was saying. His own heartbeat was too loud, his labored breath, his body's final attempts to hold on to life.

"That's why the gate let him in. That's why he was faster than I." Nerron's throaty voice was getting louder, as though he could convince himself that he was the crossbow's rightful owner. He caught himself doing it, and his next words again sounded as cool and cynical as they usually did. "Well, well, who would have thought, Jacob Reckless has the Witch Slayer's blood running through him."

Jacob would have laughed had he the strength for it. "Nonsense." He barely got the word out.

"Really?" Nerron stepped back and lifted the crossbow.

"Let me shoot. Please!" Fox's desperate voice cut through the rush in Jacob's head.

"No." Nerron took aim. "How else can we prove this isn't about love?"

Fox's cry was stifled by the Waterman's hand.

And the Goyl shot.

His aim was good. The bolt struck Jacob's chest right where his blood was painting the moth on his shirt. The pain stopped his heart. *Dead. You're dead, Jacob.* But he could hear his heart. Strong, and no longer stumbling. It hadn't beat this regularly in a long time.

He opened his eyes and closed his fingers around the bolt that was sticking out of his chest. His heart hurt with every beat, but it was beating. And the wound did not bleed.

He gripped the bolt more firmly. His chest was numb, and he managed to pull it out with one tug. It didn't hurt half as much as the moth's bites, and the sharp point was clean, as though he'd pulled it out of a piece of wood instead of his own flesh.

The Bastard came toward him and took the bolt from his hand.

"Let her go," he said to the Waterman.

Fox was shivering as she knelt down by Jacob's side. Shivering with rage, fear, exhaustion. He wanted to take her away, far away from Bluebeard chambers and enchanted palaces.

Fox looked at him in disbelief as he got to his feet. The skin above his heart was flawless. Even the wound left by the moth had healed. He felt as young as on the first day he went treasure hunting with Chanute.

The Bastard looked at him with a wry smile. "That would also be a good story for the papers: Jacob Reckless has the Witch Slayer's blood."

He pulled a swindlesack over the crossbow and dropped the bolt into it.

Jacob looked at the mirror. The Bastard could be right, even if not exactly the way he thought.

"You still want to sell the crossbow to Crookback, or did Louis ruin his father's chances?"

Talk, Jacob. Play for time.

He'd made a promise to Dunbar.

Fox looked at him.

Two against two.

"What will be your price? A castle? A medal? A title?" Jacob looked at the mirror again. Fox had noticed it as well.

What if he was wrong? It was worth a try.

"Let's put it this way..." The Bastard put the swindle-sack in his pocket. "You got what you wanted. I'll get what I want."

"What if I can give you a better price? Better than anything Wilfred of Albion or the Lords of the East could offer you?"

"What could that be? I have a castle full of treasure."

"Treasure!" Jacob shrugged disdainfully. "You can't fool me. You care about that as little as I do."

The Bastard kept his eyes on Jacob. The Goyl liked to claim they could read human faces like open books. "What are you getting at?"

"That the Preachers are right."

The thin mouth stretched into a sneer. "The gateway to heaven."

"I wouldn't call it heaven." Jacob felt his regained life like a drug. He had cheated death, so why not the Bastard? "I think you're right about the blood," he said, "but it's got nothing to do with kinship. It's just that Guismond and I came from the same place."

The Waterman grunted impatiently. He was probably already picturing the girl to whom he would offer Guismond's treasures in some damp cave. He was going to read her every wish from her eyes, but he'd never let her go.

"They are going to be here soon," Eaumbre whispered. "The Dwarfs... Crookback's men... every self-respecting treasure hunter. They will all come, but we can still shift most of the stuff."

"Then why are you still standing there?" the Bastard replied. "Take what you want, and go. It's all yours."

The Waterman gave Jacob a six-eyed glance that seemed to know exactly how many of his kind Jacob and Fox had hunted down and cheated of their quarry.

"I wouldn't trust them if I were you," he whispered to Nerron. Then he turned and disappeared through the door into the audience chamber without looking around again.

Nerron stayed silent until the Waterman's steps had receded. He looked at the pictures around them. His eyes stopped on the silver archway and Guismond's knights flooding through it. Jacob caught a brief glimpse of a child's yearning on the speckled face. He even nearly regretted that he couldn't let the Goyl have what he longed for. But Dunbar was right. Some things should never be found, and if they were found, then their next hiding place had to be better than the first. He stepped over

Guismond's body. Where was all that life coming from that he suddenly felt coursing through his veins? Was some of it the Witch Slayer's? Not a pleasant thought.

"I'm sure you know them as well as I do," he said, slowly walking toward the mirror. "The stories about Guismond's origins. That he was a King's bastard, the child of a Witch, the son of a golden-haired Devil. Nobody ever figured out that he simply came from another world."

Jacob stopped next to the mirror.

"This is it," he said. "The door you've been looking for."

Nerron's face melted into the dark glass as he stepped to Jacob's side. Jacob saw how much the Goyl wanted to believe him. He had learned to read the speckled face.

"Prove it, Fox," he said.

Of course she knew what he was planning. It wasn't hard to guess. But Fox shrank from the mirror.

"No. You do it." The fear in her voice was not pretend. For a moment, Jacob worried she wouldn't follow him. But she'd also made a promise to Dunbar, just as he had.

Nerron's eyes met his on the dark glass.

The best...

Jacob wouldn't have minded letting him claim the title. Just a pity the Bastard also wanted the crossbow.

"Go on, then," Nerron said, "prove it."

Nerron didn't notice how Fox moved closer to his side. All he saw was the mirror.

Jacob pressed his hand on the glass.

66. ONE INSTANT

One instant. Jacob disappeared and the Bastard forgot where or who he was. And what he was carrying in his pocket. Just one instant. But that was enough for the vixen. More than enough.

Fox was at the mirror before he could grab her. She had the sack in her hand. His angry howl pierced her ears as she put her hand on the glass.

And then it was all gone.

The Goyl.

The enchanted palace.

Her entire world.

67. THE OTHER SIDE

Fox turned around and Jacob took her hand. He remembered the feeling, that first time your own world disappeared and you found yourself in a different one. The dizziness. The question whether one was dreaming or awake. He was sorry he couldn't give her more time.

Jacob pulled her away from the mirror and smashed the dark glass with his pistol handle. He hacked away at it until the silver frame held nothing but a few sharp-edged shards. Fox flinched with every strike, as though it were her world he was smashing to pieces. She clutched the sack with the crossbow, holding on to the only thing still connecting her to her world. Jacob was surprised the sack's magic was still working.

"Where are we?" Fox whispered.

Yes, where?

Around them it was so dark that Jacob barely saw his own hands. He stumbled over a cable, and when he tried to steady himself, his hand touched heavy velvet.

"Kto tu jest?"

The floodlight that flared up above them was so bright that Fox pressed her hands to her eyes. The pieces of the mirror crunched under her boots as she stepped backward and got tangled in a black curtain. Jacob grabbed her arm and pulled her to his side.

A stage. A table, a lamp, two chairs, and between them the mirror. A prop. Nothing else. How had it gotten here? Had it been hidden for years among dusty theater props? Had anybody used it since Guismond passed through with his knights, or had it kept its secret since? How had the Witch Slayer gotten hold of it? So many questions. The same ones Jacob had asked himself countless times about the other mirror. Where did they come from? How many were there? And who made them? For a long time, he'd searched for the answers, but still the only clue he had was the piece of paper he'd found in his father's book.

Two more lights came on at his feet. Rows of red seats faded into the darkness. It was a large theater.

"Rozbiliscie Lustro!" The man stumbling toward them stopped dead when he saw the bloody outline of the moth on Jacob's shirt.

Jacob slid his hand into his pocket and gave the man his friendliest smile.

"Przykro mi. Zaplaçe za nie." That was about the extent

of his Polish—if what he'd heard was, in fact, Polish. Jacob had done some business with an antiques dealer in Warsaw, but that was a long time ago.

Luckily, he still had a half-decent coin on him, but the man eyed the gold piece warily, as though Jacob had paid him with stage money.

Just get out of here, Jacob.

He took Fox's hand and pulled her toward the stage steps. He still felt like a reborn man.

Dressing rooms. Another staircase. A dark foyer and a row of glass doors. Jacob found one that wasn't locked. The air that greeted him and Fox was heavy with the smells and sounds of his world.

Fox stared aghast at the four-lane road in front of them. The lights above it were so much brighter than anything in her world. A car passed them. Traffic lights tinged the asphalt red, and on the other side of the road a skyscraper stretched toward the night sky.

Jacob took the swindlesack from Fox's hand and pulled her close.

"We go back soon," he whispered to her. "I promise. I just want to check on Will and find a good hiding place for the crossbow."

She nodded and wrapped her arms around him.

It was over.

And it was all good.

68. THE RED

Jacob lived.

The moth was gone and he lived.

How?

The Red Fairy yelled her rage across the water that had borne her.

Nothing could break the most powerful curse of the Fairies. It brought death to any mortal. Eradicated them as though they never existed. Nothing else could ever bring her peace. She wanted her only memory of him to be that of his death.

Yet he lived.

The lake turned as black as the night sky, and the water showed her the weapon that had broken her sister's curse like a brittle twig.

The Red flinched.

Alder wood.

A string of flexible glass.

A mortised pattern on the gilded shaft.

No.

They were gone. For a long, long time.

All of them.

Banned into the trees that had given them their name. Not one had escaped.

The Red wanted to turn away, but there was something drifting among the lilies. She knelt down and reached for it.

It was a card.

A wilted leaf was stuck to the white paper. Startled, the Fairy pulled back her hand.

Only once before had winter come to her island.

No.

They were gone.

All of them.